Another Dawn

**Center Point
Large Print**

Also by Kathryn Cushman
and available from Center Point Large Print:

Waiting for Daybreak
Leaving Yesterday

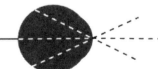

**This Large Print Book carries the
Seal of Approval of N.A.V.H.**

Another Dawn

Kathryn Cushman

CENTER POINT PUBLISHING
THORNDIKE, MAINE

This Center Point Large Print edition
is published in the year 2011 by arrangement with
Bethany House Publishers,
a division of Baker Publishing Group.

The text of this Large Print edition is unabridged.
In other aspects, this book may vary
from the original edition.
Printed in the United States of America
on permanent paper.
Set in 16-point Times New Roman type.

ISBN: 978-1-61173-059-3

Library of Congress Cataloging-in-Publication Data

Cushman, Kathryn.
Another dawn / Kathryn Cushman.
p. cm.
ISBN 978-1-61173-059-3 (library binding : alk. paper)
1. Large type books. I. Title.
PS3603.U825A79 2011b
813′.6—dc22
                                        2011001602

To Lee Cushman—

I'm glad I get to walk through this life with you.
Love you lots and lots!

In loving memory of Carl Parrish—

I'm grateful for every
single day I had with you.

Chapter 1

The Santa Barbara Wharf was the perfect place to get lost from reality for a few hours—the smell of salt air, the smiles of tourists, the Ty Warner Sea Center to enthrall my son, and the complete absence of anything resembling my normal life. We climbed out of my car and Dylan ran immediately to the safety rails lining the edge of the pier. "Look, Mama," he said as he pointed toward the churning water below.

My sandals made a contented scuffling sound against the wooden deck as I moved to his side. At the mouth of the harbor, a long blue sailboat was cutting through the water on its way into the marina, several people hurrying around its deck folding and securing the sails. Yes, this had been a brilliant idea. "Isn't that awesome?" My mood was already improving.

"Yep, now let's go pet a shark." Dylan turned and started skipping in the general direction of the Sea Center, his dark brown hair bouncing with each step.

"Dylan, wait for Mama." I hustled toward him, almost laughing with the lightness of the day. "Hold my hand, sweetie. We have to be careful of the cars."

"Aww, Mom, holding hands is for little kids." He said this with every bit of his four-year-old dignity, but he did hold up his hand for me to take. His head drooped just a fraction. "I wanted to skip."

"Well, I can skip, too. Come on, let's do it together."

"Really?" He looked at me, the left side of his mouth curled under in doubt. So completely adorable. "How come I've never seen it?"

I skipped forward in response. "Come on, slowpoke."

He laughed as he tried to skip faster than me. I was so intent on looking down and watching him that it was almost too late when I looked up and saw them.

Martin Bale and his wife, Juliana, were just ahead, their hands clasped as they looked into the window of a souvenir shop. Oh no. So much for escaping from my present reality. Well, I could still avoid it. I planted my feet, inadvertently jerking Dylan to a stop in the process.

"What's wrong, Mama?" He looked up at me with those huge chocolate eyes. "Why aren't ya skipping anymore? Is it too hard for old people to skip that long?"

Any other time I would have defended my twenty-five years as still being young. Right now, there wasn't time. "I was just thinking . . ." I looked quickly around me, grasping for an excuse that he would accept quickly enough to get us out of here without being seen. The closest building to me was also the most likely place for instantaneous success. "How about some ice cream?"

"Ice cream!" Dylan squealed the words out in the way that only a four-year-old who rarely gets junk food can scream. "Ice cream, ice cream, ice cream!" He jumped up and pumped his fist in the air, effectively removing his hand from my grasp.

"We have to do it now. Right now." I hurried toward the open door, knowing he would follow.

He didn't, just passed me in a blaze of gray T-shirt and long blue denim shorts. By the time I hurried safely inside, Dylan had already begun perusing the double row of ice-cream selections through the window. "How many scoops, Mama? Three?"

"One."

"Aw, come on. Two?" He tilted his head slightly to the side and looked up at me from behind his long, curly lashes. "Please? I've been a good bo-oy." Dylan's charm in full form was almost impossible to resist.

Still, we hadn't even had lunch yet. "I think one is more than enough."

"Aww, Mom."

I glanced through the window and saw Martin and Juliana casually strolling in our direction. We just needed to stay in here long enough for them to get to the parking lot; it shouldn't be difficult at all. Or at least it wouldn't have been if a perky-looking redhead hadn't come along. She hugged Juliana, and I could see them both talking at once like long-lost friends. This might take a while. I was going to have to stall.

"You know what, Dylan? Today's a special day. Why don't you have two scoops?"

"Woo-hoo!" He went back to looking through the curved glass. "Can I taste the pink one?"

"Sure, pardner." The man behind the counter grabbed a tiny pink spoon and pulled up a sample serving. "This one's bubblegum."

"Ooh!" Dylan's eyes grew even rounder.

I only allowed him to chew gum on special occasions and only under strict supervision. Of course ice cream and bubblegum in one package would sound extra especially like something he wanted.

"Two scoops of bubblegum, please."

I ruffled the top of his hair, looking over my shoulder to check on the Bales' progress toward the parking lot. I didn't see them anywhere— probably still talking. "Dylan, why don't you pick two flavors, instead of two scoops of one flavor?"

"I like bubblegum."

"Dylan, the whole point of getting two scoops is to get two flavors. You need to choose a second flavor if you want the second scoop." Personally, I couldn't have cared less about whether he chose one flavor or two; I just wanted to prolong the process.

"Oh-kay." His glum expression lasted about a millisecond, until he turned back to the man behind the counter with a gleam in his eye. "Can I taste the vanilla?"

"Sure can." The man handed him another sample spoon. "You want to taste the berry blitz? It goes well with bubblegum, I think."

"Sure. And can I try the orange sherbet, too?" Dylan didn't dare look my direction, knowing that I usually shut him down after a couple of samples. Since I still hadn't seen the Bales walk past, I wasn't going to do that today.

I glanced over my shoulder again and saw them walking straight toward the door of the ice-cream shop. Oh no!

"Okay, Dylan, tell the man what you want. We've got to get going." But even as I said the words, I knew it was already too late. I turned so that my back was to the door, blocking Dylan from view.

"Grace. Is that you?" Juliana's question ended my last pretense at hope.

I turned slowly. "Hi, Juliana. Hi, Martin."

"Doesn't it just figure that the one day I play hooky from work, I run into half the people I know?" Martin reached out to shake my hand. "I guess I shouldn't feel too bad, though, since you seem to be doing the same thing, hmm?"

11

Not wanting to prolong the conversation, I didn't bother to tell him that Jasmine had given me the day off to compensate for excessive overtime. I simply held up the palms of both hands and said, "Guilty."

"I always suspected there was a rebel buried somewhere in there." He nodded approvingly. "I've been telling Steve that all along, haven't I, Juls?" The question was hardly out of his mouth when his expression froze. He looked toward his wife, panic in his eyes.

Juliana's cheeks turned pink and she reached forward and hugged me. "I was so sorry to hear about you and Steve. I always thought you two were perfect for each other, didn't you, Martin?"

I held my breath with the question. I hadn't yet told Dylan that Steve and I wouldn't be getting married. This was certainly not the way I planned for him to hear about it. I turned toward him, only to find him happily sampling yet a fifth flavor of ice cream. I found myself rubbing my ring finger with my left thumb. It still felt strange to have nothing there, a sad reminder of all that had gone wrong of late.

Martin reached out to shake my hand. "Good to see you, Grace. I am sorry that things didn't work out for you two." Then, almost under his breath, he said, "And I'm *really* sorry things didn't work out with the Blue Pacific."

"What do you mean?" My voice got loud enough with this question that even Dylan and the ice-cream-counter guy stopped what they were doing and looked toward me.

"You know, the buyout. Now that you . . ." He paused, looked toward Dylan, and cleared his throat. "I thought Steve made clear that immediate family always had priority. Now that things have . . . changed with you guys, Roger's pushing the group toward investing in that boutique Phoebe wants. I hate it, because that girl has never worked a hard day in her life."

"But why won't you continue with the deal for Blue Pacific? It's a great idea."

He nodded. "I was excited about it. But once Roger got wind of what had happened . . ." Martin shifted his gaze just away from me and shrugged.

"But Jasmine has already begun making plans to move to Texas. Her son needs to be near that autism center." As the reality sank in, my panic began to rise. This was a disaster. A complete disaster. How could I ever explain to Jasmine that I had ruined everything for her, and her son?

Martin shrugged. "I know. I wish it could be different."

So did I. About a lot of things.

Dylan hurried through the door of our condo, excited to put his new dolphin snow globe on the shelf in his bedroom. The phone was ringing before I had the door closed behind me.

"Hello."

"You're never going to believe this one." Jasmine practically sang the words, something so out of character for her serious demeanor.

"What won't I believe?"

"I just had the real estate agent come look at my house, and he said that homes in this price range are starting to move right now. With a little bit of work, he thinks we should be able to get more than I was expecting."

"That's . . . great news." Jasmine obviously had not yet been told that the Blue Pacific deal had fallen through. That there was no reason to sell her house, because she was not going to be moving to Texas after all, no specialized treatment for her son. "Jasmine, have you—"

"Got to go. The Randalls just arrived. See you Monday." The phone clicked before I had the chance to finish the sentence I didn't want to finish. How could I possibly tell her that, thanks to me, her last hope for her son had just vanished?

I knew that intellectually she wouldn't blame me for this—a business deal was no reason to prolong an engagement that was doomed to fail—but this had all been my idea. Selling the Blue Pacific Bed and Breakfast had never entered her mind. Until I suggested it two weeks ago.

It had been a quiet day at work, the bed-and-breakfast only three-quarters full, with most of the guests part of a big group from back east somewhere. The husbands left for golf early every morning, the wives a few hours later for shopping and trips to the spa. There was an unusual lack of workload.

"Look at this," Jasmine had said while looking at something on her computer screen.

I walked over to see a screen full of writing, including the headline: "Full-Time Program."

"What is it?"

"It's a center in Texas that focuses on treating autism. It's a totally different approach, but I just read an article about the success they are having. I'd give anything if I could take Collin there."

"Why don't you?" I supposed I already knew the answer.

"Can't afford it. The full-time treatment option would require me moving to Texas—at least for a year or so. I'd have to pay someone to replace me here. It wouldn't work."

I knew she was right. The costs for her son's therapy already were staggering. She couldn't possibly take the extra time off work and pay an employee to take her place. "Oh, Jasmine, I'm sorry." I stared at the screen, at the picture of a father lifting his smiling four-year-old over his head. A picture that parents of the severely autistic would give anything to attain. The problem was, Jasmine had already given more than she could afford.

Half an hour later, Steve walked into the office. "Greetings, ladies." He nodded toward Jasmine, who barely looked up from the computer, still lost in her impossible dream.

"What are you doing here?" I stood from behind my desk and walked toward him, already noticing the crease in his forehead. "You look tired. Rough day?"

"As of this second, it just got a lot better." He kissed my forehead and drew me into his arms.

"What was rough about it?" I nestled against his shoulder, the wool of his sports coat rough against my cheek.

"Will you two take it outside? Some people are trying to work in here." Jasmine's teasing sounded halfhearted at best. Steve pulled away from me and looked toward her, then back at me, a question in his eye.

I shrugged in that it's-a-long-story way and took his hand. "What *are* you doing here, by the way?"

"The investment group just had a meeting at Daniel's office. I figured since I was in Ventura anyway, I'd drop in and see my favorite office manager."

"Roger still pushing for a boutique for Phoebe?"

He nodded. "Looks like it just might happen. Of course Darin and Mike would never vote against him, and the rest of us can't come up with a better proposal."

"Who knows? She's a bright girl; she could probably make it work."

"You're probably right, and there's nothing bad I can say about her . . . except she's never held anything close to a job. Everything's just been given to her. It feels risky to devote that kind of money to such an unknown."

"I see what you mean." I nodded, thinking once again what a fortunate woman I was to have landed a man who had the foresight to start an investment group straight out of college. There were eight of them, and every month they contributed money into the coffer. So far they had invested in a restaurant, which one of the partners and his wife were running, and it was doing well. Then there had been a catering facility that a couple of the wives were heavily involved in.

I looked at Jasmine and blurted out before I even thought, "Why don't you buy the Blue Pacific?"

"I didn't know it was for sale." Steve looked at Jasmine, who was just now cluing into our conversation.

"I didn't, either." She leaned toward me, resting her chin on her hand. "Do tell."

"Think of it—if Steve's group bought this place, you could move to Texas, closer to that place you've been looking at. The cost of living would be so much less expensive, you could sell your house and buy a new one with money to spare. And you wouldn't have to worry about hiring someone to replace you. I'd be ready to step in."

Jasmine offered a slow, sad nod, chin still in hand. "That's the stuff dreams are made of." She straightened up in her chair and picked up a stack of papers from her in-box. "Too bad I'm a little too old and a little too wise to believe in dreams." She picked up a pencil and made a point of looking studious over the current papers.

"Maybe I'll look into it," Steve said softly, his head tilted to the side in thought. He grasped my hand. "Shall I go pick up Dylan from preschool so you can go home and get ready for a special dinner out?"

I smiled at him. "Pizza?"

"You got it."

We both laughed.

The laughter faded from my memory, leaving behind it a gaping hole of what had once been. My engagement to Steve, Jasmine's dream of a new hope. Yep, it had been my big mouth that started this deal, and now my big mouth—or my big fight with Steve—had ended it.

Wasn't it enough that my heart was broken? Did Jasmine need to be crushed in the process? This was going to destroy her. She wouldn't blame me—I knew she wouldn't—but how could she not? She'd have to at least a little.

I suddenly dreaded going into work on Monday. Surely she would know the truth by then. It was Steve's investment group who'd made the overtures, and it was their job to tell her the bad news. I couldn't imagine having to tell her myself, or sit there and listen to her excitement growing, knowing that it wasn't going to happen. Knowing that her dream was lost.

My phone rang again. Probably Jasmine remembering something else exciting— something else that would have been wonderful if I hadn't messed everything up.

"Hey, Gracie." My sister's voice was lacking any hint of its usual perk. So unlike the Jana I knew, but it had become all the more common in the last few months. Still, I was so happy to hear her voice. She was the one constant in my life.

"Hey. You sound tired. Hannah got another ear infection?"

"Just getting over one."

Dylan had been a mostly healthy baby, but I still had vivid memories of the few times he'd been sick and up all night. Jana had lived that over and over again with Hannah. "You've really been through more than your share lately, haven't you?"

"Yes. Yes I have." There was a grim determination in her voice. "Grace . . . I didn't mean to just drop this on you, but I don't think I can do this anymore." Her voice choked for a moment. "That's why I'm calling."

A fleeting fear shot through me that she was about to tell me she was leaving Rob and Hannah and getting away from it all. I knew better, because Jana never gave up on anything, but something had changed. "What do you mean?"

"Dad's having his surgery on Monday. You remember that, right?"

"Of course." My father was having his knee replaced on Monday. Routine kind of surgery, and since Dad and I didn't talk all that much, I hadn't given it much thought.

"Well, here's the thing. He is not supposed to be home alone for a couple of weeks after. He can't stay at my house because there are too many sunken rooms and steps he'd have to go up and down. I was planning on staying over there with him, but Hannah's been sick again. All her stuff is here. I checked with a few people, but nothing has come through and I just don't have the time or energy to look anymore. Gracie, it's your turn. You need to pick up some of the slack around here. I've got more than I can handle." Her words became choked by the end of the sentence.

I'm not sure which shocked me more—my superwoman sister's need for assistance, or the fact that she'd even think to ask me. It wouldn't take a genius to know this would not be a good idea.

"Jana, I can't just take off work. I won't have any more vacation time coming to me until after September. And I think we both know that Dad and I in the same house for a couple of weeks would likely not be a pleasant mix."

"Gracie, I'm exhausted and I know this is going to come out harsh, but at this point I'm done denying the obvious. That's the problem we've got here. Every time things get unpleasant you turn and run, leaving the rest of us to deal with your part of the load. I've done it for years because I love you, but Gracie, I'm burned out and I'm fed up. You need to decide. Do you want to be part of this family or not?"

Stunned couldn't begin to cover what I felt. I'd never heard Jana speak so forcefully to anyone, especially not me. "Of course I'm part of the family. It's just—"

"Then start acting like it."

"Jana, I just don't think I can—" Hannah started crying in the background.

"I guess that means I can't count on you for help. Thanks anyway." My sister hung up the phone. Jana—the queen of sweetness and all things southern.

I'd never felt so alone in all my life.

• • •

"Um, Jasmine, I need to take a couple of weeks off work. Family emergency." My tongue was so dry, I could barely say the words into the phone.

"Oh no. What's happened? Is everything all right?"

No. Nothing is all right. Everything is ruined. "Yes, it's just that my father is having surgery on Monday, and my sister can't really stay with him afterward because my niece is sick. They just need me back there."

"Of course, if you need to go, then you should go. Emergency surgery is definitely something you need family around for."

I didn't feel overly terrible about not correcting the misconception. Of course she assumed it was an emergency, because she'd heard nothing whatsoever about my father's surgery until now. But in truth, there was an emergency. Just not the kind she thought it was. It was the patch-things-up-at-home-while-avoiding-my-boss-whose-life-I'd-just-ruined kind of emergency. The round-trip tickets at this late hour would cost more than I could afford, but at this moment, it was the least of my worries.

"Do what you need to do, but get back here as soon as you can, okay? With all this other stuff going on, I really need all the help I can get."

"I think Dad's going to need me for a couple of weeks, but I'll come back as soon as possible."

"A couple of weeks?" Jasmine choked and coughed for a few seconds. "Wow. That's longer than I'd thought. But yeah . . . you should go help with your father."

"Thanks, Jasmine. I'm . . . sorry."

After I hung up, I thought about what Jana had said. About my running away every time things got unpleasant. Well, that's not what I was doing here. I was going toward home, toward the unpleasant, to help my family. The fact that I was leaving unpleasant behind was just a coincidence. That's all it was.

Chapter 2

His outline was barely visible on the dark front porch, but I knew he was there. A single point of red fire glowing from the end of his ever-present cigarette. I turned into the driveway, and for just a brief second my headlights slid across him, then skittered away.

Oh, how I wanted to turn the car around and drive in the opposite direction. But I didn't. This was only for two weeks. How bad could it be?

I already knew the answer. Downright unbearable.

Still, this was something I was obligated to see through. I was going to prove to Jana that she was wrong about me, and if staying with my father for fourteen days accomplished that, then so be it. Best to get on with it. Even as I climbed from the car, I would be lying if I didn't admit that a large part of me hoped that things would go well enough for me to perhaps leave a few days early. Maybe . . .

The faint glow of the TV from inside the house blinked an eerie shadow as he stood and limped around the porch, his feet clomping against the wooden slats in an uneven cadence. I had parked next to the steps and as I walked closer, everything within me wanted to turn and run. Yet I couldn't. I was propelled forward.

There was so much I could say to him—the man who killed my mother—but I wouldn't voice any of those things. Instead, I came to a stop a few feet in front of him.

"Hello, Dad."

"Hello, Grace." His voice rumbled from years as a smoker, but otherwise he looked unchanged. Until I looked closer. There was pain in his eyes. I could tell it hurt just to stand. He sized me up for a minute before he asked, "Where's Dylan?"

"Backseat. Asleep."

"You planning on leaving him out here all night, or you going to bring him in?"

"I haven't decided yet." It was sarcasm, and as much as we both knew it, we also both knew there was more than a little truth to it. "I think I'll bring in the luggage first." I pulled Dylan's duffel from the trunk and tossed it on the wraparound porch, then dragged my suitcase up the three steps until I stood beside my father. "What time do they want us at the hospital Monday morning?"

"Oh, they want me there at seven, which is the most ridiculous thing I've ever heard of. I bet they won't even think about taking me back to surgery until ten or eleven. Don't know why I have to get there so early." He reached down and picked up Dylan's duffel.

"I can get that."

"So can I." He tucked it under his arm and walked toward the house.

"You're having surgery in two days. You shouldn't be carrying heavy stuff around."

"I'm having surgery on my knee. I'm not carrying anything with my knee."

"Well, it's all we need right now for you to throw your back out or something like that, just because you're being stubborn."

My father snorted. "I see you haven't lost your talent for arguing since I saw you last."

"There's a pot calling a kettle black." I rolled my suitcase toward the back door, taking a final glance toward the backseat of my rental. My son was still asleep in his car seat.

I walked into my old bedroom. It seemed so much the same as before—because of course nothing had changed. Nothing material, at least.

I heard what I assumed to be the thud of

Dylan's duffel as it hit the hardwood floor on the other side of the wall and figured I should make certain Dad hadn't gone down with it. I opened the door to the adjoining bathroom, walked across the pink-tiled floor, and into Jana's old room. I gasped when I saw the bed.

The pink quilt that had covered that bed for as long as I could remember had been replaced with a cheap bedspread emblazoned with brightly colored race cars. I looked at my father. "What happened here?"

He swiped a dismissive gesture in the general direction of the bed. "I saw this on sale at Wal-Mart the other day and picked it up. I didn't want any grandson of mine sleeping under pink flowers."

And I don't want any son of mine sleeping under some redneck obsession with speed and recklessness. Somehow, I managed to hold back the retort that was screaming to get out. These two weeks were going to be long enough without starting out with a fight in the first five minutes. "I'm sure he'll appreciate the thought."

"Of course he will." He paused for just a moment. "Unless you've turned him into one of those soft California sissy-boys like they show on the news all the time."

Oh boy. This was going to be hard. Really hard.

My father hobbled over to his chair and settled in and tried to start a conversation with Dylan, who was being extra clingy. "It's been a while since we've seen each other, hasn't it? What have you been doing since you were here last? Swimming? Soccer?"

Just then, the front door burst open, and Jana launched herself across the room toward us. "There's my sweet Dylan. Oh, my precious, come here and give Aunt Jana a hug."

Dylan shrank back into me. "No!"

"He fell asleep on the ride here from the airport and just woke up, didn't you, sweetie?" I rubbed the back of his head with my left hand and reached for my sister with the right. She looked amazing, tired but thrilled. Motherhood, so long in coming, definitely agreed with her.

She took the hand and squeezed. "Thanks for coming. Sorry I got so . . ."

"You're welcome and I'm sorry you had to." There were still issues the two of us needed to talk about—that much was obvious—but at least we were starting in a positive place.

"Yeah, Jana, and now you've gone and frightened your poor nephew to death. No wonder Grace never comes to visit." Her husband, Rob, laughed from behind her as he lugged the baby carrier through the front door. Just over six feet and broad shouldered, he had an accountant's haircut but a comedian's twinkle to his eye. He smiled at me. "Hey, Grace."

"Hey, yourself." I could scarcely breathe with

Dylan's arms wrapped so tightly around my neck. "Now, get that niece of mine over here right now so I can get a look at her."

Jana was sitting beside us now, her face barely an inch from Dylan's. "I'm sorry, sweetie. I really didn't mean to frighten you." Her voice was the perfect pitch, all honey and sweetness, and usually charmed anyone. Given the way he was squeezing the breath out of me, Dylan was one of the few remaining holdouts.

"Don't leave me, Mama." He put his head on the other shoulder, farther away from Jana, who smiled a sympathetic smile, but the look of determination did not diminish one bit from her face.

"Really, Dylan, it's okay. I'm your Auntie Jana, remember?"

"No!"

Rob came to stand in front of us. I found it amusing that in spite of the fact he'd come in lugging baby and diaper bag, his khaki pants and blue broadcloth shirt remained as unwrinkled as ever. "I don't blame you, kiddo. She scares me, too. I'm Uncle Rob, the normal one, and this is your cousin, Hannah Rose."

"Hannah Rose?" Dylan lifted his head and looked at the sweet bundle of pink in the carrier. "That's Hannah Rose? I've seen lots of pictures of her."

"I'm sure you have." Rob smiled and squatted

before him. He reached down and unbuckled his daughter and lifted her into his arms. "Your aunt Jana's been burning up the camera's memory cards faster than we can download them."

Dylan leaned forward and smiled at her. "Hi."

"Brrrbrr." She began to make a razzing noise, complete with plenty of spit.

"She's funny." Dylan slid out of my lap and knelt on the floor. "Hey, Hannah Rose, hey, girl."

Several minutes later, Rob, Dylan, and Hannah Rose were enveloped in their own little world of funny faces, noises, and excess salivation. Jana looked at the scene. "Isn't this exactly what I've spent my whole life dreaming about?" She sighed a deep, contented sigh. Only the dark circles under her eyes gave away the fact that everything wasn't perfect. "Isn't she beautiful?"

"Yes, she is," I said.

"Just like her father," Rob deadpanned and braved a swat from Jana.

I was glad in that moment that I'd decided to come here. Perhaps this trip might be just what we needed to heal my little broken family. I watched Dylan beside Hannah, animated in a way I'd never seen. I hated for it to end, even when I knew it was getting late.

"Dylan, let's brush your teeth and get your jammies on. It's time to start unwinding."

"I don't want to." Dylan whined all the way

back to his room. "I want to play with Hannah Rose."

"It's her bedtime, too, but you can come back and play with her for just a few minutes after you're ready for bed. Now, come on, let's get you moving." I looked over at Jana. "Be right back."

I led my son through my room and into our shared bathroom. "I'll go get your jammies and toothbrush. You go ahead and start getting undressed." Dylan usually moved at a snail's pace, so I knew he would likely remain fully dressed when I returned. I walked into the room and unzipped his duffel, knowing I'd put his pajamas and toiletry bag right on top for just such a moment as this.

"Wow! Cool bedspread!"

I turned to answer my son, but he raced past me and was soon bouncing on the bed. "Awesome. Vroom, vroom."

I tossed his Thomas the Tank Engine pajamas toward him. "Now put these on and get your teeth brushed. Hurry up. Hannah Rose is waiting."

"These are baby p.j.'s." He grumbled as he pulled the crew neck over his head. "I want race cars, just like my bedspread."

"You don't need race cars."

"Do too. Jason has skateboards on his."

And Jason was going to grow up to be a thug,

just like his big brother. "You like Thomas, remember? We rented some DVDs just last week."

"I was littler then." He jumped to the ground, and in truth the pajamas were a couple of inches too short for him now. "Where's my toothbrush? I want to get back to Hannah Rose."

It was the fastest I'd ever seen him get ready for anything.

After we'd finished brushing his teeth, he ran into the living room and dropped onto the floor beside Rob, right on the edge of Hannah's blanket. "Hey there, hey there," he spoke in high-pitched baby talk that I found to be adorable.

"Where's Jana and Dad?" I asked Rob.

He nodded toward the stairs. "Jana wanted to make certain he'd followed her directions explicitly in his packing, and well, you know how she is. She's up there making him show her that he really did it right."

I started up the front stairs. Memories of my childhood—sitting on these stairs, sliding down these stairs, lurking about outside my parents' room—assaulted me. I missed my mother every bit as much now as I did when she died seven years ago. Maybe more. I wanted to share the joys of motherhood with her, ask her opinions, enjoy the cute stories that only a mother can truly appreciate. When I got to the top of the stairs, the bedroom door was open. I heard my father's voice. "He seems pretty whiny, and until y'all got here he was holding on to a stuffed bear, like a girl with a doll or something. I hope she's not turning that boy into a fraidycat sissy. I mean, look at that hair. He looks like a girl; it's no wonder. Maybe you can try to talk a little sense into her."

I stopped just short of the bedroom door, holding my breath and waiting for Jana's reply. "Oh, Dad, I wouldn't go that far."

This was not exactly the defense I had hoped for from my sister. From any reasonable mother, for that matter. At this point I'd heard more than enough. I retraced a couple of steps, then walked noisily toward the door and walked through as if I'd just arrived and hadn't heard a thing. "Hey, you two. How's the suitcase look?"

Several wavy wisps of Jana's hair had come loose from her ponytail as she'd bent over Dad's suitcase. She straightened up, looking a bit embarrassed, I thought, brushed them out of the way, and shook her head. "All I can say is, it's a good thing I checked."

"Hmph."

"You'll thank me later."

"Right."

The three of us made our way back down the stairs, Dad taking one at a time. We found Dylan on the blanket beside Hannah, tickling her chin with his finger.

"Hey, Grace and Dylan, I'm working in Hannah's class tomorrow at church," Jana said. "Do you two want to help me? We could spend some time together, just hanging out."

Rob looked up. "Tomorrow's a good day for it, too. Our pastor is out of town and Deacon Ross is doing the preaching." He scratched his chin. "Maybe I'll help in the nursery, too." Rob tickled Hannah's tummy and she giggled.

"Let me try, Uncle Rob." Dylan reached over to his cousin's stomach and soon she was giggling and snorting. In spite of the cuteness of the moment, my earlier optimism about somehow rebuilding this family had started to fade.

Jana was watching me with expectant eyes. If taking care of Dad was the first test, going to church seemed like the second. I wondered briefly how many more she would arrange for me. How many times I'd need to prove myself to her.

"We'll be there," I said.

The prodigal sister returned.

Chapter 3

"Look at me, Hannah Rose." Dylan's voice bounced off the pink-and-blue-striped wallpaper of the church nursery. He made a face, turned a somersault, then made another face—anything he thought might get a giggle out of his baby cousin. He was proving rather successful.

"Da da da da," Hannah gurgled.

"Hey, Mama, I think she's trying to say Dylan," he called over to me.

Jana grinned down from the rocker where she sat giving Kelsey Whyte a bottle. "You know what? I think so, too. It's amazing." She waited until Dylan turned away before she whispered to me, "Better not tell Rob that Da-da is actually Dylan. I think he'd be upset."

I laughed. "Yeah, the truth hurts sometimes." I watched Dylan's animated antics around the blanket. "I've never seen him like this. When he's around Hannah it's like a new, confident Dylan emerges from beneath his usual shy self."

"Thanks for helping me in the nursery today."

"I'm glad you asked." All morning long I'd been trying to get the courage to start a deeper conversation but hadn't yet found it. Until the phone call a couple of days ago, it had never entered my mind how Jana felt. But for now, we were doing what my family tended to do . . . carrying on surface conversations, pretending like nothing had happened. Jana and I would have lots of time to talk next week while Dad was in the hospital.

"It's always good to have an extra set of hands when working with babies." She looked toward

Dylan. "Or two. He's so cute with them, and I can't believe how much he has grown."

"Yeah, way too much, if you ask me. It's amazing how fast it goes by. You keep that in mind and enjoy this time while it's here."

"Believe me, I am. I am." Her voice, its cherubic sweetness, was intensified. "She's such a gift, I'm not going to take one single minute for granted." Jana and Rob had spent years and thousands of dollars, and more heartbreak than most people could bear, in an effort to become parents.

I looked at Hannah's tiny fingers, her chubby little cheeks, and love welled up in me with the same intensity I felt toward my own son. "I'm so glad to finally see my beautiful niece in person."

"I wish you could have come sooner." Was there an inflection of accusation in her tone? She had asked me to come after Hannah was born and "help her figure this baby stuff out." Jana had always been so self-assured, I'd never really considered that she might have been serious. Until now. I began to wonder just how many times I'd let her down over the last few years.

"I . . . wish I could have, too."

Jana put Kelsey into a bouncy seat and began to twirl a butterfly on the bar in front of her. "So how're things going with you and Dad?"

I looked at my sister's too-innocent face. The

35

usual wavy strands of blond hair had escaped from her ponytail and danced around her eyes as if they, too, were enjoying the joke.

"Here, I'll do it for her, Aunt Jana." Dylan dove into position and began to simultaneously bounce Kelsey and twirl the toys on the rack. Kelsey cackled and Dylan worked all the harder.

"How do you *think* it's going?" I asked, trying to keep my voice low enough that Dylan wouldn't hear too much, but not so low as to make him think there was a secret and maybe he should pay attention.

He did glance my way for just a second before turning back to his charge. "Bouncy, bouncy, bouncy," he singsonged as Kelsey cooed.

I leaned closer to Jana and whispered, "If he tells me my son needs a haircut one more time, I swear I'll . . ." Truth was, I didn't know what I'd do. Probably nothing, as usual.

She looked toward the door, the dark circles beneath her eyes not quite concealed under her makeup. "I wish Steve could have come with you. He and Rob get along so well."

"Yes, they do." I swallowed hard and pointed at my empty left finger. "Unfortunately, I can't say the same about the two of us."

"Oh, Gracie." Jana put her hand to her throat. "I can't believe I didn't notice that."

I couldn't believe it, either. The words *Jana* and *details* were practically synonymous. The poor thing really was exhausted. "You've got a lot on your mind."

"Yes I do, but still . . ."

I shrugged. "You've never seen me wearing it, so it wouldn't seem that strange to you that it is missing, I suppose."

She was shaking her head as if trying to return things back to their proper order. She reached over and took my hand then. "I am sorry. I had no idea. I wouldn't have called and gone off on—"

I squeezed her hand. "I'm glad you did. We need to talk through some things during this visit. I'm just glad you told my oblivious self that there was a problem."

"Obviously, I fall into that oblivious category, too, although I'd never realized just how much so until this very moment. What happened? When did it happen?" Her voice had picked up a bit of its usual perk now. She was Jana the mender, ready to tackle my problems. It was good to see a bit of the old spark.

Knowing that she would pry the answers out of me eventually, it was likely better to go ahead and get it done with. I had finally told Dylan about the breakup, but I hadn't shared details. At this point he was occupied with Kelsey, so it seemed safe enough to talk. "Monday night."

Surprise overtook her. I knew what was coming, so I waved her off.

"I didn't tell you because you would've let me stay in California. And as for what happened, well, let's just say I'm just not sure . . . I don't know if I can trust him. It makes me nervous." I rubbed the back of my left hand. "You know me, when I get nervous, I tend to get a little crazy."

"You tend to bolt, you mean. I played right into your hands, didn't I? When I called and demanded that you come out here, it gave you the excuse you needed to run away from the problem."

I shook my head. "No, I'm not running away from the problem." Not the one she was thinking of, anyway. "There's nothing left to run from. It's over." The words hurt; it was as if saying them made the situation undeniably real. Still, I found myself somewhat comforted that I was finally having this conversation with my sister.

"I don't believe that. Steve loves you; anyone could see that."

"I messed everything up and I don't know what to do about it."

"So you were mean and downright ornery?"

"I wouldn't go that far."

"Yes, you would. You have. If it were anything less than that, you would have already told me about it." Cuteness. That is Jana's quality that is the downfall of everyone around her. I looked at those big blue eyes, her hair with just the right amount of wave to it that it always looked a little messy, and her dimpled cheeks that were nothing short of angelic.

"You know me entirely too well."

"Of course I do." She looked smug.

"Hey, Paisha, what ya doing?" Dylan moved across the floor to the next baby.

Paisha was wearing pink pants, a pink sweater, and a pink hat. She was up on all fours, every ounce of pinkness rocking back and forth, poised on the brink of crawling.

Dylan knelt hands and knees beside her. "You just put one hand out in front. Like this, see?" He moved his hand out. "Now, move your leg forward, put that leg on the other side so you don't fall over. See?" He moved his left knee forward. "Now, just repeat."

Paisha rocked all the harder. "Hee, hee." She gurgled.

"That's right, you're almost doing it. Now, just pick up your hand, see." Dylan reached over and put his left hand under her stomach, to hold her up, then with his right hand, he picked up her right arm and moved it forward and set it back down. She propelled herself forward and fell, in spite of Dylan's steadying hand.

"Come on, let's try again. You almost had it, I know you can do it." Dylan had his face only inches from hers.

Paisha looked at him for a moment, a sort of grin on her face, then rolled over on her back and started playing with pink-sock-ensconced feet. Crawling lesson over.

Emma Sanders began to cry, so I picked her up out of the baby swing and rocked her slowly back and forth. "What's the matter now, sweetheart?"

Jana picked up Ryan and began to rock him, as well. "Start back at the beginning. What exactly happened?" She spoke in baby talk, the way most women do when they talk to babies, and although she never looked away from Ryan, I knew the words were directed toward me.

I glanced toward Dylan, who was now busy following Hunter as he commando-crawled toward the back wall. I whispered, "He'd been at the conference in Los Angeles all day. I was wondering if he was going to stop by for dinner on his way back to Santa Barbara that night, so I called several times. It went straight to voice mail, which is not surprising, since he was probably in a meeting. I never left a message, but he always calls me when he sees my caller ID on the missed calls. He never did.

"So, just as I was starting dinner, I called one last time. It was on the fourth ring and I was just about to hang up when he finally answered. There was a lot of noise in the background.

"I said, 'Hi. It's me. I've been trying to reach you.'

"He said something to the effect of, 'Really? I

guess I haven't even looked at my missed calls.' His voice got really quiet. 'It's been a crazy day, I'll tell you that.' "

She waited.

"And then I heard people cheer and a woman's voice asking for some peanuts. He was at a Dodgers game. With another woman."

"Oh, Grace." She patted my hand, but then her eyes narrowed. "So he confessed."

"He said a bunch of people from the conference were at the game. Including Daria, this insanely beautiful client of his. He got defensive when I asked what other people were there, and we yelled some—me mostly—and hung up."

I looked down at Emma, whose eyes were closing with each downward stroke of the rocker. "Needless to say, the conversation the next day did not go well. He was mad at me for being so jealous all the time; I was mad at him for being . . . well, I don't know, untrustworthy, I guess."

"You've been together for a couple of years. Has he done anything that would lead you to believe you can't trust him?" Jana bounced Ryan on her knees.

I shook my head. "Not that I know of. But the point is, I'm perfectly fine on my own. If we were to get married, if Steve really became part of Dylan's life, and then he decided he was happier without us, well, I just couldn't stand it. I couldn't watch my son go through something

41

like that. It nearly crushed me as a twenty-year-old. How can I expect a child to survive something like that?"

"Just because Chase was a jerk doesn't mean every man is. Rob and I have been together through some really hard times. I mean, you know, you were there—at least on the other end of the phone line for hours at a time—during all the infertility treatment and the miscarriages. You know how hormonal I got. He was a rock through the entire time."

"You"—I stood with Emma and carried her to the nearest crib—"did manage to land one of the only perfect men around. Unfortunately, that took one of them off the market and greatly decreased the odds for the rest of us."

"Perfect? No. But wonderful, yes. I think there are still a few more out there. In fact, I'd go out on a limb here and say that Steve definitely qualifies."

"Maybe he did. But, like I said, that doesn't matter anymore. It's over."

Chapter 4

"If you're going for a walk, hurry back. That boy of yours wakes up kinda whiny. I don't blame you, necessarily. That's what happens when you raise a boy with no men in the house. They just don't learn to man up."

The last thing I needed on a Monday morning was this from my father. "Man up? You think a four-year-old needs to learn to man up?" How my eyeballs remained inside my face at this point, I don't know, because my entire head was about to spontaneously combust.

"I didn't mean it that way, exactly. What I meant was, if there was a man in the house, Dylan would be a lot less emotional, too. Wouldn't be carrying that stuffed bear around with him."

Not quite six in the morning, and I'd already listened to half an hour's worth of Dad's tirades against politicians, fat-cat doctors, and most anyone who wasn't like Dad. That's when I'd come up with the idea of going for a quick walk. I'd decided I needed to get out of here if I were going to play the role of the caring daughter at the hospital today. I pushed back from the table. "I'll keep my walk short." What I really wanted to do was grab my son, race out the door, and never come back.

Twelve more days, only twelve more days. I needed to do this. I was going to prove to Jana that I didn't always bolt when things got hard. And I didn't. I'd kept my son, in spite of the fact that there were other options available, and I'd done a good job of raising him so far. That should've counted for something.

"Mama, I don't feel so good." Dylan's voice

came from the hallway behind me. It was extra high-pitched, and I didn't have to wonder what my dad thought of it.

I turned around, surprised to see that Dylan's face did seem perhaps a bit flushed. "Oh, Dylan, what feels bad?" I sat back down and extended my arms toward my son, chancing a quick glance toward my father.

His expression was every bit as smug and disapproving as I expected. He looked from me, to Dylan, to Frederick—Dylan's bear—and I could read his thoughts now as easily as if he'd spoken out loud. *Whiner.*

Dylan crawled into my lap and laid his head on my shoulder. "Everything. Well, my nose is runny and . . ." He started coughing.

Great. A bad cold was all we needed at this point. "I knew I shouldn't have let you play in that sandbox yesterday." I thought of the little plastic turtle. It had a lid, but even if it was always covered, kids with all their germs digging into the same small bit of sand—well, it couldn't be very hygienic. I felt his forehead. "You don't feel terribly hot. You probably just caught a cold. Let's go get you some juice. Does your tummy feel okay?"

"I think so."

I removed him from my lap and set him on the seat beside mine, careful not to look at my father again. I went to the refrigerator and pulled out the organic apple juice I'd had to drive all the way to Lawrenceburg yesterday to find. "You drink a little of this, okay?"

"'Kay." He leaned over and laid his head on my father's shoulder. "Hi, Grandpa."

"Hey there, little man. Having trouble getting in gear this morning?"

"You know what, Dylan? You probably shouldn't sit so near your grandfather. We don't want him to catch your cold. After all, he's having surgery on his knee today."

Dylan slid over, folded his arms on the table, and rested his forehead against them. "I'm tired."

I was ready for my dad to spit out something about manning up, and how he'd already slept half the day away, but he didn't. Instead, he looked at Dylan with concern in his eyes, then looked up at me. "What's the matter with him?"

"A bad cold, I guess." I put my hand on Dylan's forehead again. "He's maybe a little warm. Do you have a thermometer?"

"I'm sure there's one around here somewhere. Your mom was always and forever checking y'alls temperatures." He stared out in the distance as if seeing the scene. "Look up in that cabinet above the sink. I'd bet that's where it is."

I pulled a chair from the kitchen table and climbed up on it to see what might be inside the cabinet. Memories flashed through my mind of watching my mother standing on this very chair, rummaging through this same cabinet, while saying things like, "Oh, darlin', don't you worry. You'll be feeling better in no time," or, "Judging from the look of that knee, I'd say you slide into first base with more effort than anyone out there." I missed the comforting sweetness of her voice. Jana had inherited it, along with our mother's wispy blond hair, leaving me with Dad's gravelly speech and stick-straight black hair. Those were the only two things we had in common.

Inside the cabinet, there were several dusty prescription bottles, along with some long-expired Tylenol and Aspirin. Toward the back, there was a small wooden bowl. I pulled it out and climbed down so I could more easily view the contents. I found a nice supply of Band-Aids, ancient Neosporin, and what looked like a black plastic pen. I unscrewed the cap and pulled out an old mercury-filled glass thermometer. "You know what? Maybe this afternoon I'll run to the pharmacy and pick him up some Echinacea, lemon juice, and honey. While I'm there, I'll get a digital thermometer."

"What's wrong with that one?"

"It's got mercury in it."

"So what? It's inside a tube of glass."

"Well, if that glass breaks, it's a very big deal."

"I seem to recall breaking a few of those things over the years. Only problem I remember was it was hard to clean up, 'cause it all sort of came apart in little liquid balls. What do you think is going to happen? He's going to lean down and lick it up? I tell you what. Every single kid you were raised around and went to school with had their temperature taken with one of these thermometers. Far as I know, they're all alive to tell the tale."

"Yes, and I guess we should drive around without seat belts and air bags just because that's the way you used to do it. Just because I never had a problem with a broken mercury thermometer doesn't mean that Dylan won't."

"Ah, parents are so uptight about those things these days." My dad leaned back in his chair and rubbed his right knee. "When you were little, we let kids be kids. We didn't run around with antibacterial wipes, and we gave you vegetables from gardens that had fertilizer in them. Kids today, they're growing up soft."

"So you think we should pump our foods full of chemicals and smear our kids with germs?"

Dad ignored me.

"Bah. It's just like those narcotics they'll send home with me from the hospital. You don't have to be a particularly smart person to know that those things can be addictive. Don't mean I'm not going to take something when I need it just because there's a little risk. That's what we need more of these days, a little common sense and self-restraint."

I set Dylan's juice on the table beside him. It was in a blue plastic cup shaped like a snail, with a straw coming up from the back of his shell. Dylan didn't lift his head.

"Hey, darling, do you think you could eat a little toast? We've got to get Grandpa to the hospital for his surgery here in a little while."

Dylan looked up. "Okay. Will Hannah Rose be at the hospital, too?"

"Yes, she will. But you know what? Since you're not feeling well, you need to stay away from her today, okay? We don't want her getting sick."

"Lord knows that kid has been sick enough."

This was a fact I knew well. Hannah had been plagued with colic for the first few months; now it was recurrent ear infections.

"I can play with her, right? As long as I don't get in her face?"

I turned toward Dylan and pulled his hair back from his cheek. "You can dance around like you did yesterday and see if you can make her laugh again, but you can't touch her or get near her. Okay?"

"Okay, Mama." He put his head down on the table again.

I reached forward and put my hand on his forehead, even though I'd already done so several times. "You know what? I think I'll go get some liquid Tylenol out of my carryon just in case." I never gave Dylan medication unless I knew for certain there was a valid reason to do so. But, with no safe thermometer, and my father's impending surgery, I figured this morning might be the time to bend the rules.

Chapter 5

Jana, Rob, and Hannah were already at the hospital when we arrived. It was still not quite light outside, and they stood waiting just inside the sliding glass doors of the main entrance.

Rob was in his usual dark suit for work at the bank, looking neatly pressed and completely at ease, even while holding Hannah under one arm and the diaper bag on the other shoulder. He smiled when he saw us, as Jana rushed over, a concerned look on her face. "So, Dad, are you all ready?"

My father nodded toward the small duffel in his hand. "Yeah, got my knee packed and ready to go."

"What about your list of current medications? And the rest of the items I suggested you pack—the ones I wrote on that sticky note for you?"

"Yes, I got it all. It's plain ridiculous, if you ask me. Don't know why I have to bother to pack a bag. They'll make me wear one of those ugly hospital gowns the entire time, and they always give you a little kit with a toothbrush and toothpaste. Nothing else I can't do without for a few days."

"Da-ad." Jana's southern drawl always made two syllables out of the word. This time, she said it with such exaggerated rebuke that it was almost three.

He held up his left hand in surrender. "Yes, I've got everything on that list you gave me."

"That's what I like to hear." Jana looked at me and shook her head. "Honestly, I'm glad you're here. I'm tired of being the nagger."

"I'm tired of that, too." Rob kissed the top of Jana's head as he said it. "One more reason Hannah and I are glad that her favorite auntie is here."

"Well, too bad for you. Since Grace will be taking over Dad-nagging duty for a couple of weeks, I'll have extra nagging saved up for you." She stuck out her tongue in a playful way. I could only hope my being here was good for their marriage in some way.

"Great, just great." Rob looked down at his daughter, who was resting in the crook of his arm. "Did you hear that, Hannah? Things are going to get pretty bad for us." He lifted her up and blew raspberries against her stomach.

She squealed in delight. "Da-da."

"That's right, I'm your Da-da, yes I am." He blew against her stomach again, resulting in an all-out chuckle.

"Hannah Rose, you're funny." Dylan made his own razzing sound.

I put a restraining hand on his shoulder. "Remember, honey, don't get too close."

"Oh, Mama, I feel much better now." This statement confirmed to me that he must truly have been a bit warm. The Tylenol had kicked in, and he was more or less back to his old self.

"Are you not feeling well, darling?" Jana looked toward Dylan with concern.

I ruffled his hair. "Nothing terrible. He woke up with a little cough and runny nose this morning, maybe a tad warm. I told him to keep a safe distance from Hannah just in case."

Dylan's chin began to quiver. "I feel better, honest. I want to play with Hannah Rose."

Rob leaned forward so he and Dylan were face-to-face. "You've been such a good cousin to Hannah ever since you got here. Jana was just telling me about how good you were with the kids in the nursery yesterday, and now you're being so responsible about not making Hannah sick. I'm thinking we might have to hire you as a nanny once you get all better."

"What's a nanny?" Dylan asked.

"Someone that helps take care of kids, just like you've been doing since you've been here. If you stayed at our house all the time, Hannah would be well taken care of, and Jana and I might even be able to have a conversation from time to time, without being interrupted by this noisemaker." He touched Hannah's nose.

"I'll do it. Can I, Mom?" He looked at me, his brown hair hanging a little too low over his eyes.

"Honey, I think we live a bit too far away for that. But you can be her special helper while we're in Shoal Creek—at least after we're sure you're feeling better. How about that?"

"Aww, okay."

Jana took hold of my father's left arm. "It's time to get Daddy back into pre-op. Rob, you'll take the kids into the waiting room. Right?"

"Aye, aye, *mon capitaine.*" He saluted Jana, then looked toward Dylan. "All right, Sergeant Master Dylan, we have our marching orders. We are to assemble the troops—well, the troop—and remove her from behind these enemy lines."

"Yes, sir. Let's get this space ranger safely into her home galaxy and away from the forces of the evil emperor Zurg." Dylan offered back his best Buzz Lightyear salute.

Rob looked a bit confused at the cosmic talk but didn't let it stop him. "Right. You must be the advanced scouting ranger who leads us forward. See that sign right there? The one that says surgery waiting area and the arrow?"

Dylan nodded. "The blue one that starts with the letter *S*?" Dylan was proud of the fact that he knew his letters already. So was I.

"That's right. You've got to look for signs

exactly like that and follow the arrows until we arrive at the designated location."

"Follow me." Dylan marched down the hall in his most dignified, soldierly walk.

Rob followed behind him, then turned to call over his shoulder, "Don't worry about us. I'll keep them both under control."

None of us had a clue just how out of control things were going to get.

"I wonder what Rob and the kids are up to?" Jana said a few hours later as we sat in the post-op waiting room. She looked toward the door for the hundredth time since we'd arrived.

"I'm sure he has them well under control." I laughed. "Or not. Perhaps Dylan has tied him up somewhere, and even now he and Hannah are making a break for that new ice-cream parlor downtown."

Jana laughed outright. "You say that as a joke, but it doesn't sound that far off from you at that age."

"Hey, I wasn't that bad." Even as I said it, I knew I kind of was.

"Flibberdijibbit. That's what Mom used to call you. Remember?" Jana bobbed her head. "That pretty much sums it up."

"I believe Dad's term was more like delinquent." My mother was the only person who ever believed in me—really believed in me. To

Dad I was just someone who was never quite enough of anything—not driven enough, not serious enough, not hardworking enough.

"I think a few of your teenage stunts added several grays to his hair, that's for sure."

"Not my fault. Teenage rebellion was the only subject where I could reach my true potential. I never could measure up to my big sister in any other area, so I figured I might as well have some fun. No one should be forced to walk in the shadow of such glowing perfection."

"Bah." Jana made a dismissive gesture with her left hand. "You have never not measured up to anyone, let alone me."

"Spoken like a painfully modest valedictorian."

"Mrs. Graham?" A man in blue surgical scrubs entered the waiting room.

"Yes." Jana and I both answered at once, not bothering to correct our names.

He came and sat across from us. "Your father is out of surgery. Everything went according to plan. I'm very pleased at the outcome. Given how bad his knee had gotten, I think he will begin to see significantly improved mobility and comfort almost immediately."

"That's great." Jana nodded. "Can we go see him now?"

"He'll be in recovery for another hour or so." He stood. "They'll let you know as soon as they are ready to move him to a room."

"Thank you, Dr. James." Jana watched him walk out the door, then turned toward me, arms folded.

"Okay, maybe I had you in grade-point average, but that was the only way. You were always the one everybody wanted to be around. The popular girl. I'll bet if Dylan tried to pull half the stuff you did, you'd have an all-out meltdown."

"It's a different world out in California, Jana. It's not Shoal Creek. He could get swallowed up out there. I just want to raise him as best I can. Teach him the value of being healthy and safe."

"Of getting a good education so he can be a productive citizen," Jana said in a mock gruff voice as she leaned forward to slam her fist on the magazine table.

I burst out laughing. She was doing a pretty amazing impersonation of my father—using the exact same words and motions that had been shouted at me time and time again. Then it occurred to me—she was also doing an imitation of me. I was becoming like the one person I never wanted to be like.

No. It couldn't be true.

Could it?

I stood up and stretched as though I hadn't a care about anything. "Let's go see if we can find Rob and the kids. He probably needs a break about now."

• • •

I awoke to a dark room and the song "Paperback Writer" blaring through the darkness. I had no idea where I was or what was happening, but the faint glow of my cell phone as it vibrated on the bedside table pulled me into action. I reached for it out of instinct. "Hello?"

"Check your email." The voice on the other end of the phone sounded excited.

"Huh? Who is this?"

"Well, who do you think it is? Grace, are you okay?"

Reality was slowly returning, and with it came recognition. "Jasmine?"

"Yeah."

"What's the matter? What time is it?" Even as the questions slid off my tongue, I realized I knew what was the matter. She'd found out.

I'd spent the last couple of days trying to decide how I would handle this moment. Finally, I'd come to the conclusion that I should say as little as possible, and in the little bit that I did say, try to say nothing that would give away the fact that I knew this was coming.

"Nothing's the matter and it's nine thirty."

I reached for the lamp on the bedside table and flipped it on. "Jasmine, you do realize that nine thirty in California is eleven thirty here in Tennessee, right? I spent the day at the hospital with my father."

There was a bit of a pause. "Oops."

"What were you saying about my email?"

"My real estate agent has been talking to an agent near Houston. He sent me a dozen pictures of some of the prettiest houses you've ever seen. You were right about the housing prices. These places are perfect."

I rubbed my forehead, the truth of the situation here in full force now. "Don't you think it's better not to get your hopes up? What if your house doesn't sell for a while?"

"My agent says houses like mine are in the only price range moving. He expects it to sell. Especially now that I'm having the guest bathroom redone."

"You're what?"

"Well, not completely redone, but you remember how out-of-date it is, right?"

"Jasmine, can you afford this right now?" I knew the answer was no.

"He told me that a $10,000 investment now could mean a $20,000 increase in sales price. Seems like a good deal to me."

And it seemed like a disaster to me. "Jasmine, have you talked . . ." I couldn't finish the sentence. I didn't want to be the one to tell her that her dream was ruined. Not now, as groggy as I still felt. "I'm just saying you should use caution, you know, until things move a little more forward with the Blue Pacific deal."

"This is my one chance, Grace. And you're sounding like *I* usually sound, so lighten up."

"Well, you usually sound pretty smart."

"What has gotten into you? I think I'll let you get back to sleep and we'll talk again in the next day or two, when you're back to yourself." She hung up before I could reply.

I immediately dialed Steve's number. We hadn't talked since the breakup, and I wasn't quite sure even how to begin this conversation. It rang once, twice, three times, and I realized it was about to go to voice mail. Was he avoiding me? Or was he out somewhere on a work night? Having dinner with someone—Daria, perhaps? I shook my head to knock the same questions out of it that were always there and waited for the beep after his message.

"Hey, it's me. Listen, I ran into Martin a few days ago and he told me that the Blue Pacific deal is off. I'm in Tennessee right now, but I just talked to Jasmine. She has no idea. She has hired someone to remodel her bathroom to make her house sell for a better price. Could someone please let her know? Soon?" There was so much more I could have said. "I miss you. I'm sorry." But what was I sorry for? For doubting his intentions? Well, considering the fact that he wasn't answering his phone at nine thirty on a Monday night, those doubts seemed entirely justified. No, there was nothing more to be said between us, because nothing had changed.

The next morning Dylan seemed to feel a little worse. His cough grew more persistent; his temperature edged a bit higher. "Mama, can we please go over and play with Hannah Rose after we visit Grandpa in the hospital? I won't make her sick, I promise."

Dylan's eyes were enormous in normal situations, but when he did his full-blown, most sincere, most yearning expression, they were gigantic pools of liquid chocolate that even the hardest heart could not ignore. And I didn't want to ignore them. I wanted to spend time with my sister and my niece even more than Dylan did. But we couldn't. It wasn't responsible and I knew it.

Dad was well tended at the hospital; he could do without my visits for a day or two if necessary. So I had made the heartbreaking decision to stay home with Dylan until his fever went away.

Unfortunately, the day went by and then another with no improvement. I took to cleaning out my old closet and scrubbing kitchen cabinets just to pass the time. As I worked, I worried about Dad's knee—in spite of the encouraging updates Jana phoned in once or twice a day—and I wondered why Jasmine hadn't called me yet. Was she too devastated to talk about it? Did she blame me? I wanted so badly to pick up the phone and call her, but since I wasn't supposed to know anything, all I could do was to wait it out.

When Dad arrived home from the hospital late Thursday evening, we still hadn't left the house and Dylan was feeling worse than ever.

Dad hobbled through the door on his walker, took one look at Dylan lying on the couch, and said, "He still under the weather? Maybe he needs some fresh air."

"Dad, he's running a fever. A hundred and two this morning."

Dad nodded. "Did you give him something for it?"

Did he really think I was that big of a moron? "I did give him something. Even Tylenol isn't bringing his temperature completely back to normal anymore."

"Hmph." Dad dropped into his recliner.

"I'll put your bag away, Charles." Rob walked down the hallway and I followed. He looked over his shoulder at me. "You sure you're going to be able to handle this?"

"No." I sat down on the bed. "It's such a bummer Dylan is sick. We could have all spent a lot of time together this trip. A little family rebonding, you know."

"And now you're stuck all alone dealing with your father, in pain and on narcotics. Not a nice combination, is it?"

"You can say that again. I'd say he's in one of the grumpiest moods I've ever seen him in—and from my father that is saying a lot." I sort of laughed. "You tell that sister of mine she better appreciate this." I regretted the words right after I'd said them. I realized how little I'd shown appreciation for all the years that she'd been here carrying all the family burdens. Still, she had always been Dad's favorite.

"Oh, believe me, she knows." He sat beside me. "I know the two of you have some things to work through right now, but it's all going to work out just fine."

Rob had always been a calm voice of reason. He and Jana had just gotten engaged when Mom got sick, and I couldn't count the ways he'd helped during that time.

I reached over and gave him a hug. "Hopefully, both boy and beast will be feeling better by the weekend. We'll get together then."

"Count on it." Rob saluted. "I better get back to work before someone notices I'm missing."

"See you later. Thanks for driving him home." I watched him leave, dreading the next few days. How I hoped Dylan got better soon. I didn't think I could stand this otherwise.

I walked back into the living room to find my father's eyes about half closed. Good, maybe he would go on to sleep.

"Did you get my stuff put in my room?"

"Yeah, well, the guest room, anyway."

"Guest room?"

"Dad, we talked about this." The master suite was the one and only room on the second floor. It had been off limits to us as kids—officer's quarters, Dad had called it. Now it was off limits to him as well. "You can't go up the stairs to the master bedroom for at least a couple of weeks. Remember, Jana got you all set up in the guest room?"

"It's noisy there, on the front of the house."

"It also has a private bath. But, if you'd rather, take my room, then. I'll sleep in the guest room."

"I'm not taking your room. That's an even dumber idea than putting me in the guest room."

"Oh, Dad."

Dylan had been lying on the couch, taking in this whole scene with wide-eyed interest. "You want to sleep in my room, Grandpa? It's got a really cool bedspread. I think you'd like it there."

Dad actually smiled at this. "Thanks for the offer, but that bedspread is special just for you. I guess I'll have to learn to make do in the guest room."

I had always tried really hard to shield Dylan from the strained relationship between my father and me, but much more of Dad's current mood and Dylan would know all. I walked over to the couch and sat beside him. "Come on, honey. Let me run you a nice bath."

"I'm tired."

"I know you are. You can go to bed right after, okay? It'll help you relax."

"Okay." He held up his arms for me to carry him, something I knew would fry my dad.

I scooped him up, casting a glare in the direction of my father as I did. Let him think what he wanted, but I was not going to make my sick child walk to the tub just so he could learn to man up.

I set Dylan on the toilet lid while I turned on the water and checked the temperature. "Okay, honey, now let's get you undressed." I pulled the T-shirt over his head, and as his hair pulled away from his face, I noticed what looked like a rash. "Oh, Dylan!"

"What?" He looked puzzled.

"On the side of your face—it just looks like a rash. I don't see anything on your shoulders or chest. Let me see your back." I checked his back, his legs, everywhere, and saw no sign of anything. "It's probably a reaction to those sheets. Grandpa doesn't use the same good laundry detergent we use. I'm afraid your little body doesn't know how to respond when confronted with all those chemicals."

It made sense that it would bother him, since he'd been lying down for most of the week, either in his bed, or on the couch, but he'd had his race-car pillow with him the whole time.

"Maybe tomorrow I'll run to the store and get the good stuff, huh?"

"Sure," Dylan answered, but he had long since tuned me out. He sat in the tub and leaned his head against the wall. "Can I get out and go to bed now?"

"Really soon, sweetie." I washed, dried, and clothed him as quickly as possible.

He fell asleep almost instantly once he climbed into the bed, the little race cars covering both him and Frederick. I sat and watched him sleep for a long time. I wanted to be sure he was okay. And I was in no hurry to deal with my father right now.

Chapter 6

Early Friday morning I sat in the kitchen planning my outings for the day, enjoying the peace for what little time there was left of it. I was hoping the narcotics would help Dad to sleep in. He needed the rest and I needed the quiet.

Between Dad's grumpiness and Dylan's sickness, I had little hope that today might be anything other than just plain hard. I walked through my room and the adjoining bathroom so I could peek at my son—just to reassure myself, I suppose. The morning sun was shining through the pink curtains and it cast a reddish light across his face. Funny how the pink lace seemed even more distinct now that the bedspread was in such direct contrast. I wondered if Dad had noticed it, too. Probably. I was guessing there would be sterile white blinds in here the next time we came home.

It concerned me that Dylan's face seemed so especially red. I supposed it was a combination of the glow from the curtains and a bit of lingering fever. Still, he slept soundly. He could do just fine without me for a little longer, so I tiptoed out to the kitchen determined to enjoy what few minutes of quiet I had left.

Thump. Thump-thump. Thump.

The sound of my father's walker banging across the guest room—or perhaps into the bathroom door—let me know that my moments of peace had just come to an end. After one especially loud thump, everything went quiet. Time to go check on him.

I stood outside the guest room, knocked lightly, and turned the knob. *Tried* to turn it would be more accurate. It was locked and barely moved with the pressure. "Dad?" I leaned close to the door and cupped my hands against it.

"Don't need no help." His voice came from well inside—the bathroom, I guessed. "Just get on about your business while I get on about mine." And that was the end of that.

"Mama?" Dylan's scratchy voice sounded from

somewhere behind me. It was followed by a volley of coughing.

"I'm sorry we woke you up. How you feeling, sweetie?" I turned around to see my son padding down the hall, Frederick the bear in one hand. In that moment I realized it hadn't been a funny light cast by the curtains. On his forehead and all around his hairline was a solid rash, and his whole face looked flushed. I put my hand on his forehead. "You're burning up."

I picked him up and carried him into the kitchen, where I set him on the counter closest to the medicines. I pulled out the digital thermometer, which I had purchased at the local pharmacy a few days ago. "Put this under your tongue and let's wait for the music," I said. This particular thermometer was the kind that beeped when the reading was complete. The slower the ending beeps, the lower the temperature. I waited nervously, hoping for slow. Really slow.

A rapid staccato of high-pitched beeping soon filled the morning air. This was not going to be good news.

One hundred three point four.

"Okay, buddy, time for some more of that good cherry medicine. Okay?"

" 'Kay." He didn't say anything else, just rubbed his eyes, which also looked red and irritated.

"I'm sorry, buddy. You're having a hard time

getting over this thing, aren't you?" I handed him a small measuring cup full of thick red liquid. "Drink this. It'll make you feel better."

"'Kay." He drank the Tylenol without comment, then held out the cup for me to take away. "I don't feel good, Mama."

"I know, sweetie, I know." I looked at my watch. It was seven thirty here, which meant it was only five thirty back in California. His pediatrician wouldn't be in the office for another three hours. I supposed there was nothing of an emergency in a rash, so I carried him into the living room, where his pallet was still set up from the day before. "How about some juice? Or water?"

He shook his head. "I don't want anything."

As his fever had grown higher over the last few days, his appetite had gotten significantly smaller. I didn't want to force food, supposing that his stomach was just telling him it couldn't handle anything right now, but I was starting to worry about dehydration. "You need to drink something. Do you want water or juice?"

"Neither."

"How about Sprite?" I knew this would get him. I never allowed him to drink soda, but Dad had gone out and bought a twelve-pack before we came, thinking it was perfectly fine since there wasn't caffeine in it. Just sugar and chemicals.

Dylan looked up at me, a bit of a light in his eyes. "We've got Sprite?"

"Yes we do." I was already moving toward the pantry door.

"No thank you."

"No thank you?" I asked. "I thought you loved Sprite."

"I just don't want any right now."

That sealed it. The answering service would have to page the doctor, but something was wrong. I needed to do something to help my son, and I needed to do it now. I called into the office and soon found myself connected with the call center.

"Children's Medical Clinic, what is the nature of your call?"

"My son is a patient of Dr. Conrad. He's had a fever for five days, which seems to be getting worse, and this morning his face is covered with a rash." I made certain I mentioned the five-day thing. The general rule of thumb at our doctor's office was fevers less than three days were not considered urgent unless there were other factors involved—pulling at ears, wheezing, and so on.

"At what number can Dr. Conrad reach you?"

I gave her my cell number, thankful to find out it was my own pediatrician on call. She was a no-nonsense doctor, never got alarmed at anything, but followed through on everything—from the most to the least significant symptom.

"Thank you. I'll page the doctor."

Five minutes later the phone rang. "Yes, this is Dr. Conrad. Can you tell me what is going on with Dylan?"

"I'm visiting my family in Tennessee, and he's had a fever since Monday. It started out kind of low-grade, runny nose, cough. I thought it was just a cold. For the last day or so, he's been feeling worse, and this morning his temp is one hundred three point four, and he woke up with a rash on his face."

"What does it look like?"

"A rash, you know, flat, red, lots of specks that are kind of joining together in one big red blotch on his forehead."

"Besides his cough, does he have any respiratory symptoms? Wheezing? Difficulty breathing?"

"No, nothing like that."

"Does he have a sore throat?"

"No."

"This sounds like what we've been seeing a lot of in the office lately. Viruses that cause rashes are a dime a dozen these days, and our waiting room has been full of those kids the last few weeks. The best thing to do is treat his fever with acetaminophen and ibuprofen, make sure he stays hydrated, and have him get plenty of rest. Keep him away from other kids and make sure you wash your hands a lot. When will you be back here?"

"Not for another week."

"Since he's had a fever for five days, you could take him to a local pediatrician there, but I suspect she would say the same thing. The current virus we've been seeing at the office tends to run its course in about a week. If his fever isn't gone by Monday, you should take him in. If he should develop any more troubling symptoms in the meanwhile, you should also find someone local and get him seen."

"Thanks, Dr. Conrad." I hung up the phone a bit relieved. This wasn't some terrible, awful disease; it was just a dime-a-dozen virus that would all be over soon. Just a couple more days and things would be getting better.

My father shuffled into the kitchen, his walker making a low-pitched squeaking noise with each step. He looked at Dylan lying there on the living room couch. "Where'd that rash come from?"

I shrugged. "Some kind of virus, I guess. I just got off the phone with our doctor back in California. She said there are lots of viruses going around now, and several of them come complete with a rash. Apparently, we are the lucky recipients of that variety."

"Ahh, that's too bad. I feel sorry for the poor kid."

"Me, too."

"Guess it doesn't surprise me none, though."

"Oh? And why is that?"

He shrugged. "It's just the way you watch over every little thing he does—no sweets, no fast food, you use antibacterial hand wipes about every fifteen seconds, don't let him climb trees or nothing. By the time something from real life gets near him, he don't stand a chance. Let him fight through some stuff. Let him get used to germs, figure out a way to deal with it."

At this point I'd listened to my father's criticisms of my overprotective mothering more than I could possibly stand. I stood up and leaned on the table so that I was towering over him. "Your theory doesn't work, and you of all people should know that. Mom sure never got used to a little smoke, did she?"

My father's face went ash white, but he didn't respond. It seemed as though my words had found their mark. I went to sit beside my son on the couch.

Chapter 7

We avoided each other over the next few hours, and soon the weight of silence became too much for me.

"I think I'm going to run a few errands while your physical therapist is here. Is there anything you need me to get for you?" We were doing our usual thing after trading harsh words: pretending that it never happened. Not in a warm, all-is-forgiven way, just a terse, refusing-to-back-down kind of truce.

He was sitting back in his recliner. I could tell by his flushed face that the exertion of getting there had been painful, but he wasn't about to admit that. "How about picking up a pack of those chocolate sandwich cookies we always used to get? I've been craving those things all day, and I'll bet Dylan likes them, too, right?"

At the mention of cookies, Dylan lifted his head. "What cookies?"

I looked at my father. "You know we don't eat those kinds of foods."

"For the love of all things blue, what's one little cookie going to hurt?"

"That's the rule and it's final. Next week when Dylan's better, we'll drive over to Lawrenceburg and get some organic ingredients so I can make healthy treats for us all."

"I want a cookie. Just one, Mama, please, just one."

The fact that he was actually willing to eat something made me almost reconsider my stance. Then I thought of how much sicker all that sugar and saturated fat would make him feel in the long run. "Sorry, buddy."

"Grandpa said I could. This is his house. He makes the rules, right?" Dylan turned his gaze over toward my father, obviously hoping for backup.

My father nodded. "Sounds right to me. I tell you what, your mother ate plenty of those things when she was your age, and it don't seem like it hurt her none, now, did it?" He was going to play this for all it was worth, his way of getting back at me for my earlier comment.

"Dad, you know—"

The doorbell rang, and likely saved me from saying something that would've plunged us in deeper. I opened the door and found a smiling young woman. Thirtyish, I suppose, with short blond hair, a perky smile, and the perfect posture of someone with complete confidence in her ability.

"Hello, I'm Shannon Volmar. I'm here to see Charles Graham."

"Yes, you are." I smiled at her as I opened the door, then whispered under my breath, "Good luck."

She smiled in return. "That bad, huh?"

"Oh yeah."

I pulled my car to the curb in the old city square. Until this week, I hadn't been here in ten years, and it was amazing how many things had changed, and yet how many refused to change at all. The building that used to house my favorite clothing store now said Antiques on a faded sign out front. It was dark inside, and a sign on the door said Open By Appointment Only.

I walked past Moore's Shoes—that place had been there forever. They still displayed Stride Rites in the window just as they had when I was a kid. Maybe I would bring Dylan back here later when he was feeling better and do a little shopping. He could use a new pair of athletic shoes.

Then I reached the weathered brown bricks of the old movie theater. Once again the sight of it brought back a wave of memories. It had been mostly shut down since about my eighth-grade year, but I'd seen plenty of movies here as a kid.

I looked up at the marquee, no longer aglow with hundreds of light bulbs. It said Theater Center Shops in dark blue script where the names of movies had once been posted in big red letters.

I entered what once had been the theater lobby and saw about a dozen round tables. The old snack bar remained in place but was now apparently a coffee counter. The place was almost full. I took the three steps that led to the old theater entrance. There were now two sets of doors. One said Daybreak Apothecary, the other Beuerlein Travel Agency.

There was the faintest hint of the smell of buttered popcorn, although I saw no sign of a popcorn machine at the coffee shop counter. Perhaps the smell was so well burrowed into the heart of this place that it could never go away. Or perhaps it was just nostalgia on my part.

I could still remember sitting up in the balcony with Melanie Ledbetter, large popcorn between us, when we noticed that Mrs. Lumpkins—the meanest first-grade teacher at our school—was right below us. We started dropping popcorn, one kernel at a time, then ducking beneath the half wall. We'd hit her at least a half dozen times when the theater manager nabbed us and made us go down and apologize, then sent us home. I suppose it was a good thing we'd been second-graders by then, or Mrs. Lumpkins would have made the rest of our school year miserable.

Even now, I was glad it was my mother who got that call instead of my dad. Her lecture had been stern enough, and I'd lost privileges for longer than I thought fair at the time, but I never doubted, even in the midst of it all, that she loved me. My father, on the other hand, well . . . Dad was never satisfied with my realizing I'd made a mistake. He always pushed and pushed until I came to understand that *I* was the mistake.

I shook my head to clear the thought and pulled open the door into the pharmacy. It was the most unusual store I'd ever seen. The old giant round wall lights had been incorporated right into the design of the place, with polished wood and a tidy appearance making it feel a bit like a cathedral, I thought.

They had a fairly decent-sized over-the-counter section, and I had been thrilled on my earlier visit to find that they had a large selection of herbal remedies. I stood perusing them when I heard a voice behind me say, "Can I help you find something?"

She looked to be a few years younger than I was, and had the most beautiful wavy red hair I'd ever seen. It was elegant and yet untamed all at the same time.

"My son has a virus. I need some more Tylenol for his fever, but I was looking to see what else might help him."

"You've come to the right place, and you happen to be talking to the right person. I make a pretty mean herbal tea combo, if I do say so myself. How old is your son?"

"Four."

"Hmm, that changes things. For most adults or bigger kids, I'd mix up some oolong tea, but it's got too much caffeine for the youngsters. I could whip up some of my famous cold-and-flu-fighter recipe. It contains peppermint leaf—it's got some antiviral properties and can help you sweat out toxins—some elder, both flowers and berries, which seem to help the body fight off flu viruses, and a bit of ginger for aches and nausea."

"How does it taste, though? I wonder if I could get him to drink it."

"I always suggest adding a little honey after you're done steeping. A little sweetness goes a long way. Right?"

"Right. How much is it?"

She shook her head. "We just opened our tea dispensary last month. I always give the first sample free along with a tea ball. You take it home and try it. If your son will drink it, and if you think it's helping, give me a call and I'll make up a full batch."

"Sounds perfect."

"Good. It's settled, then. My name's Dawn, by the way."

"I'm Grace."

"Pretty name. Well, come on back here and have a seat." She directed me toward a little cubby in the back wall of the store, which had a couple of barstools and a counter with sugar, honey, stirrers, and a few other things. She unlocked a cabinet and removed several sealed containers. It wasn't long before she was scooping and mixing our own special herbal tea.

"Mixing some of your famous tea, Dawn? Honestly, I don't think we fill nearly as many prescriptions as we used to, now that you're curing half the town with your herbal remedies." A beautiful blonde who was obviously about six months pregnant approached, wearing the cutest blue sundress I thought I'd ever seen.

Dawn laughed but didn't look up from her work. "Well, you're the one who insisted I further my education. And I guess that it's a good thing I did, since your worrywart husband thinks you're standing on your feet too much."

The blonde laughed. "He's pretty adorable, isn't he?" She nodded at me. "Enjoy your tea." As cliché as it was to say, she really did look radiant.

I don't think I ever looked that way when I was pregnant with Dylan. Of course, this woman had several things that made it easier, I supposed. An education, a stable career, and the adorable husband. I'd had none of those things. Within two days of finding out I was pregnant, Chase was out of the picture and I no longer had a boyfriend, much less an overprotective, adorable one. The real kicker, though, was having no mother.

There are few times in life that a girl needs a mother more than when she's expecting her first child, especially when that girl is little more than a child herself. I'd been twenty years old, frightened half to death, and all alone. It still topped the list of reasons I couldn't forgive my father for killing her.

"Here you go." Dawn handed me a little bag full of tea leaves. "Now, steep this for ten minutes, add a little honey, and I bet it'll have him feeling better in no time."

"I hope so."

"Come on over and I'll ring up that Tylenol for you so you can be on your way."

"Thanks so much."

"You're very welcome."

I walked out the door, past The Christian Bookstore, which had been on the square for as long as I could remember and had been a favorite haunt during my teenage years. I thought of going in to buy a book for Dylan, since we hadn't exactly been regulars at church lately, but decided to wait until he was feeling better and bring him down here so he could pick it out himself.

Next to it was the sign for the upstairs offices of a couple of lawyers and *The Shoal Creek Advocate*, the town newspaper. "Grace Graham, is that really you?"

I turned toward the voice and found myself looking into a face straight out of the past. A face that was perfect then and was perfect now. Patti Fox. I couldn't even pretend not to recognize her, because she hadn't changed one single bit since high school. Not one freckle, not one extra pound, and of course, not even the hint of a future wrinkle. "Hi, Patti. How are you?" I did not want to stand here and have this conversation, but I couldn't think of a polite way to get out of it.

"I'm well." She flipped her hand out and down. "Wow, you look absolutely terrific. I bet people tell you that you look like Sandra Bullock all the time, don't they?"

"Hardly." Okay, I'd maybe heard it once or twice, but to agree would end up requiring me to say something about her looking like Paris Hilton, and I wasn't going to go there. Instead, I blurted out the first thing that came to mind. "What are you doing here?"

She pointed toward the doors I'd just been looking at. "I'm the proud new owner of *The Shoal Creek Advocate*."

"Really?" I looked toward Patti, the golden highlights in her blond hair glistening in the sunlight. "I've been out of touch a bit. Dad never tells me anything, but I'm surprised Jana didn't mention it. Good for you."

"Yep, the timing was right. I was working for a PR firm up in Nashville, but you know me, I've never been one to take orders from people very well. I wanted to be my own boss. I came home to visit my mother one weekend and ran into old Mr. Baumgartner at Shoney's. You remember him from journalism class, right?"

I nodded but said nothing. I didn't want to think about journalism class, or Patti's current success, or the way she and her friends used to snicker behind my back. From the moment she'd arrived at the end of our junior year, she'd made my life miserable in one way or the other.

"Yes, we just started talking about old times and kind of catching up with each other. He told me he was ready to sell *The Advocate* and retire, but he hadn't found the right buyer—since it had been in his family for several decades, he didn't want to turn it over to just anyone, you know."

"And you were just the perfect one." Of course she would be.

She shrugged. "I don't know about perfect, but I'm sure glad it worked out the way it did. I cleaned out most of my savings account and started on this new venture. I'm out pounding the pavement trying to get advertisers, between writing articles and editing."

"Sounds hectic."

"I'll say. We just went from being twice weekly to daily. This economy is not really the right time to do that, but, I don't know, I just felt like it was something I was supposed to do—just as surely as I was supposed to buy the paper."

"Really? Just felt like it, huh?" The freedom of changing careers just because she felt like it did not in any way serve to ease my dislike of her.

"Yeah. Most people think I'm crazy buying a newspaper in today's world. Folks around here sure love their paper, though. I'm bringing some things online, too, trying to expand. I started a TalkBack blog for readers a couple of weeks ago. It's been really interesting to see the feedback we get from our stories. I've taken to printing portions of it in the next day's newspaper, since some of our customers haven't quite figured out the Internet yet. It's been so well received, I'm just amazed."

"That's great. Well, I've got to get back now."

"Of course you do. I didn't mean to talk your head off."

"It was good seeing you." It seemed like a polite way to end the conversation, in spite of the complete lack of truthfulness behind the words. I turned toward the parking area.

"Did you know I just moved down the street from your father?" She fell into step beside me. "Remember the house the Frakers used to live in a few doors down? How long are you in town? I'd love to have you over for dinner."

Normally I would have struggled for some excuse to avoid the invitation, but today's wretched home life had at least one silver lining. "Oh, thanks so much for the thought, but my father just had surgery and my son is sick, so I'm more or less confined to the house."

"That's too bad. I'd really like to talk to you sometime." She paused for a moment and I got the impression she was trying to decide whether or not to say what it was she wanted to say. She finally sighed. "If there's ever anything I can do to help you, let me know. Okay?"

"Sure." I moved toward my parking spot. "Good luck with the paper." I got in the car, glad to be heading home and as far as possible from Patti Fox.

Chapter 8

When I returned home, Dylan was lying on an old quilt in the middle of the den floor, a couple of pillows situated around him and his cup of juice within arm's reach. The Disney Channel was having an all-morning *Handy Manny* marathon, which suited him just fine. "Hi, Mom."

My father was sitting on the couch, reading a *Field & Stream* magazine. He looked up and said, "The kid has hardly moved since you've been gone. Don't know when I've seen him so quiet."

"How'd your therapy go?"

"Ridiculous. It's absolutely ridiculous that she wants me to do all these stupid exercises—trying to get me to bend my knee way in—you'd think she'd get a clue from the fact that I just had surgery to understand that's not going to happen. She even wants to assign what she calls homework. Give me a break. What did people do a hundred years ago before there were these fancy physical therapists?"

"A hundred years ago they didn't have the technology to replace knees to begin with, so you just would've been a cripple."

"Hmph. Modern medicine's just trying to outsmart itself, that's all."

I looked away from my father and toward my son, now fully engrossed in the show. "Okay, kiddo. I've got some things for you, but first of all, let's see how you're doing." I put my hand to his forehead, relieved that he didn't feel particularly warm. Maybe things were finally looking up. Still, I gave him the thermometer and ten seconds later was rewarded with a series of single beeps. Ninety-nine point four. My doctor would call that a borderline fever. Nothing to get excited about.

I knew we still had a dose of Tylenol on board, and his rash looked possibly a bit worse. "I'll be right back." I went into the kitchen where I'd left the bag from the pharmacy.

"Did you get the bubblegum-flavored stuff?" He sat up and looked at me, completely turning his back on the TV.

I know a lot of kids refuse to take medication of any kind because they hate the taste. Dylan was the exception to this rule. Although he'd rarely needed medicine because we lived such a healthy lifestyle, on the occasions that ibuprofen or acetaminophen were called for, he was one happy boy. The two rounds of amoxicillin a few months ago had put him over the moon, and had him faking an earache for days afterward.

"I got the cherry kind." I purposely picked the flavor I knew he liked the least because I didn't want him to drag this thing out just to get another spoonful of medicine. "The good news is, I brought you something else that you can drink, too. The nice lady at the pharmacy made some special tea for you."

"Tea? Blah. I want the cherry stuff."

"How do you know it's blah? You haven't tasted it yet."

"I've tasted your tea when we're home. It's yucky."

I drank decaffeinated green tea almost every day. I didn't particularly like it, but I knew it was high in antioxidants, and of course the fact that it was rumored to help people maintain a lean body weight was always a bonus, especially living so close to the beach. "Well, this is a different kind of tea. It helps people with viruses feel better."

I set some water to boil and after the tea was ready, I leaned forward and sniffed. It had a fairly strong herbal smell. Dylan would immediately be on high alert. Being the practiced mother that I am, I knew how to fight this. I carried the tea, the honey, and a spoon into the den so that he could see what I was doing. "I thought we could put some honey in your tea, just for a little treat. What do you think?"

"Honey, really?" Dylan loved his honey.

"Yep, honey." I made a point of holding the honey bottle high above the mug so that he could see the thick golden syrup as it cascaded from the container into his cup. I stirred, then handed it to him. "What do you think?"

He took a sip, scrunched up his nose, and said, "Not very good."

"I'll add a touch more honey, okay?"

"Just take it away. Don't want it."

"Take just a few more sips. Okay? Here, I'm putting a little more honey in."

He watched another squeeze of honey melt into the mug. "Okay. I'll try." He took another sip, made a face, then took another. "Can I watch *Handy Manny* now?"

"Are you sure you don't want to go out into the backyard? Maybe get some fresh air?"

"No thank you." He lay back down and effectively tuned me out. Discussion over.

My father looked over his magazine. "Why don't you go get some of that fresh air? You've been talking about going for a run ever since you've been here. Neither of us men is planning on budging from our spots in the foreseeable future, so you might as well enjoy some peace and quiet while you've got the chance."

It wasn't a bad idea. "Yeah, maybe I'll do that."

Five minutes later, I was running through the old streets in my neighborhood, memories floating all around me with each *thwap* my feet pounded against the sidewalk. I'd learned to ride without training wheels at this very corner. At that time it had been an empty lot. Now a brick ranch-style home and a Greyhound-bus-sized RV occupied the space. I turned the corner, remembered all the water-balloon battles we'd had right here on Robin Street. I remembered the time one boy had thrown rocks instead of balloons, and hit that bully Skip Higdon right upside the head—a head which subsequently required five stitches and shut down most of the neighborhood fun for a good month. Still, it knocked a good bit of the overt meanness right out of Skip Higdon. Yep, that had been a good summer.

As I rounded the last corner toward home I passed the Frakers' house. Patti's house.

As much as I disliked the thought of her living in *my* neighborhood, I did find some consolation in the fact that it was a 1960s brick ranch-style, instead of the grand mansion I would have assumed she would live in by now. Of course, she was still plenty young and still beautiful. Getting what she wanted had never been a problem, so I had no doubt she would work her way into something better in no time at all.

I could still remember the phone call from my friend Brenna. "I just saw Jared getting ice cream with that new girl, Patti Fox. She was all over him, and he was returning the favor." And just like that, the first boy who had ever said he loved me, the first boy I'd ever loved in return, proved unfaithful. And he certainly wouldn't be the last.

I ended back at Dad's driveway, promising myself to do whatever it took to avoid her for the rest of the trip. Given the current situation, I didn't think it would be that hard.

The garbage trucks had already made their morning rounds, so I rolled Dad's two trash cans up the driveway and to their place just behind the trelliswork outside the garage. I scanned farther down the backyard and saw Mrs. Fellows sitting on the wrought-iron bench out by the crab apple tree, and I walked toward her.

She waved when she saw me coming. "Hello there, Gracie. It's so good to see you home again. Tell me, how is your father doing? I'd be more than a little surprised if you didn't tell me that he is rebelling against all his at-home physical therapy."

"There's no need for surprise here." I smiled at her. "Honestly, it's almost like having a second child."

She laughed. "Yep, stubborn men and children. They have a lot in common."

"Unfortunately my son has been sick since Monday."

"Oh, really? I'm sorry I didn't realize that, dear, or I would have brought some soup over or something. Maybe tomorrow I'll do that. Okay?"

"Oh, you don't have to."

"I know, I want to. Your father made it more

than clear he didn't want any kind of babying, as he called it, but he didn't say a word about your son. It'll just make me feel better if I do something to help." Matter settled.

I smiled at not only the sweetness of sitting out here with one of my mother's oldest and dearest friends, but also the thought of how much her coming over with soup would annoy Dad. "Are you getting ready to plant something new?" I pointed toward the area beneath the tree. The entire root area was surrounded by mulch, which was lined by a circle of stones—standing upright, rather than lying flat like most landscape stones. I knew that this middle area held bulbs that would bloom at random times and in random colors. Since the circle was on both properties, she and my mother had tended this together. For the past seven years it had been left to Mrs. Fellows alone.

"No. I just like to come out here and think sometimes. Oh, how this place reminds me of your mother and the day we decided to put this circle around this tree."

"I remember when y'all did that. I came home from school one day, and the two of you were back here, covered head to toe in potting soil, and you had a wheelbarrow full of those big rocks that seemed at the time like they weighed a ton. You were out there having such a good time. I thought you'd both lost it. It's funny, I don't really have any memories of the two of you together before that."

"That's because we never were." She reached her hand down to touch one of the rocks. "Oh, that was a special time."

"Special, like how?"

"Your mother and I had had an ongoing feud ever since your parents moved in here. I'm ashamed to even admit it now, but fact was, I'd grown up in hard times, and even though I know it's not an excuse, well, I didn't want people taking what was mine. This crab apple tree is on my property, even though it hangs over yours, and I was convinced your mother was sneaking over here and stealing the fruit. After Jana and you came along, you two would cut the corner of my backyard on your way to the creek."

The backyards in our neighborhood were not fenced. Most were bordered about halfway back by a row of shrubs, then were open to each other. The crab apple tree sat just beyond the hedgerow on Mrs. Fellows's side, and although I had no memory of this, I was certain we'd cut through her backyard many a time. It was, after all, the fastest way to the creek. "I don't doubt that we did."

"I contended that you were walking right across the roots and damaging the tree. Then, on more than one occasion, I saw the two of you eating apples, which I assumed were mine."

She shook her head then and pointed at several apples scattered around the circle. "The Good Lord knows that fruit made just as big a mess in your yard as it did mine. The tree always sort of leaned your direction. Anyway, your mother and I had long since quit speaking, except when there were accusations flying."

"Really?" I searched all my memories, trying desperately to find a single episode that led me to believe that the two of them were anything but the best of friends. There were none that I could remember. "Mama never mentioned any of this."

"Likely not. Your mama was not the kind of person who went around stirring up trouble. She might have been mad at me, but she wasn't one to pass it on—'specially to her own kids."

"So what made you two decide to put in these flowers and become friends all of a sudden?" I'd always kind of wondered at their friendship, considering their almost twenty-year age difference.

"As you are well aware, we went to the same church, as lots of people do in this town. There was a women's Bible study we were both going to. It was awkward for us both to be there, to say the least, but I was secretly praying God would show her just how wrong she was and maybe make her come beg me for forgiveness." She laughed. "Maybe she was doing the same thing, although that doesn't really sound much like her."

"Ha. I can remember sitting in Sunday school and praying the same thing about a few people." Patti Fox came immediately to mind, but I didn't say as much. In more recent years, it had been my father.

"That's our old human nature, I suppose. It's not pretty, but it's the unfortunate truth too much of the time."

"So what happened?"

"One day we heard the story about Gilgal."

"Gilgal?" I looked at the tree, utterly confused. "Am I supposed to know what that is?"

"Likely not, it doesn't get taught too often. You remember when Moses led the Israelites out of Egypt, right?"

I really didn't want to hear a Bible story, but I was curious enough about what had happened between Mrs. Fellows and my mother to go along with it. For now, at least. "Yeah."

"He parted the Red Sea to get them safely away from the pursuing Egyptian army, and away they went toward the land God had promised to them. But they didn't quite make it. Do you remember why?"

It had been a long time since my Sunday school days. "I remember they wandered around in the wilderness for forty years."

"That's right. Because when they got just outside the Promised Land, they sent in spies. Twelve of them. And they came back with clusters of grapes, so huge that it took two men to carry them. They also came back with the story that the people in the land were huge. The spies said they looked like grasshoppers compared to them and it was more or less hopeless." She pressed her lips together. "It's always harder to have faith when the problem is staring us in the face."

I laughed. "I guess there's quite a bit of truth to that."

"So the people decided they wouldn't go in. It looked too hard. The people started complaining. 'I want to go back to Egypt. Life was better as a slave than being out here.' Better as slaves?" She shook her head. "Can you imagine? 'Course, it's easy to call them crazy, but I'm sure we've all done something similar at times."

"I guess so." She had more or less lost me, but I was trying to hang in there, if only for politeness' sake.

"So, forty years later, God brought Joshua and Caleb and the next generation to Gilgal. Long story short, it was sort of where they got a 'do-over.' "

"A do-over?"

"Yep, complete with God parting the water for them again—the Jordan River, this time. They took some stones out of the middle of the river and stood them up in remembrance." Finally she stood up, bending over and stretching out her knees. "Oh, I'm getting way too old for this." She smiled down at me. "The place where they camped was called Gilgal, which means 'circle.' I guess some people believe they actually put the stones in a circle, though I don't know if it's true or not. Either way, it was the place where the Israelites came full circle. Understand?"

"Sort of."

"It was their fresh start. A new beginning in spite of the mistakes made in the past. So the afternoon after we heard that story in Bible study, your mother came home with a bag of mulch, and the next thing I knew, she was out here by this tree, putting the stuff out here. I came running out, thinking she was surely doing something awful, and demanded an explanation.

" 'Mrs. Fellows,' she said, 'I have never taken an apple from your tree, nor, to my knowledge, have my children. But they do walk across your lawn and I know you are concerned that it is damaging the tree roots, and I know that it is your yard, so you shouldn't have my kids walking through it, so this is my way of starting over with this whole thing. I'm putting the mulch around the tree as my symbol of my promise to you that I will do my utmost to keep my children away from here.'

"All that time I'd thought it would feel really satisfying to have her realize just how wrong she was, but in that moment, I just started bawling. It wasn't until then I realized how selfish and wrong I'd been. I was the one who needed to start over, to make a different choice, but there she was, humble as could be, asking me if she could start fresh.

"I went and got a shovel and helped her with the mulch. By the time we were finished, we decided to put some landscaping stones around it to help hold in the moisture. She started laying them around the circle, but I stopped her. I said, 'What do you think of this?' and I turned one of the stones up on its end, making it a standing stone, if you will, just like they used at Gilgal."

I looked at the circle of upright stones, seeing them in such a completely different way than I ever had before. How I missed my mother in that moment. What an incredible woman she had been, and through Mrs. Fellows's reverie I realized that there was even more to her than I had known. "So what made y'all decide to plant other things in the circle as well?"

She laughed. "It looked kind of funny, with just the stones stood up around the tree. And you remember old Mrs. Fouch down the street? She was such a teller of tall tales, we could both just picture her telling everyone how we were doing some sort of occult rituals out here, or something. We decided to increase the circumference so there was some topsoil on both properties and make it kind of a raised flower bed. It was the only way to play it safe."

I laughed. "And it seems to have worked, because until now, I never even thought to ask the question about it."

"You know what? You're only the second person to have ever asked."

"Really? Who is the other?"

"Young lady that just moved in down the street a while back. Sweet little thing she is, too. Her name's Patti. Patti Fox."

Now, didn't that just figure? Of all people, Patti Fox had known the secret of my mother's garden before I did. "Oh."

"You know her?"

"Yeah, we went to school together." *And she made my life miserable.*

"I declare, the timing of telling her that story was definitely providential. It was a story she needed to hear. Who knows?" She shrugged. "Maybe God brings the question to mind to the person He knows most needs to hear it." She looked at me and winked. "Something you need to do over?"

I laughed, but it was more a laugh of discomfort than humor. I definitely needed to start over with Jana. And maybe my father—although I wasn't particularly convinced that was worth the effort of attempting. "Lots of things."

"Well, now you know there is a chance. One

thing you've got to remember about my story, though."

"What's that?"

"When the water parted in the Jordan for the second crossing, the water didn't part until the priests put their feet in it. They had to actually move forward in faith and put their feet in the water before they saw any results."

Knock. Knock. Knock.

I followed the sound to the back door, wondering which of the neighbors I would find there. I pulled back the lace curtains from the kitchen door and peeked out, hoping I wasn't about to get stuck in a long conversation.

Rob smiled when he saw me. "Hey, you."

I pulled open the door and gave him a hug. "Hey, yourself. What are you doing here?"

"I was on the way home from work and thought I'd stop by and check on things." He brought his voice to a whisper. "You know, make sure Charles and you haven't killed each other yet."

"You think you're being funny. Come on in. Dylan and Dad are both sacked out in front of the TV in the den, so we can go in the living room and talk."

He took a step forward, then stopped. "No, I'd better not."

"Why?"

"Jana made me promise I wouldn't catch

anything. She said if I caught Dylan's flu and brought it home to Hannah . . ." He took a step backward. "Let's just say the words *slow,* and *painful,* and *death* were all used in the sentence. Since everyone's asleep anyway, how about we sit outside?"

I laughed. "Sure. I guess I don't much blame her."

The wraparound porch had a total of six rocking chairs down the length of it. I took the closest one and Rob took the one beside it. "So Jana tells me he's not getting better, and now he has a rash or something?" Jana hadn't been by since Dylan got sick, but she called for updates every few hours.

"Yeah, just on his face. I guess that kind of virus is going around right now, but what lousy timing for us, huh?"

"Yes, it is." He rocked for another minute. "So Jana also tells me that you and Steve broke up."

I stopped rocking then and looked at him. "Aha! She sent you here to talk about this, didn't she? I can hear her now—'Go see if you can talk some sense into that hardheaded sister of mine.'" I tried my best to imitate the higher pitch and sweeter accent of my sister, but it came out sounding rather nasal and irritating.

"You know your sister pretty well." Rob rocked and laughed in perfect rhythm.

"And I know you. She may have bullied you

into coming over here, but being the peacemaker that you are, you've been dying to get over here and see if you can't help figure this all out."

"Well, I do have to say, I've known you a long time, and I sure thought Steve was the perfect guy for you."

"You just say that because Steve wears a sports coat and even an occasional tie if the situation calls for it." I tugged at the sleeve of his neatly pressed suit. "This is not about him being perfect for me; it's about male fashion."

"I think I'm insulted. You know I don't care about that." He put his feet up on the porch rail. "I'm as laid-back as the next guy. Although I think we could all agree that we are relieved you finally found someone who favors something besides flip-flops and baggy shorts. But that is beside the point."

"What is the point, then?"

"You love him, right?"

"Yeah." I couldn't look toward him. "But where's it going to lead?"

"Well, I'd say if you stick to the usual plan, the answer to that would involve marriage, kids, and old age."

"Or . . . infidelity and abandonment."

"I've spent a fair amount of time with him—a couple of vacations in California, that ski trip to Mammoth, and when he came here a couple of Christmases ago—plus emails and phone calls in the interim. From what I've seen, I don't think Steve's that kind of guy. Do you?"

I shrugged. "I don't know. Sometimes I do and sometimes I don't. And I don't want to find out the truth the hard way like I did last time."

"You can't let Chase ruin the rest of your life for you."

We both rocked in silence for a while. Finally, Rob said, "Jana says Steve is your trifecta of perfection."

"Trifecta?" I burst out laughing. "Only Jana would compare relationships to racehorses. What exactly is the trifecta of perfection?"

"Let's see, what did she say? He loves your son"—he held up one finger—"he is responsible and has a good job"—he held up the second finger—"and this one is Jana's, not mine, he is . . . what does she say . . . gorgeous." He put his third finger in the air. "She says that about me, too, right? The gorgeous part, I mean?"

"Oh, all the time."

"That's what I thought." He nodded smugly. "So now back to our subject. When are you going to give that guy a call? You know you really want to."

I did. But then again, I didn't. I had no idea what I wanted anymore.

"Okay, Rob, I think we've had enough of a serious talk that you can go home now and tell Jana you've done your part."

He wiped his brow in mock relief. "Thank goodness. I hate all this mushy talk."

I reached over and squeezed his elbow. "You really are the best. I'm glad my sister found you."

Chapter 9

My cell phone started singing "Paperback Writer" from its spot on the coffee table. I tensed as I reached forward to grab it. Time to face the facts. I took a deep breath before I slid it open. "Hello, Jasmine."

"I know you asked for two weeks, but is there any way you can come back a few days early?"

Of course she probably needed my help with lots of things now that she knew the deal had fallen through. Had she really found out only today? I couldn't believe that Steve and his group would have let this go for so long. I wanted to do anything I could to help her, but I looked at my son, lying on the floor and covered in an ever-growing rash, and my father—his leg outstretched, still barely able to get up and down by himself. "I really don't think that's a possibility. What's wrong?" Like I didn't know the answer to that one.

"Well, for one thing, the Oates family is due here in a couple of days."

"There's nothing about that statement that

entices me to hurry back." I rubbed the back of my neck. "Have you put away the crystal and fine china from the shelves in the hallway? Last year, I found some of the kids juggling several pieces from there."

"Believe me, I remember it clearly. Those kids are a nightmare."

"My point exactly." I realized then that there was more than one thing I'd managed to run from in taking this trip now.

"The real reason I'm calling is Mr. and Mrs. Pilcher. They're due to arrive this afternoon and I know they have a list of requests for their suite, but I can't find it anywhere. Do you know where we keep it?"

"Yes, I do. It's in my file drawer, under the customer file, letter *P*, but don't bother looking for it. Them, I know by heart."

She exhaled in relief. "You have no idea how stressful it's been around here lately."

"It was unlucky timing on our part that the Pilchers should decide they want to visit the weekend before the Oates family arrives. Our pickiest guests back to back with our most destructive guests."

"Tell me about it. I'm living that nightmare right now."

"Take a deep breath. It'll be fine."

"Let's have the list."

"They want the Sunshine Suite, of course, and

Rosalea knows to have it extra spotless for them. Fresh flowers should be beside the bed, on the coffee table and the dining table, as well as a small arrangement by the claw-footed tub. These need to be changed daily. A box of Patchi chocolates—I've got them in my office already, just look on my desk—should be in the suite to greet them, and extra towels in the bathroom. Make sure the French door is streak free and that the lanai is spotless."

"They are so particular. It would really be helpful if you were here now, Mrs. Pilcher seems to like you."

"You'll do fine. She's really a nice lady as long as you make certain everything is done according to her specifications. Speaking of which, Chef Jonathan should already have a memo about Mr. Pilcher's lactose intolerance to make certain he plans the morning menu accordingly. The housekeepers need to be invisible. Last time, we had Kristyn page them when she saw the Pilchers leaving the property so the room could get cleaned without them running into each other."

"Got it. I'll go double-check the suite right now."

I found it strange that she hadn't even mentioned the buyout.

"Great. Uh, Jasmine, are you . . . is everything else okay?"

"Not really." She paused. "I promised myself I

wasn't going to unload my troubles on you this week. I know you've got problems of your own there. But you did ask."

"What's going on?" I waited for what I knew was coming.

"The bathroom remodel has Collin all out of his routine. You know what a change in routine does to his meltdown threshold. It has been a nightmare. I've had to miss large chunks of a couple of workdays because of extreme escalations. Without you here, and with me not fully here, this week has been a nightmare all around."

"Your bathroom remodel . . . it's still going on?"

"Well, yeah. What, did you think it would be finished in a day or two?"

"No, I guess not."

She still didn't know. A week after I'd found out and she still didn't know. "Have you heard any more from your real estate agent?" Surely there had been some sort of indication by now that the deal was falling through.

"Funny you should mention that. She called today and told me that the Wadley Foundation had been making inquiries about buying this place. Isn't that the strangest thing? I've never even thought of listing it for sale, and now two different investment groups have become interested within a month of each other."

My hopes began to rise with this last statement. Perhaps there would be a backup deal if things went bad. "The Wadley Foundation? I've never heard of them."

"I don't think you want to, either. I did a little research. They're known for buying a place like ours, then dismissing the entire staff and bringing in their own people. It's a good thing we won't have to deal with the likes of them."

"Yes, it is." This was getting worse by the second.

"Listen, I was serious when I said things are really hard here right now. Please, if there's any way, try and come back as soon as you can."

"I'll try my best." I hung up the phone and shook my head. Why hadn't they told her?

"Why does your cell phone always play that bone-jangling song when your boss calls? Any other time it just rings." My father had one eye partially opened and pointed in my general direction as he lay back in his recliner.

"I did it as a joke, Dad. Get it? I get a call from work, but I'd rather be a paperback writer?"

He shook his head as if this were all complete nonsense. "What'd she want?"

"She called to ask if I could come back early, but I think all she really needed was a little moral support."

My father said, "That right there is the problem with parents being too soft on their kids. That girl never had to work for anything in her life.

Now her parents retire and give her the business, and she can't handle it. So she decides to cash out, but in the meantime she leans on someone like you, someone whose parents actually instilled a little work ethic in her."

"Dad, she's got other issues. Lots of them." More than even she knew.

"We've all got issues, but that don't keep most of us from pulling our own weight."

"She's in intensive therapy sessions with her son three days a week, occupational and speech therapy after that. She pulls her weight in a different way."

"By letting everyone around her pick up the slack. What if you decided you wanted to get Dylan in Harvard and the best way to do that was to go to class with him three days a week? You think she'd be so understanding about that?"

"It's not the same thing." I could have continued to argue with him that most of us don't have a severely autistic son. Jasmine's life on a daily basis was hard; there was never any other way about it. I really wanted to say all of this to my father, to scream at him until he understood.

But having promised myself that I wasn't going to spend this entire trip arguing with him, I changed tacks. "Yeah, too bad you don't own a hotel on the beach in Ventura. You've given me all the tools I need to run the place; you just haven't given me the place."

"You want a place like that, you've got to work and earn it. It means so much more when you build your business yourself. Didn't nobody give me nothing. I worked hard and earned everything I've got."

"So you're saying if Jana and I had been boys, and we became plumbers, you wouldn't have passed the business down to us?"

He shook his head. "I'd have made you buy into it, like Billy and Sam just did, even though they've been with me twenty years. It would have been easy to hand the place over to them, but I know by them investing their money in it, they'll be more likely to take care of the business I built. I didn't want to turn it over to someone who was going to let the place go."

"Jasmine's not letting the place go, Dad; she's just overwhelmed."

"When you're running a business, you don't have time to be overwhelmed. You've just got to keep plugging away."

Plugging away.

How many times had I heard that phrase through my childhood? Too many to count, that was for sure.

I thought back to the elementary school science fair. I had been in the third grade, Jana in the sixth, and I had found the most advanced experiment I could find, involving heat conduction and different types of insulation material. I had no idea what most of it meant, but it sounded really official and splashy, and I'd written up a bunch of scientific facts. Jana, on the other hand, had done an experiment about which household surfaces tended to harbor more bacteria.

The night of the science fair I was pretty certain I would win the blue ribbon for my class. My write-up and display board were all so highly scientific. Jana's experiment had taken a lot of time, but there was nothing really intellectual about her research, other than ordering some Petri dishes and swabbing several surfaces in neighborhood homes. I didn't expect her to place at all. Finally, this would be the night I would hear my father say the words I'd heard him say to Jana on countless occasions: "I'm proud of you." I skipped over to the school cafeteria turned science lab. "Come on, Mama, come on, Daddy, hurry up. Hurry up." I couldn't wait to see the award hanging from my display.

The sixth-grade experiments were at the front of the room. As soon as my father saw Jana's, with the giant blue ribbon attached to it, he'd put both hands on her shoulders. "That's my girl." He picked her up and swung her around.

"Let's go see the third-grade stuff. Come on, everybody." I'd dragged my mother by the hand toward the appropriate section. The first thing I saw when we got there was the blue ribbon practically glowing on Roberto Langston's project. *No, it couldn't be.* Next to his, the red ribbon hung on Mimi Forrester's Clean Drinking Water exhibit. Mine, three display boards down, held the brown "honorable mention" ribbon.

My father tousled my hair and said, "You'll just have to work a little harder next year, sport. You've got to keep plugging away if you're ever going to reach your goals." An hour later, I could hardly feel my feet as I trudged home behind my family. Jana was walking beside my father, carrying the blue ribbon in her hand.

I'd spent year after year from that moment trying to do something to earn his love—at least his approval. It wasn't until my senior year of high school—the year he killed my mother—that I decided I didn't care anymore.

Chapter 10

By Saturday morning, the rash had begun to spread down Dylan's neck and trunk. His fever remained high and there seemed to be no end in sight. As I walked to the end of the driveway to bring in the morning paper, I debated calling Dylan's doctor again, but decided that first I should do what every modern mother does when her child is sick—search the Internet for answers. First problem I had to face—I needed to find the Internet.

Once again, I cursed the fact that my father not only didn't have a wireless connection, he didn't even own a computer. I'd have to take my laptop and go into town. Unfortunately, I had no idea where.

I bent over to pick up the paper, remembering my encounter with the new owner yesterday. This was Patti Fox's paper. I grasped the paper between my thumb and index finger, holding the whole thing at arm's length, trying to avoid contact as much as possible. Yes, it was a childish thing to do, but I couldn't seem to help myself.

"Hey there. Did your paper get wet or something?" Patti's voice was coming from the sidewalk directly in front of our house.

I looked up to see her in jogging clothes and a high ponytail, stretching her left leg behind her. She obviously had just finished a run, but of course she hadn't broken a sweat. I lowered my arm to my side and said, "No, I just thought I saw a bug."

"Welcome to Tennessee. Home to some of the biggest and creepiest insects known to man." She nodded toward the house. "How's your dad and your son feeling?"

"Not so great, unfortunately, so I better get back inside." But just then, I realized that Patti might have the information I needed. "Hey, do you by chance know where the closest WiFi hotspot is to here?"

"No smart phone, eh?" She smiled.

"Well—"

Just as I was considering throwing my paper at her pretentious blond head, she said, "Me neither. Hard to afford on a budget."

For just a brief second I felt a smidgen of kinship with her. It lasted only long enough for me to remember the words she and her friends had written in shaving cream on my windshield in the summer after my junior year. Time to move on from here, so I redirected the topic. "I was thinking the library?" I took a step toward the house as I asked the question, wanting to send the message that this conversation was drawing to a close.

"There is WiFi at the library but their hours are limited. There's a coffee shop on the square that has wireless but it's always packed. I'll tell you the best place to go, especially from this neighborhood, it's Krystal."

"The fast-food place?"

She nodded. "You got it. They've got free WiFi, and it's only a couple of blocks from here."

"WiFi at a burger joint?"

She laughed. "I think you'll be surprised at what you find there. You walk in, and probably a third of the tables are full of laptops. It's the small-town equivalent to a Starbucks, I suppose."

"Well, thanks for the info. I better be going." I took a few more steps toward the house.

"Okay. Don't forget to check out the TalkBack blog while you're online."

"Sure thing." I said this without even a hint of sincerity as I dove inside the front door.

I put the paper on the kitchen table in front of my father. "Dad, I'm going to drive over to Krystal for a little while."

"Krystal? I didn't think you ate fast food anymore."

"I'm not going to eat. I'm going to take my laptop over there and use the Internet. It's the closest place to your house where I can get an Internet connection."

"Don't seem right to me, to use their Internet and not buy any food from them."

"I'll buy a cup of coffee. Make you feel better?"

He shrugged. "Guess so. I'm thinking maybe you should buy some corn pups and fries for your son—" he cleared his throat and continued before I had time to shut him down—"and for your poor old father who has been cooped up in this house for far too long."

"I won't get any for Dylan, but I'll bring you back some if you want. What would you like?"

"How about four corn pups and a large fry?"

"Four?"

His face took on a totally fake expression of innocence. "I'm really hungry."

I knew what he was going to do. He was going to eat a couple of the miniature corn dogs, declare that he was full, and then give them to Dylan, all in the name of not wasting food. Any other time I would have argued with him, but right now, all the fight was knocked clean out of me. "Fine."

I got in my rental car and drove to the fast-food restaurant I'd loved as a kid. The kind of place I'd learned too much about in recent years and decided to avoid at all costs with Dylan, hoping to teach him the benefits of a healthy lifestyle.

So I ordered my cup of decaf, then sat at a table against the windows. It amazed me to see how full this place was, and just as Patti had predicted, laptops were present in plentiful supply. A family with small children was at the table next to me, eating miniature square burgers and fries. On the other side, there was a large group of mostly senior citizens who had pulled several tables together. They were talking and laughing and having a grand time. It was hard to concentrate with all the noise.

When I finally settled into my Internet search, I got a plethora of responses. There was one site, though, that I found especially helpful. It described different scenarios in children where rashes appear and what might accompany them. There were hives, and eczema, and then there was a whole page devoted to viral rashes. Sure enough, just like the pediatrician had said, these were the most common suddenly appearing rashes. It even said if your child has a fever and then breaks out in a rash, it is probably one of these harmless viruses and there's nothing to be concerned about; just treat him symptomatically.

There was a list of a few viruses which could be identified by the particular kind of rash—chicken pox, Fifth disease, coxsackie—none of which matched what Dylan had. Roseola had some similarities, three days of fever before the rash, for instance, but it specifically stated that the fever usually broke when the rash started. Well, we'd had two days of rash and no end of fever in sight. But still, it was similar enough to assure me that Dylan indeed did have some sort of virus, and I promised myself to quit worrying about it. This new resolution lasted for all of fifteen minutes.

When I arrived home, bag of greasy food in tow, I took one look at my son and immediately started worrying again. I took his temperature and it was still a hundred and three in spite of a dose of Tylenol a couple of hours ago, and his rash had moved all down his body. This could not be a regular virus. Something was wrong. Really wrong.

Since it was Saturday and all regular medical offices were closed, I loaded him into the rental car and drove him to the local walk-in medical clinic. The building was brand-new—something we rarely saw in seaside California—with gray tile in the entranceway, a tasteful berber carpet in the waiting room, and granite counters at the reception desk. It all smelled of fresh paint, carpet glue, and disinfectant.

Thankfully, there was only one other person in the waiting room—an overweight middle-aged woman with a rhinestone-studded shirt and earrings the size of Texas. She nodded toward Dylan. "He doesn't look like he's feeling so good."

I rubbed his back. "Not at all. It's been a rough week."

"Bless his heart." She shook her head and continued to look at Dylan, his head resting on my shoulder. "Bless his sweet little heart. I remember when mine were that age. It was so hard when they got sick. I always wished I could be sick in their place."

"I know what you mean."

Just then a nurse came to the door. "Mrs. Steepleton?"

The woman used her hands against the chair arms to struggle to a standing position, but then turned and pointed at Dylan. "That young man there looks like he's feeling a bit worse than I am. Why don't you take him back first? My sore knees can wait a few more minutes."

"Are you sure?"

"Of course." The woman dropped back into her seat.

"Thank you," I said as I scooped Dylan up in my arms. "Thank you so much."

"Don't mention it, honey. You just get that little one well."

The nurse coaxed Dylan out of a death grip on my neck long enough to take his weight and temperature and told us the doctor would be right in. Less than a minute later, I heard the chart rustling outside the exam room and the door opened soon after.

Dr. Crawford was young. In fact, he looked younger than me, which was impossible. He wouldn't have had time to complete college and med school and be practicing. Would he?

He shone a flashlight in Dylan's eyes and with a gloved hand pulled down the bottom lid. "Looks like he has a bit of viral conjunctivitis." He put a tip on the flashlight and looked into Dylan's ears. "Ears are perfect." He ejected the tip into the trash. "Take a few deep breaths for me, Dylan."

Dylan took a slow, deep breath, then another, and another, while the doctor moved his stethoscope all around Dylan's chest and back. "Lungs are clear."

"What does that mean?"

He shook his head. "Probably viral. There are a couple of things we need to consider with a rash and high fever. Has Dylan been bitten by a tick recently that you know of?"

I shook my head. "Never."

"Rocky Mountain spotted fever is endemic to this area. It comes from a tick bite and causes a rash and high fever. However, the rash usually occurs on the wrists and ankles, and Dylan doesn't really have any rash in those places."

"So you don't think that's what it is?"

"No. I also don't think it's the other possibility, scarlet fever, but why don't we do a rapid strep test and just see if it shows anything?"

"Okay."

He brought in what looked like a long Q-tip. "Now, Dylan, when I say 'go,' you open your mouth real wide for me and stick out your tongue. Okay?"

" 'Kay."

"Go."

Dylan threw back his head, opened his mouth, and stuck his tongue way out. The large Q-tip went inside his mouth and kept going. He started gagging, and the doctor pulled it out and looked at me. "Just give me a few minutes."

"Okay." And Dylan and I were left alone in the exam room.

"That hurt, Mama. Why did you let him do that?"

"He had to, honey, to see if he could find out what is wrong with you."

"I don't like that doctor. Dr. Conrad never pokes things in my throat."

"You've never had a rash like this when Dr. Conrad was around."

"She wouldn't poke me anyway." He folded his arms across his chest in a show of complete indignation. "The doctors here aren't very nice."

"I'm sorry, kiddo." I kissed the top of his head and rocked back and forth as best I could in a straight-backed chair. "So sorry." I began to hum softly, no real tune, just a comforting sort of sound.

Dr. Crawford came back into the room. "The test came back negative. I suspect this is a virus that will be self-limiting. Here's my card. Please do call the clinic if he gets worse, or if he's not better by Monday."

"Thank you." I walked from the waiting room angry at myself. Dr. Conrad had said this exact thing, my Internet search had agreed, and yet I had wasted the money for a doctor's visit anyway.

I drove home berating myself. Yet still, when I looked in the rearview mirror and saw Dylan in the backseat, I knew how sick he was. How could I not err on the side of caution?

As we pulled into the driveway, Mrs. Fellows was just making her way up onto the front porch. She saw my car and turned to walk toward us. "Hi, Grace. How's that boy of yours?"

"Still not very good, unfortunately. We're just getting back from a trip to the doctor. He says it's a virus that should pass. I hope it does."

I opened the back door and reached in to unbuckle Dylan from his car seat. "Come on, darling." I hefted him up onto my hip, admittedly a bit eased by the pediatrician's assessment. Just a virus; it would pass. Dylan would be better soon.

"I brought some chicken and dumplings and some homemade cookies. Hopefully that will make him feel better."

Dylan lifted his head from my shoulder to look at her. "Thanks for the cookies." His head dropped against my shoulder again.

I looked toward Mrs. Fellows, waiting for her smiling response to my son's good manners. Instead, I saw her put her hand over her mouth, just covering a gasp.

"Mrs. Fellows. Are you all right?"

She lowered her hand from her mouth and pointed at Dylan with it. "I declare, that's something I never thought I'd live to see again."

She had my full attention now. "What?"

"Measles. That child has the measles."

Chapter 11

My hand was trembling as I looked at the business card I held and tried to push the correct numbers on the phone. The phone rang four times before someone finally answered. "Shoal Creek Walk-In Clinic. Can you hold, please?"

"Uh—" Muzak was coming through the line before I had the chance to attempt an answer. A thin film of sweat was forming on the palm of my right hand, so I changed the phone to my left hand and wiped the right on my shorts.

"This is Christi. May I help you?"

"Uh, yes. This is Grace Graham. I was just in there a few minutes ago with my son, Dylan."

"Oh, right. The rash."

"Yes." The rest of what I needed to say was right there, waiting to come out. But I couldn't bring myself to say the words. "Uh . . ."

"Did you have a question?" There was definite annoyance in her voice now.

"Well, it's just that my neighbor . . . when I pulled into the driveway, my father's next-door neighbor was outside. She's older—eightyish I guess—and she saw Dylan and said she thinks he has the measles."

"Measles?" I could almost hear the tolerant smile in her voice. "Don't you worry one bit about that. With today's vaccines, it's almost impossible that he could have the measles."

"Well, that's maybe not totally true. You see, Dylan's never received a vaccination."

"Never?"

"No."

"At all?"

"No."

"For anything?"

"None."

"Oh my." She paused for just a moment. "Let me put you on hold and go talk to the doctor for a minute. Okay?"

Muzak filled the line again. It gave me time to try and remember my research on the MMR vaccine and the reasons that it wasn't necessary to give. Measles was a fairly benign virus, as I recalled, and what Dylan was experiencing now was as bad as it got. At least I hoped that's what I recalled.

Well, a week or so of fever and rash sure beat a lifetime of autism. I thought of Jasmine and Collin's life and had no regrets for my choice. I knew there were plenty of parents who would disagree, but since they would have vaccinated their children, thereby making them safe from catching this, there shouldn't be any problem.

For the first time since we arrived, I was grateful that we hadn't seen Jana and Hannah since Monday. I was also now somewhat thankful that Jana did not share my concerns about vaccines. As much as I had lectured her about mindlessly allowing the doctors to put all sorts of microbes and foreign chemicals into her baby's tiny body, now I admit I felt a bit of relief in knowing that Hannah was safe. I wouldn't want to be responsible for making Hannah sick.

"Ms. Graham, this is Dr. Crawford."

"Hello, Dr. Crawford. My neighbor saw my son and thinks . . ."

"Yes, I heard. With your son's vaccination history, or rather lack of one, it is possible your neighbor could be right. The only way to confirm that—and we do need to confirm it—is to draw some blood from Dylan. The only place we have the proper medium is at the hospital. Can you take Dylan to the lab there? I'll call them and tell them you're coming."

"O-okay." My entire body had gone numb.

"Now listen, this is important. Measles is a highly contagious virus, we do *not* want you in the lobby with a bunch of other people if Dylan truly has been infected. I'll make some calls so that they'll be ready for you. Do not, under any circumstances, bring him into the building until you've heard back from me with instructions on what they're going to do."

He took my cell phone number and told me to start a full list of people Dylan had had contact with while contagious.

This was the first bright thought in this whole

situation. Dylan hadn't left the house since Monday afternoon. Although he had been running a fever then, he hadn't gone near anyone. At least that was one problem we didn't have.

Chapter 12

Mrs. Fulton had known I was pregnant and desperate when she hired me to work at the Blue Pacific. I had trouble understanding why she was so generous about the whole thing—when my father and my so-called friends were certainly less sympathetic. I didn't have to wonder for long. My first day at work was the day I met Jasmine. And Collin. He had been four then, the same age Dylan was now.

The front office of the bed-and-breakfast was nothing like the rest of the house—done up in Victorian elegance, quiet, serene. It looked like any other office in the city might look, two small oak desks crammed in a too-tight space, each stacked with papers, computer screens sending an odd glow, the smell of stale coffee wafting through the air.

The phone was ringing and ringing. Mrs. Fulton looked at the girl behind the desk. "Elizabeth, I just received a call from Jasmine. I don't think she's going to make it in today."

"But, Mrs. Fulton, we need her. We're

swamped in here. The phone's ringing off the hook, this is the end of the month, all the invoices are due. We have that big group arriving from Arizona this weekend."

"I know, I know. We're just going to have to muddle through as best we can. Grace will help answer the phones. You won't mind staying a little late tonight, will you, dear?" She looked toward me, and her expression was so sweet, so utterly guileless that I couldn't have refused her anything.

"I don't mind."

"Thank you so much. I knew we could count on you. Now, settle in at this desk right here. Elizabeth will show you what to do."

"Mrs. Fulton, I have plans for tonight. This is not fair." Elizabeth twisted her dark hair around her finger and glared at Mrs. Fulton, apparently not the least bit uncomfortable to have this conversation in front of me. The new girl.

Mrs. Fulton nodded briefly and I saw the hint of moisture in her eyes. "Unfortunately, there are a lot of things about this life that aren't fair. The sooner you learn that, the better off you'll be." She walked out of the room as if the matter were completely settled.

The door had barely closed behind her when Elizabeth looked at me. "Jasmine is already half an hour late. Owner's daughter or not, she needs to show up to work, just like the rest of us. I wish

I could decide I just wouldn't come in on a day when I'm running a half hour late." She shook her head. "She was supposed to go to the market this morning and pick up some nonperishables that Chef Jonathan needs for breakfast in the morning. I am *not* running out for flour and sugar during my time off, mark my words."

I pictured this Jasmine girl, a spoiled rich brat, still in her pajamas, maybe just now waking up to decide she couldn't make it in today. Even though I'd never met her, I instantly disliked her.

Two hours of total chaos later, when the office clamor had finally begun to calm a bit, *she* walked through the door. Her hair was short and curly, almost frizzy, and she wore a long brown skirt and a yellow tank top. She didn't look remotely like the glamour-puss I'd been picturing. I'll never, for as long as I live, forget the look on her face. Her eyes were red and puffy from where she'd obviously been crying, but beyond that, her expression was completely hollow. As if her entire soul had fled from her, leaving nothing but this shell. "I brought in the supplies for the kitchen. Can someone help me unload them?"

Elizabeth refused to even look up at her. "I've got to finish these invoices."

I stood. "Uh, I'll help."

She looked toward me. "You must be the new girl."

"Yeah, I'm Grace."

"Well, Grace, how about following me? We've got some stuff to unload from the back of the SUV parked around back by the kitchen."

"I need her to help in here." Elizabeth snarled the words in an I've-been-at-work-all-day-while-you-haven't sort of way.

Jasmine didn't bother to look at her. She turned and walked through the office door, calling over her shoulder, "I think you can spare her for just a few minutes."

Not knowing what else to do, I followed after Jasmine. I was just to the door when Elizabeth called from behind me, "She would've had all the time you need if you'd bothered to show up for work today."

Jasmine wheeled around, almost knocking me over in the process. I backed up so she could reenter the office. She crossed her arms across her chest and leaned on the doorway, frowning toward Elizabeth, something like a dare in her eyes. "You want to know why I was late?"

"I'm guessing I already do."

"Oh, somehow I doubt that you came up with this one."

I took a step backward, wondering if I should continue to stand here or return to sitting at the desk. Or should I walk out of the room and go unload the SUV and leave these two to work out their differences? Since Jasmine was blocking the door, this one wasn't really an option.

"I took Collin with me into Trader Joe's." Jasmine looked at me then and said, "My son is autistic. Fluorescent lights and crowded places don't make for a good combination with him. They tend to stimulate his already overstimulated mind."

I nodded as if I understood, but in truth I didn't. Yet.

"Right from the get-go, he was fussy, so I shopped as fast as I could. He saw some candy near the checkout that he wanted, but I'd already written the check and there was a line behind me. Collin went crazy on our way out of the store."

She paused a minute and began to pick at her thumbnail. "Elizabeth, you've seen Collin when he's in meltdown mode; you know how ugly it can get. I think it is safe to say that this was one of his bigger melts. So . . ." She looked up toward the ceiling, staring as if seeing the scene projected against the white paint. "I grabbed him out of the cart, and he was flailing and screaming at full tilt now. 'No! No! No go!' "

Jasmine went silent and rubbed her hand across her face. Elizabeth's irritation had cooled enough that she looked at me and said, "Collin doesn't use many words. 'No' is one he has perfected."

My stomach flipped picturing the scene. I thought about the baby growing inside me and wondered what my future held. Was this what motherhood might look like for me, as well?

"Yes he has." Jasmine sighed. "He was kicking at me as hard as he could and hitting at me, although I was holding his arms against his side. I got him in the car and managed to buckle him in, but he was still screaming, kicking, and hitting, shouting 'no.'

"I walked around to the back of the car, tossing the stuff in as fast as I could because I wanted to get out of there. I put the last bag in and closed the hatch and drove out of the parking lot. Fast. Meanwhile, Collin was kicking the back of the seat, hitting himself, hitting the windows, flailing like he was hurt." She shook her head, biting her bottom lip in what I assumed was an effort to retain control.

"I made it about three blocks before I noticed blue lights in my rearview mirror." She rubbed her temple between her thumb and middle finger, effectively covering her eyes in the process. "It seems that several people in the parking lot who witnessed the scene had called 9-1-1 and reported a kidnapping in progress."

A kidnapping? I couldn't understand how a child's tantrum could be mistaken for a kidnapping. Once again, Elizabeth looked at me and spoke. "Collin is four; he's big for his age and looks at least six. No one expects these kinds of tantrums from a six-year-old."

Jasmine dropped her hand and looked up. "So that's why it took me until now to make it here.

Between calming Collin, and then calming myself, I just couldn't do it." She looked directly toward Elizabeth. "I'm sorry I bailed on you today."

Elizabeth nodded. "Come on, let's go empty your car."

That first day and many others since with Collin replayed in my memory as I drove Dylan to the hospital. I hadn't told Dad where we were going or why—there'd be a lecture I couldn't bear at the moment—just drove as fast as I could, formulating with each mile a list of reasons for not having vaccinated my son.

But as it turns out, nobody even took the time to ask. Then.

As we'd been told, a lab technician was waiting for us on the sidewalk at the back corner of the hospital. She was wearing what looked like a large yellow gown, and a mask covered the lower half of her face. "My name is Emily. I'm the lab tech who will be working with Dylan today." She held out a couple of yellow gowns and masks. "We'll need both of you to put these on before we go in."

"Only girls wear yellow. That's yucky." Dylan coughed as he hid himself behind my legs.

Emily held up one of the yellow gowns. "Haven't you ever seen a doctor on TV, Dylan? They wear these things all the time."

"Real doctors? Like when they do surgery?" He reached out his hand to touch the gown.

"Yep. Or see patients that might have certain germs." Emily nodded encouragingly. "Someone might even see you wearing this and think you work here, so absolutely no performing surgery today, no matter what they ask you to do. Okay?"

"'Kay." He put the mask on his face, but he was coughing and it made it difficult for him to take a deep breath. Still, he was totally enthralled with the whole idea of looking like a doctor, so he became very cooperative in the process in spite of the fact that he was sick. I hurried into my mask and gown. We followed Emily inside, through a series of corridors until we reached a door labeled Critical Care Unit.

Just the sight of it took my breath. "Why are we going in there?"

"We need a negative pressure room so we don't spread any germs around."

"Oh." I couldn't think of a more intelligent response.

Emily looked to be about my age, but cuter and far more put together. She led us through the unit, and into a room with a double set of doors. She pressed the nurse call button. "Will you let Dr. Mabry know I've got Dylan Graham in the negative pressure room?"

"I just talked to him. He asked that you wait until he gets there to draw anything."

"Will do."

She looked at me. "The on-call pediatrician will be in to check him out in just a minute. I think he wants to take a look before we start drawing labs, just in case there's something else he wants to add when he sees him." She looked toward Dylan. "No one wants to poke twice if you could save the second one by being thorough."

"Okay." It was as if my mind had ceased to function. Somehow I sputtered, "I took him to the clinic this morning. The doctor there didn't mention measles, but my elderly neighbor, she thought it might . . ."

Emily's gloved hand reached out and squeezed my arm. "Don't you worry. We'll get to the bottom of this. He's going to be okay."

I nodded numbly. Dylan climbed into my lap, coughing inside his mask. "I want to go home."

Me too, buddy, me too. "Don't worry, we'll be out of here before you know it. I'll bet we'll make it home in time to watch *Clifford the Big Red Dog.*"

"Well, what exactly do we have going on in here?" A man in a yellow suit and mask entered the room. His shock of gray hair and the smile lines around his eyes led me to believe that he was close to sixty. Somehow in this situation, his advanced age comforted me. He walked over to us. "You must be Dylan. I'm Dr. Mabry, and if you don't mind, I want to take a closer look at your spots."

" 'Kay." Dylan didn't move, so Dr. Mabry was forced to lean closer and examine him on my shoulder. He looked first at Dylan's forehead and neck, then pulled back the sleeve on his yellow gown before looking back up toward Emily. "This rash could very well be measles. It certainly looks like it."

He pulled out a flashlight from his pocket. "Open your mouth for me, Dylan."

"You're not going to poke one of those things into my throat, are you?"

"Nope, no poking. Just looking."

Dylan's mouth remained firmly closed. Dr. Mabry held up one empty hand, the other hand holding only the flashlight. "See. I don't have anything. Promise."

Dylan finally opened his mouth, and Dr. Mabry leaned forward and looked inside. He looked at me and nodded toward Dylan's outstretched tongue. "I would say what we are looking at here could be what is left of Koplik's spots. Have you noticed these bluish white spots in his mouth over the last few days? Looks kind of like salt granules?"

I shook my head, ashamed and surprised that I could have missed something. "What are they?"

"They are called Koplik's spots. They usually appear a few days before the rash breaks out, and they are diagnostic for measles. Unfortunately for us, they go away about the time the rash starts, so it's not terribly clear at this point." He pulled his flashlight back and pulled down the bottom lid of Dylan's right eye, which was red. "Yep, just what I would have expected." He let go and put his flashlight back into his white lab coat. "I've not seen a case of measles in a long, long time. But your son . . ." He sounded more intrigued at having a real-life specimen than accusatory toward me for not vaccinating. "He's got all the classic hallmarks. We need to proceed with the strong assumption that he does have the measles and go from there."

He looked at Emily. "I'm going to put in a quick call to Dr. Welton. I saw his car out back. I'd really like him to come take a look. In the meantime, I'll order the labs so you can get started." He picked up a clipboard from the counter on the far wall, spent some time writing on the top paper, then handed it to Emily.

"Who is Dr. Welton?" I asked.

"He's our infectious disease specialist. He drives down from Nashville one day a week to see patients in the clinic." Dr. Mabry removed his glasses and wiped them against his sleeve. "He's only in town today because last night we admitted a young lady with an unusual infection and he came to check on her. It's our good fortune that he happens to be here."

Emily pushed Dylan's sleeve way back and pulled out a strip of what looked like red rubber. "Dylan, I'm going to tie this around your upper arm for just a minute. Okay? It'll be a little tight, but I won't keep it on for long. Can you squeeze this ball really hard for me?" She reached inside her yellow gown and pulled a rubber ball from her lab coat pocket.

"I guess so." Dylan gripped the ball without further comment, at least until a few seconds later when he saw the needle. He started screaming, an all-out bloodcurdling scream. "No! No! No!" The sound echoed off the walls until I was certain the glass windows would shatter.

It took three of us—Emily, Dr. Mabry, and me—to hold him. I kept Dylan in my lap and hugged him tightly, trying to keep him still. All the while he was screaming, "No, no! Mama, help me! Mama, don't let them!"

I felt myself getting sick at my stomach. Holding him still when all I really wanted to do was to pull him away from all this was the hardest thing I'd ever had to do. "It's okay, Dylan. Just calm down. It will all be over with soon." There was no way he could hear me over his own screams, but I continued to repeat the words, just because that's what a mother does.

"Okay, everyone ready?" The nurse thumped her gloved hand on the vein at the crook of

Dylan's arm. "One, two, three, a little stick."

"Owww! Owww! That hurts!" Dylan's screams got louder and the strength of his fight tripled. He thrashed and convulsed like nothing I'd ever seen.

"Got it," Emily said. Then she pulled loose the elastic tourniquet she'd tied around his arm to help pump up the vein. "Almost over, Dylan."

I looked down to see red liquid flowing into the syringe. She changed tubes a couple of times, then pulled out the needle. Finally, this trauma was coming to an end.

A few moments later, Dylan had a SpongeBob Band-Aid over a rolled piece of white gauze on his arm. He was still crying, but the screams had stopped now. He looked at me. "Why did you let them do that?"

"I'm sorry, honey. I'm sorry."

"I didn't have to look hard to find this group. I heard the yelling all the way down the hall." Another yellow-clad man, this one very tall, had entered the room. "What have we got here, Richard?" He looked toward the other doctor.

Dr. Mabry gestured toward Dylan. "Take a look and see what you think."

Dylan shrunk against me. "Don't touch me."

"It's okay. I promise not to hurt you. I just want to take a quick look. Okay?"

Dylan held on tight, but the doctor reached forward and pulled Dylan's hair back from his face to look at the rash. He then looked at the arm sporting the SpongeBob Band-Aid. "Measles. It has to be." He looked at me then. "Have you been in Oregon recently? Particularly in the Ashland area?"

I shook my head. "No. We live in Ventura, California. I haven't been anywhere other than there and here."

"When did the rash start?"

"Thursday night."

"And when did you fly here?"

"Last Friday."

"Well, that's a piece of good news. He wouldn't have been contagious on the flight, which would have made this an epidemiological nightmare. You haven't been anywhere else, you say?"

"Nowhere."

"Hmmm. Well, for now you need to keep him completely isolated from everyone. Stay confined to your property, absolutely nowhere else. Understand?"

"Yes."

"In the meantime, you need to think about everyone you've had contact with in the last week or so."

"The only places we've been this week were church last Sunday—that was the day before the fever started. And on Monday, he was running a low-grade fever and coughing. We sat in the surgical waiting room while my father had knee-replacement surgery. He didn't get a rash until Thursday night, so we should be good. Right?"

"Waiting room? In this hospital?" Dr. Welton ceased his examination of Dylan's spots and looked at me.

I nodded.

He turned his attention toward Dr. Mabry. "We need to notify infection control. All medical personnel who were in the facility that day need to have documentation of adequate vaccination or they will have to be put on leave until they can otherwise prove immunity."

"But that was three days before the rash started," I said, certain these doctors were overreacting.

"Unfortunately, with measles, the patient is contagious for about four days before the rash starts. That's usually a day or so before any significant symptoms show up. And, since measles is one of the most infectious diseases around, anyone you get near during that time is exposed. Possibly the people at church on Sunday, definitely the people you came in contact with at the hospital. I'll get in touch with the health department and let them know what we suspect."

People put on leave from work? What exactly had we just unleashed?

"Did you go anywhere else besides the waiting

area while you were here?" Dr. Welton was focused on me now.

"The cafeteria, the gift shop, and we walked over toward the newborn nursery, but they have that hallway locked off now, so we couldn't go in there."

"Well, that's certainly a good thing. We don't want babies exposed; that would be a worse-case scenario."

My mind was wildly flashing from scene to scene of what had occurred over the last week. One scene in particular kept playing through my mind. "Umm, Doctor . . ." My tongue was so dry I could barely speak. "You should probably be aware that at church Sunday we worked in the nursery. My niece and five other babies were in there, but I know my sister has chosen to vaccinate. I'm assuming the rest of them have, too. So they should all be fine, right?"

"When you're saying babies, what age are we talking about?"

"There weren't any newborns, but none of them were walking yet. I'd say the range was six months to a year."

Even the mask could not disguise the panic in Dr. Welton's eyes. "Sunday would be right on the cusp of whether or not he was contagious. Let's just pray that he wasn't yet, because babies usually aren't given their measles immunizations until between twelve and fifteen months. If Dylan was infectious on Sunday, and he may very well have been, it is highly possible that every single child in that room will come down with the measles."

"Oh no." My body went numb. I looked at Dylan. "My niece has a lot of ear infections. I hate the thought of adding what Dylan has been through this week to her problems."

Dr. Welton said, "If all those babies experience what Dylan has been through, and nothing more, I will be thankful."

"What do you mean?"

"Measles can be quite serious in infants. Lots more possibilities for complications."

"Isn't there something you can do to stop it?"

"Not now." He shook his head. "If we find out about exposure within seventy-two hours, we can actually give the exposed person the vaccine with pretty good results. We're considerably past that point. After three days but up until six days after exposure, we can give a shot of immune globulin, which is somewhat protective. What time were you in the nursery?"

"Ten until eleven."

The doctor looked at his watch. "It's four o'clock. Past the deadline." He and Dr. Mabry exchanged a meaningful glance. He looked at me. "At this point, we're just going to have to wait it out and hope for the best. In the meantime, we need to contact the mothers of all those babies. Best case, they get put on quarantine for what turns out to be no good reason. Worst case . . . well, let's not even go there."

Chapter 13

As I pulled into my father's driveway, a feeling of relief—of safety—washed over me. Strange how this place that had felt like such a prison to me only hours ago was suddenly the only refuge I had.

My father was nowhere in sight when Dylan and I came through the back door and into the empty kitchen. I got Dylan settled in the living room, then returned to the kitchen and simply stared at the phone. I did not want to make this call. But if I didn't do it now, she might hear from the health department first, and that would only make matters worse. I finally removed the black plastic handset from the base and punched in her number.

"Hi, Jana, it's me."

"Hey there. I was just about to give you a call. How's Dylan feelin' today? I hope he's better. We all really need to spend some time together."

"Umm, not so much."

"Really? Does he have an ear infection or

something? I've never heard of the flu lasting this long."

I really did not want to continue this conversation. I did not want to be in this situation at all, but that wasn't a choice I had anymore. "Well, here's the thing. We've just arrived home from the hospital."

"Hospital?" Her voice squeaked with concern. "Oh, my goodness, is he all right?"

I dropped into my old chair at the kitchen table. The one I'd sat in beside Jana for so many years while we talked about swings, and boys, and life dreams. And now it had come to this. "We're not certain yet, but it appears that he potentially has the measles."

"Mea-sles?" She drew the word out long and slow. "Oh, wow. Oh, Gracie, I am so sorry. So very sorry. That must be so awful for him and you."

The fact that she didn't use this time for an I-told-you-so moment was a true testament to my sister's class and good grace. I wondered if she would still be so gracious when she heard the rest of what I had to say. "I think someone from the health department will be calling you soon."

"Calling me?" She almost whispered the question. "Why?"

"They are trying to reach everyone he came into contact with during the contagious phase."

"But we haven't even seen you since Monday, and we kept a good distance then."

"I know. It's just that apparently . . . the contagious phase in measles starts several days before the rash, maybe even before he had a fever. That could make it . . . possibly Sunday."

"Oh no." The other end of the line went silent, but I could hear her practically hyperventilating. "Sunday." She barely mumbled the word. "Surely not." Again, this was whispered, and I suspected meant more for herself than me. Finally, she said, "So what are we supposed to do?"

"Unfortunately, it seems that they figured out what was wrong with Dylan too late to give Hannah and the other babies any kind of preventative treatment. At this point, the doctor said we just have to wait it out. And, Jana?"

"Yeah?"

"The health department will be calling all the other mothers. I think they're going to impose some sort of a quarantine; I'm not sure."

"Oh, my poor Hannah. Those poor darling babies and their mamas." She paused, absorbing the implications, I supposed. "Some of those women are single mothers. How are they supposed to do a quarantine?"

"I don't know, Jana. I wish there was something I could say, something to make this better."

"I'll tell you what you can say. Tell me you

haven't brought measles to my baby. To all those sweet babies."

"You know I would never, ever have put her in danger like that. If I'd had any idea at all that Dylan had the measles—or anything at all, for that matter—I would never have let him near her."

"That's the choice you made, though, isn't it?" She waited quietly.

"What do you mean?"

"Well, there's no reason to go there right now, is there? I'll get off the phone and call the other mothers from church. Better they hear it from me than from some public health official."

"Maybe I should do it. It will give me a chance to—"

"You know what? I think it's best that I call them." Her voice was tight, controlled, completely lacking in the usual southern sweetness. "This is awful. This is terrible. This is . . . this is . . ." She went quiet again.

"I'm so sorry." There was so much more I wanted to say, but I chose to simply wait her out.

Finally, she whispered, "What have you done?"

I didn't think I wanted to know the answer. The phone disconnected with a click. Apparently Jana didn't want to know, either.

"Well, well. Sounds like we've got ourselves a bit of a mess here, doesn't it?" Dad had come into the room behind me while I was talking.

"You heard?"

"I heard enough." He let go of his walker and shuffled forward to grasp the kitchen counter. "I wonder how many people he exposed?"

"We haven't really been anywhere other than church and the waiting room at the hospital. Thankfully, there weren't any small children in the waiting room that day. Problem is, all those kids at church were too young to have been immunized, and now they're talking putting employees on leave from the hospital if they can't prove immunity."

"Oh boy." He shuffled over to his kitchen chair and lowered himself in. "What about when you went to the doctor's office this morning?"

"I hadn't even thought of that." I picked up the phone and called the number they'd given me for the health department. "This is Grace Graham. It just occurred to me that we went to the walk-in clinic this morning. The doctor there thought it was just a virus, so we didn't take any precautions."

"Uh-oh." The man whistled. "Was the waiting room full, do you remember?"

"No. There was just one other lady. She was older, very nice—let us go in front of her." I pictured her kind face, remembered the way she'd put us ahead of her own convenience. "She should be all right, right? She was probably close to sixty, so she would have been vaccinated, right?"

"Most likely. The problem with measles is that

the droplets remain in the air for a couple of hours. So if someone walked into the waiting room an hour behind you, there is still a possibility the disease could have spread."

"Oh." Just when I'd thought it wasn't possible for me to feel worse, I did. It was then that I truly began to wonder just how many people my choices were going to affect.

Chapter 14

Dr. Welton called a few hours later. "Ms. Graham, I've contacted the health department and the CDC. We all agree that we should proceed with this as a confirmed case of measles. The blood will not be back until early next week, but at this point, the likelihood is high enough that we need to proceed accordingly."

I had known this was likely, but the shock of absolute reality hit. Hard. I focused every bit of my attention—at least the part of my brain that was still functioning—on dealing with what needed to be done next. "All right. What should I be doing now?"

"Keep Dylan at home. Don't let him leave the property at all. His fever should start to go down by tomorrow, if it hasn't already, and the rash will begin to fade. After four days of the rash, he won't be contagious anymore. It started Thursday night, right?"

"Yes."

"Why don't we say stay in until Tuesday morning, just to be certain?"

"Okay."

"Were you planning on flying home sometime this week?"

"Not until Saturday."

"He should be fine to fly by then. Just fine. We've got the list of people Dylan might have come in contact with and have made the appropriate notifications. Have you thought of anything else?"

"No."

"That's good. We're also trying to piece together where this came from. Everyone agrees that it is a bit too much of a coincidence that there is an outbreak on the West Coast—not California maybe, but close enough at about the time Dylan contracted the disease. They've sent the blood off for genetic typing to see if there is a connection. In the meantime, you told me that you have not been to Oregon, or anywhere farther north than Ventura, is that correct?"

"Yes."

"Patients usually get sick ten to fourteen days after exposure. Can you remember anything at all from a couple of weeks ago that might give us a clue?"

I closed my eyes and tried to remember. "We're just coming out of the slow season, so the inn where I work hasn't been at capacity. There haven't been any children at all, mostly adult getaways. I flew out here a little more than a week ago, so I suppose it could have been someone on the airplane."

"That could be true, if he developed the disease quickly. I hope that is not the case, because if there was someone contagious on that plane it could make for a much larger outbreak. I'll be in touch. Remember, you need to keep Dylan at home."

"Not a problem."

I hung up the phone and put my head onto my folded arms on the table. This really was happening. I just prayed that Dylan hadn't been contagious that day in the nursery.

Dylan fell asleep in front of the television with an untouched apple juice beside him. I walked out into the backyard and over to the crab apple tree. I looked at the stones and thought about fresh starts and new beginnings. That's what this trip had been about for me, I supposed, coming to some sort of peace with my father, and rebuilding my relationship with my sister. Starting over. Now it was too late. A fresh start was no longer possible for me. I'd messed things up too badly.

Jasmine needed me at home, needed help with the inn. Perhaps I would see if I could get my airline tickets moved up to next Wednesday. There was no reason to waste my time here, working on what could not be fixed. Dad would be fine to get along without me in a couple of days—I was sure of that—and my early departure might make this easier on all concerned.

I thought about Jana, and her statement that I always ran when things got hard. At this point, I was pretty certain she would be more than happy to see me run out of here for good. She wasn't going to want anything to do with me.

"What'd the doctor say?" Mrs. Fellows had come up behind me without my noticing.

I looked at her and shrugged, trying to blink back the moisture that had gathered in my eyes. "Looks like you were right. It's the measles."

She nodded. "I thought so. I had measles when I was a kid, but I don't remember much about it other than my brother and I had them at the same time, and they put us in a dark room, curtains drawn, because the light hurt our eyes." She was studying my face, no doubt noticing the hint of tears. She walked closer and patted my arm. "We all came through just fine in the end, so don't you worry overmuch about it."

"Dylan's going to be fine; I'm pretty sure of that. Problem is, it's possible that we infected a whole nursery of babies at church Sunday. None of them were old enough to have been vaccinated yet. Measles is especially dangerous for babies, and my niece is one of them, and if they all get sick, I don't know what I'll do." I dropped onto one of the wrought-iron benches and began to cry. "My sister is furious with me right now, and how can I blame her? Her baby might get sick because of a decision I made. Not one *she* made, one *I* made." I shook my head and rocked back and forth. "What are the odds? No one ever gets measles in America anymore. Why should I risk having my son injured by the chemicals in those vaccines?"

"There's more to that story we talked about the other day that might help you answer some of these questions you're asking."

"About you and Mom?"

"No, those folks at Gilgal."

I was not in the mood to hear Bible stories right now. "I probably should get back into the house."

"It'll just take a minute." She came to sit beside me and put her hand on my back.

"What is it, then?" I figured the sooner she started, the sooner she would be done.

"The Israelites made a pact with the people of Gibeon—something they shouldn't have done—but that part of the story is for another time. Right now what you need to know is that the city of Gibeon was attacked and Israel was obligated to help."

"I'm not sure how that ties in with a measles epidemic."

"Well, like I said, they shouldn't have made the treaty in the first place. At the time they were probably mad at themselves, especially mad at their leaders. They had made a decision, a wrong one, and now lots of people were stuck paying the consequences."

"So, basically, this story is about how wrong I am for not vaccinating." I definitely did not want to hear this.

"Didn't say that. Because there was some downright trickery involved in their decision to make a treaty. So they could also say, 'This is really not my fault; why should I have to pay the consequences for this?' Kind of like what you were just saying about not putting chemicals into your child's body. Those 'it's my fault, I blew it' thoughts fighting with those 'it's not my fault, why am I having to deal with this' kind of arguments can rip you apart. You know what I mean?"

I nodded.

"Thought you might." She clasped her hands together on her lap. "But you know what? It's not so important what got them to the situation; it's important what they were going to do now that they were in it. They chose to go forward and do the right thing, even though it wasn't necessarily in their best interest.

"So off they went to help this country who was now surrounded. They had to march all night, hour after hour. When they finally arrived the next morning, you can only imagine how exhausted they were, physically and emotionally, and now they saw that the city was situated so that it was going to be an uphill fight."

I shook my head. "I'm not sure I want to hear the rest of this. I want the hard part to be over. I don't think I can take the equivalent of an all-night march and an uphill fight in my near future." Even as I said the words, I supposed they both were likely to happen.

"None of us think we can when we look at a whole big picture like that. I think that's one of the reasons God just shows us one thing at a time. First the march, then the uphill. But the good news is, once Israel got to Gibeon, they took the enemy by surprise. Still, an uphill battle is never an easy thing, but you can imagine how the all-night march had made it doubly hard. All could have been lost, but God did a couple of incredible things for them."

"Like what?"

"First of all, He sent a hailstorm. With hailstones so large, they were landing on the enemy troops and killing them. In fact, more men were killed by the hail than by the sword that day. Can you imagine that?"

"If He was able to do that all along—destroy

the enemy by hailstones, I mean—take care of the whole situation by himself, why didn't He just drop the hailstones on the enemy before the all-night march and leave the Israelites safe and at home? And maybe at the same time, He could squash this measles virus before it goes anywhere else. For that matter, why didn't He squash it before it got to Dylan?"

"Sometimes we've got some things we need to learn. You take these lessons with you and apply them to the next uphill battle in your life. The next time things got hard for them, I'm betting they had a lot more confidence that God could handle it than they did before. Don't you think?"

"I'm sure, but I still think He could have done that while they were in the comfort of their own homes. They would have still remembered."

"You think so? In my experience, easy answers are often easily forgotten."

I thought about that and slowly shook my head. Maybe so, but it was all still irrelevant to what was happening here. "I suppose you're right. I wish God still did things like that. He could make Dylan all better and stop the disease from spreading to anyone else. Especially those little babies from the nursery on Sunday."

"Honey, He still can. He still can. But don't forget to ask about healing hearts in the meantime. Maybe those hailstones are needed to squash some hurts from the past, built-up anger, fear and insecurity, things like that. Point is, you've got to keep marching, moving in the right direction. You march forward with what little you've got left, determined to do what He's telling you that you need to do, and you pray, pray, pray. Knowing that He can do more than you ever imagine or dream about."

I doubted God would put much of an ear to my prayers. I was an unwed mother, had attended church sporadically at best for the past five years. I wasn't the kind of person God would listen to; I was certain of that. I stood up, ready to get away from the pervading sense of guilt and failure. "Thank you, Mrs. Fellows." *Yeah, thanks for making me feel worse than I already did.*

"Not at all, not at all."

I turned and walked back toward the house. I considered the story of the army and the hailstones, and my hope faded with each thought of it. Everyone knew that God didn't work like that anymore. I was the only one I could depend on, and I didn't have the strength or resources needed to fight this battle.

Chapter 15

Dylan was sound asleep, his little face and body so red with the rash that I could hardly recognize him. I put my hand to his forehead and thought that he did perhaps feel a little cooler.

Dad was laid back in the recliner, snoring. I pulled the cell phone out of my pocket, walked into my bedroom, and shut the door. Even as I hit number three on my speed dial, I wondered if Steve would answer the phone when he saw my name on caller ID. Actually, that's not true. I knew he would if he was available. Mad at me or not, he didn't play games like that.

"Hi, Grace."

"Hi." I suddenly couldn't make myself say more. Mr. Jefferson's lawn mower roared from across the street, the old clock on my dresser ticked off each second, but I couldn't form a single sound.

Finally, Steve broke the silence. "So . . . I heard you were back in Tennessee. How are things going with your dad?"

"Not so great, unfortunately." I took a breath so I wouldn't choke up. It didn't help overmuch. "I mean, he's doing okay, I guess, and we're getting along . . ." *Deep breath. Get through this.* ". . . I guess as well as can be expected. The problem is . . . it appears as though Dylan has the measles."

"Oh, Grace." He paused for a moment, the way he always did when he was changing lines of thought. "Where'd he pick that up?" The tone of his voice had completely changed. He was focused on me now, ready to at least offer a shoulder in spite of the sea of trouble that churned beneath us. I loved him for that. What I

154

wouldn't give to have him here right now. Well, there was no reason to continue that line of thought. *Focus on the point.*

"No idea. They're trying to figure it out now. I guess I just thought you'd want to know. The bad news is, he probably exposed several babies, including Hannah."

He whistled low. "How long until you know for sure whether or not they got it?"

"Three or four days. I don't know what I'll do if there's an outbreak. It will be my fault."

"I'm sorry, Grace. I know that's got to be so hard for you. I'm glad Jana and you are so close. That will make things easier, right?"

That's when I realized just how far the last week had separated us. He didn't know about Jana's phone call, any of it. The only reason he even knew I was in Tennessee was because of the message I'd left him earlier this week. He didn't know that what little rapport I'd managed to rebuild with my sister had been smashed to bits already, that it was time to cut my losses and retreat. Back to . . . nothing. Still, I had no right to dump all that on him, so I simply said, "Yeah, I guess you're right."

"Good. Hey, I got your message earlier this week. I talked to Darin—he was supposed to contact both Jasmine and her real estate agent. He had planned to wait until we knew for sure, but I told him to go ahead and make the calls."

"Knew for sure?"

"The group hasn't met officially yet. I'm still holding out hope the deal will go through."

"Really? I thought . . . I mean Martin said . . ."

"It'll be a tough sell, but it's not totally out of the question. Still, Darin said he would put them on the alert that there might be a problem." He paused. "I'll be in touch. Maybe after you get back we can talk. Hmm?"

There was nothing I wanted more. And nothing I needed less. I couldn't afford to get tangled up in this emotionally right now. "I'll probably be pretty busy, but maybe sometime we could talk."

"Well, good-bye, Grace."

Chapter 16

A few silent hours passed and I put Dylan to bed for the night. His fever hadn't worsened, but his rash still looked awful. As soon as he was tucked into bed, my father's home phone started ringing. I ran into the kitchen to snatch it up before it woke up Dylan. "Hello?"

"Grace?"

"Yes." I didn't recognize the female voice on the other end of the line.

"This is Patti Fox."

"Hi, Patti." She was the last person I wanted to talk to right now. "I'm sorry, but this is a really bad time, I can't really talk now."

"I know it is, and I'm so sorry. Unfortunately, that's also the reason I'm calling."

"What do you mean?"

"The paper is running a story tomorrow about the potential measles outbreak. I'd really like to be fair in our coverage. Would you like to tell your side of the story?"

I couldn't keep in my surprise. "How did you find out so quickly?"

"Once parents started getting calls from the health department and hospital employees started getting notified by their supervisors, my phone started ringing. Quite a bit, actually." The tone of her voice showed absolutely no hint of condescension, but I knew what she was thinking.

"Yes, I suppose it would." Of all the people to have this kind of power over me, Patti Fox was not the person I would have chosen. I pictured her gloating, thinking how my predicament would increase her circulation. The same hate I'd felt toward her in high school surged anew through my veins. "My side of the story? You want my side of the story? Well, my side of the story is that I've got a sick little boy."

"I know that your son has been quite ill. What I'm asking is, do you have anything that you would like any of the parents whose children may have been exposed to know? About your choice not to vaccinate?"

"I . . ." I considered telling her what she could do with her newspaper. I could slam down the phone right now and be done with this. But, somewhere deep inside me, a small voice whispered that this might be my only chance to tell my side of this story. Collin's side. I figured I owed Jasmine at least that much, and I wanted the truth to be known. I began to consider what I might say, what might make a difference. "I did a lot of research before Dylan was born. Those vaccines aren't safe, and since most of those diseases are rare now, it was a risk I was not willing to take with my son."

"So your decision was based on scientific research?"

"Yes. And . . . my boss is a member of a group that I've gotten to know. Parents whose children have been vaccine-injured—my boss's son is autistic. I've seen videos of him as a bright one-year-old, saying dozens of words, walking early, bright-eyed and friendly. After he got his MMR shot he developed a fever. A few days later, he quit speaking. Even as a seven-year-old he speaks little. His mother has never heard him say 'I love you,' but she has heard him scream for hours; she's seen him hit himself in the head over and over again."

"So, you decided you'd rather risk the virus than the vaccine?"

"Yes, I guess that's it in a nutshell."

"Just one more question." She paused for just a moment and then said, "The measles and autism link was widely noted after an article in the medical journal *The Lancet* back in 1998, where Dr. Andrew Wakefield found measles in the guts of several autistic children. This led him to the conclusion that the measles themselves perhaps played a role in the development of autism. Were you aware of that article when you made your decision not to vaccinate?"

"Yes." The vaguest sense of relief began to surround me. She had done her homework; she would understand the truth for what it was.

"Are you aware that since then, *The Lancet* has retracted the article? And, in fact, Dr. Wakefield has lost his license to practice medicine in Britain at this time?"

Or not. I could barely form the words to a response. "I've heard about the article retraction, but not the second part."

"Well, knowing that, does it make you wish you'd chosen differently?"

I pictured Collin, on the floor banging his head and screaming over the tiniest deviation from his normal routine. I thought of Jasmine's story of exactly how and when that started, and the story of every other mother in her support group was similar. And there were hundreds and thousands more who told the same story—online, and in the magazines Jasmine read. I realized I didn't care what the popular scientific theory was at the moment; I cared about what I could see with my own eyes. "No. No, I wouldn't."

"I have to say, that answer surprises me a little."

I knew that tomorrow's article was going to be a bloodbath as far as I was concerned, but having come to my previous conclusion, I was not going to beg otherwise. I was in the right, no matter what Patti said about me. "If you spent some time with my boss's son, it probably wouldn't."

"Thanks for answering my questions, Grace. Please feel free to contact me with anything else you want to add at any time."

Fair treatment. Right. In the clarity of hindsight, I regretted that I'd talked to her. I should have said, "No comment," hung up the phone, and let her make what she would of that. Well, it was too late to change it now. It was too late to change a lot of things.

Chapter 17

My father looked up when I walked into the den, where he sat watching the ESPN nightly recap. "Who was that on the phone?"

"You don't want to know." I shook my head, wishing for some relief from the myriad of thoughts and fears and hopes that were circling around in there. "Dad, I'm going to Krystal again really quick. I won't be gone long."

"Okay."

I parked beside the entrance and, on a whim, pulled out my laptop while I was still in the car. I opened it and searched for available connections. I was happy to see that I had a signal—weak, but still useful—right here in the car. I rolled the driver's-side window about a quarter of the way down, hoping to combat the heat and humidity with at least a bit of a breeze.

I opened Google and typed in the words *baby* and *measles* and *symptoms*. I knew what to expect from a four-year-old, but I wasn't clear on exactly what could happen in the babies we might have exposed. The first site I went to started with the words, "Measles is one of the most dangerous diseases for babies." The car's interior was suffocating. I couldn't get a deep breath no matter how hard I tried; the oxygen just seemed pressed out of me. I skimmed on down until I saw the words, "Before vaccinations, measles used to kill millions of children around the world."

Oh no. Oh no. Please, God, please don't let those babies have measles. I took a deep breath and looked farther down the page, wondering just how bad it could be. I stopped at the line that said, "Measles is caused by a combination of two different body humors." *Body humors?* I almost wept with relief. Obviously this was not a legitimate medical Web site.

I went back to Google and tried again. The next site detailed how the droplets of measles stay active for a couple of hours outside the body. Dr. Welton had said the same thing. "A non-immunized person with a close exposure has a very high likelihood of contracting the disease, upwards of ninety percent." Very high likelihood? Ninety percent? I pictured the babies from Sunday school—there had been six, counting Hannah. If Dylan was contagious that day, and if this Web site was correct, then at least five of them would soon be sick, maybe all six.

I skimmed on down to read the information under the heading "Possible Complications." I loved the opening line. "A complete and uncomplicated recovery is expected for most otherwise healthy children." I liked that a lot. It did go on to list a few of the more serious side effects that could happen—pneumonia, meningitis, and inflammation of the brain. Awful, terrible complications. But if these only happened rarely, the odds were in our favor, right?

The final sentence in the section took my breath away. "Children under the age of five are most at risk for serious complications." Each child exposed at the church was well under five years old.

Still, these complications were rare. I was going to have to depend on that.

One last thing before I turned off the computer. I typed in the words *Oregon measles*. Since the doctor had asked if we'd been there, I assumed there must be a reason.

The page was filled with links. I chose one from a local news station.

```
"Ninety families affected so far
by local quarantine, authorities
say more will follow."
```

I clicked on the article.

```
Ashland, Oregon, home to the
Shakespeare Festival and a well-
off and highly educated
majority, has one of the lowest
vaccination rates in the
country. Parents here opt for
organic food and a natural
lifestyle.
```

Well, hooray for the parents in Ashland. I couldn't have agreed with their priorities more. But how did they go from healthy lifestyle to ninety families in quarantine? *Ninety?* Just the thought of it was staggering. I scanned farther down the article.

For many, that healthy lifestyle includes the absence of what they feel are toxins in vaccines. Physicians say it was just a matter of time before this outbreak happened.

Health officials are now telling us that the outbreak started when a family from Switzerland paid a visit to Ashland. The family took in a rendition of *Hamlet*, a couple of nice dinners, and a trip to a local park. They left town before their own child showed signs of the disease, and when children here first started getting sick, due to the rarity of measles, it took the doctors several days to determine what was wrong. Since several of the exposed children had not been vaccinated, nor had their friends or siblings, the spread was rapid and unabated.

So far, one of the infected children, an infant too young to have received the vaccine, has been hospitalized due to high fever and extreme dehydration. Doctors here say they expect more to follow.

Oh no. Oh no, no, no. Surely not. Surely this was not going to happen here. Surely I hadn't brought this on the families of Shoal Creek.

I started the car, but instead of heading straight home, I pulled into the drive-through line. "I need six cheeseburgers and two large fries."

On the drive to my father's house, I ate three of the burgers and at least half of one of the fries, never tasting a bite. I pulled into the driveway and ran to the bushes, feeling my stomach preparing to heave. Whether from the unaccustomed greasy food or the guilt, I couldn't say.

Chapter 18

I schlepped out the front door, down the porch steps, and across the path on the lawn to the sidewalk. *The Shoal Creek Advocate* lay in an innocent-looking loose roll, held together by a thin rubber band. I picked it up and hurried back inside, waiting until the door was closed behind me before I slid the elastic off the end.

Will Shoal Creek Become the Next Ashland?

There has been an apparent case of measles reported by local health officials. Although the case is not yet confirmed, it shows all the hallmarks of the disease. Authorities are expecting confirmation by late this week. Until that time, several families in town have been notified that their child has likely been exposed and should be considered contagious and under quarantine.

This disease entered our community when a former resident came to visit her family in the Shoal Creek area. . . .

I skimmed down to the next paragraph, looking for something I didn't already know.

Anyone who was in Shoal Creek General Hospital on Monday, May 2, may also have been exposed. If you fall into that category, please contact your physician immediately for further instructions.

In Ashland, Oregon, more than two dozen children have been infected with the virus in the last few weeks. Many of these cases are school-aged children whose parents chose not to vaccinate.

I knew more than I cared to know about what was happening in Ashland, so I skimmed down the article to see what else it said. To see how bad Patti was planning to make me look.

Quick measles facts: Measles is one of the most highly contagious viruses known to man. . . .

I started skimming again. The list was matter-of-fact, telling the reader what to look for, the dangerous complications, and so on. Not one word of condemnation voiced. But I knew the readers would supply plenty of that.

I thought about the TalkBack blog that Patti had told me about, and wondered what kind of response this article would ignite there. I wasn't certain I wanted to know.

I called Jana. "Hey, it's me. How are things?"

"So far, so good. Hannah's still feeling fine; her temp is normal. I talked to a couple of the other mothers this morning; they all say the same."

"That is great news." And it was great news. It was also way too early for celebrating yet. We all knew that.

"Jana, I'm really sorry about all this. I would never have brought this to you if I'd had any idea at all."

"I know you wouldn't." Her voice was kind,

back to herself. "Serves me right for bullying you into coming out here in the first place. I don't know why I've been so insistent that you remain a part of this family when you've so obviously wanted otherwise for a long time now."

This is the conversation I'd hoped we could have over coffee sometime during my visit here. Not now. Not in the middle of all this. But this was all we were likely to have this visit. I needed to move forward. "That's not true."

"Isn't it?" Her voice got quiet.

"Well, maybe I thought I didn't for a while, but I know better now. I was hurt, and . . ."

"We all were, honey. The difference is, we stayed put and you ran off."

"I didn't run off; I went to college."

"Until the day you up and told us you were going to Santa Barbara City College, I don't think I'd ever heard anything come out of your mouth other than the fact that you were going to the University of Tennessee to study Creative Writing and Literature."

"Well, you weren't listening so much my senior year then, because Mom and I had been talking about UCSB and film studies."

"Yeah, but you were just saying that to tick off Dad, and I know it. I knew what you two were up to. Dad didn't think Creative Writing and Literature would get you a real job, so you and Mom concocted that whole scheme just to show him it could be worse. Even Dad would have to agree that Tennessee and writing were better than California and films."

"He bought it hook, line, and sinker, too." I could still remember watching my father's face turn a bright red when I showed him the brochure. "It never really had the desired effect, though. I think it just made him that much more determined to make me pick a real major that would get me a real job." I thought about my life. "I guess he won that battle, didn't he? Here I am, an office manager at a small inn."

"Who rarely comes home to see her family."

"You were already out of the house and engaged by the time Mama died. You weren't stuck here, living with the person who killed her. I was so angry with him I just couldn't stay here and look at him. And I did come home, a couple of Christmases ago."

"Because Rob wanted to see you and Dylan enough that he bought your tickets with his frequent flyer miles."

"He volunteered. I didn't ask for that."

"Because you didn't even want to come and see your family."

"Because I couldn't afford it. Honestly, Jana, that's all I need, an amateur shrink for a sister."

She got quiet for a minute, and I thought she might have hung up. Then she said, "Honey, he lost her, too."

That argument had never held weight for me. It wasn't going to start now. "He lost her—we all did—because of *his* bad decisions. No one had to lose her."

"I'm not sure you're the right person to be making that argument anymore. Maybe you should think about that."

And I did think about it. I could think of nothing else. Still, I knew I had made the right decision for my son. The question was, at what price?

Chapter 19

In spite of myself, I barely waited until Monday's newspaper hit the ground before I rushed out to pick it up. I ripped off the rubber band and started reading. It didn't take long to find out what I didn't want to know. The TalkBack section was three full pages long, and considering that this comprised about a third of the total length of the paper, I saw this as a bad sign. The first entry was almost a full column long, and it was titled "Fruitcake Medicine."

Former Shoal Creek resident Grace Graham has lived in California for the past five years. During that time, she attended college without bothering to graduate, had a son without bothering to marry his father, and apparently bought into all the Hollywood starlet hype that vaccinations are bad for our children without bothering to think about how that choice might affect others.

As a mother I can appreciate wanting to do what is best for your child. However, what I cannot appreciate is when you get that information from people like Jenny McCarthy, a former Playboy bunny, instead of from the CDC and other respected medical sources.

How dare this person presume to know why I made the choices I made? She had no idea of what had shaped my decision. She had no idea about Collin. Or Roger. Or Jessica.

Unfortunately for the rest of us—responsible parents who do vaccinate our children—her son has exposed numerous vulnerable members of the population. Being one of those parents who is now waiting with a sick dread, wondering just how bad it will be for my daughter, I say to myself, why? Why would another mother have put me in this situation? The answer, well, it's something I have yet to figure out.

Anonymous

This letter had come from someone in the church nursery. From a parent whose baby I had watched while she enjoyed an hour of sitting, listening, and relaxing.

But I knew that none of that would matter now. All that mattered is that I had made a choice that was putting her baby at risk. For a mother, nothing else would matter. As much as I hated to be the brunt of this, it was logic that I couldn't dispute.

I looked at the next one, not sure why I was going to put myself through more of this.

Who Is Responsible?

My neighbor is one of the babies that has been exposed. For the next three weeks his parents have to keep him inside his own home. Unless, of course, he is lucky enough to break with a rash before then, at which time we're told he will be allowed back into the public four days later. His mother works full-time; his father works full-time. They are each having to give up work hours to stay home with their infant son because they are no longer allowed to take him to the day care, which has three other infants, due to fear of exposure. Who, I ask, should be responsible for the financial loss they are suffering right now?

I submit that vaccination should be a choice a parent is allowed to make. However, the people who choose not to vaccinate should be held financially responsible for the havoc they cause in the lives of the rest of us who actually do the responsible thing.

sallysmom

I decided I wasn't ready to read the other comments just yet.

I spent the next hours idly paging through an old paperback mystery and toiling over the crossword puzzle in the paper. The only page of *The Advocate* I could bear to keep in front of me. Finally, my cell phone rang to break up the monotony and I checked the caller ID on my cell. Steve. I needed to let it go to voice mail, to get him out of my life for good. Then again, he might be calling about the Blue Pacific deal, and that was something I needed to know. Of course, I could get that answer from voice mail if I didn't pick up. I let it go to the fourth ring when I finally decided I really wanted, needed, to answer. "Hello."

"Are things going better today?"

"Hardly." I looked out the window and I could see smoke wafting past the corner of the house, where my father was rocking and enjoying yet another cigarette. "I can't wait to get out of here. I'm so tired of all of it—it's not enough that Dylan is sick. My father is refusing to even attempt his physical therapy assignments, he's grumpy as all get out, and if I have to watch that man smoke one more cigarette, so help me, I'm going to lose it." Another reason I shouldn't have answered. For some reason, no matter how much I tried not to, I always unloaded every single bit of my anger and frustration on Steve. No wonder he wanted to be around Daria.

He laughed. "He just had surgery; he's gone from being a complete do-it-yourself kind of guy to being dependent, even if only for a brief time. I think you could maybe cut him a little slack, don't you?"

"I'm certainly not getting any." I looked at the

paper, folded on the table. "The local newspaper here has a blog. For their non-computer-savvy customers, they put the choicest comments in the paper. You should see what the people are saying about me."

"I'm guessing you're not the most popular mommy on the block right now."

"That's the understatement of the year. I'm thinking of writing a letter to the editor, but I doubt she'd print it. I just wish those people could stop for one minute in all their self-righteous indignation and see my side of this story for what it is."

"Sometimes it's hard to see both sides of the story when someone you love is being hurt by one of the sides, huh?"

"I know that."

"I'm just thinking . . . it sounds a lot like you and your father, doesn't it?"

"No. That's completely different."

"You think? He made the decision he considered best for him—willing to accept the risk of the consequences. He just wasn't thinking that those consequences might extend to other people, as well."

"You know what? I think it's best for both of us if we just make this a clean break. We're obviously going in different directions."

"You're doing it again."

"Doing what?"

"Every time you get under pressure, you react by pushing everyone—including me—away. You come up with all sorts of crazy excuses to make it seem reasonable."

"I do not."

"Take the Dodgers game, for instance. You know I was there with a bunch of people from the office. Daria was one of them, sure, but so was Randall Dickson and Matt Jenkins. She was just an excuse, because you don't want to admit you are afraid. Why can't you realize that some things are worth staying put and fighting for?"

His words reminded me of Jana's, about how I always ran away. That wasn't true. I had just learned, the hard way, to remove myself from unhealthy situations. I needed to spend my time and my energy on my son and on forging healthy relationships. The only problem with that—at this point I didn't have any healthy relationships left.

Chapter 20

Steve's phone call left me even more frazzled than before and it was all I could do to keep from pacing the house. I hadn't committed a crime, and yet it felt like I was under house arrest. I'd barely even stepped outside for days, and now we were running out of juice, bread, and milk. I needed to go to the grocery store, but I didn't want to go in the middle of the day. It was bound to be full of people, likely some of whom had read the paper and would recognize me. So I waited until a little after seven.

I hurried through the aisles, grabbing the first "no sugar added" apple juice I saw on the shelf and tossing it in the cart, then power-walked up the bread aisle. An uncomfortable sensation of being watched began to crawl up my spine. I looked around me and saw no one but a teenage boy looking at pastries and an older woman squeezing the loaves of white bread. Still, the feeling didn't lessen.

There was only one cashier on duty in the full-service lane tonight, and she spoke so loud I could hear her throughout most of the store. "What kind of recipe you gonna use this in?" "You gonna fry this chicken or grill it?" "Did you hear about Norma Jean?"

Never before had I fully appreciated the self-checkout at a grocery store the way I did right now. I hurried over to it, making a point to keep my eyes averted from the loud-talking cashier. I did not want to attract attention of any kind.

I scanned the organic milk, listening to the *beep* as it went across. The bread was next. *Beep.* Juice. *Beep.*

I was just sliding my credit card into the appropriate slot when I heard the cashier's voice again. "Really? She's the one? Are you sure?"

Though I couldn't be certain, it didn't take a genius to guess whom they were talking about.

I hurried out of the store and rushed over to my rental car. There was a torn piece of white paper under the windshield. I snatched it up, threw my groceries into the backseat, then locked the door and turned the ignition before unfolding the paper.

It was written in blue ink, in neat printing.

Go back to California where you belong. You're not welcome here.

I glanced in my rearview mirror as I pulled from the parking lot. Nothing seemed unusual, but the note under my windshield had multiplied the discomfort I'd felt earlier in the store.

It wasn't a long ride home, but I got caught at the second light on the one and only main road through town. Again I looked in the mirror. There was a large red pickup truck behind me. I couldn't see the driver due to the glare of headlights. Could it be the note writer?

I wanna be a paperback writer. Paperback writer.

I jumped so hard my leg hit the steering wheel. I snatched up my cell phone from the side pocket of my purse. "Hello."

"You knew, didn't you?" Jasmine's voice was cold and flat.

"Knew what?" It was a weak attempt at a cover-up at best, but it was all I could muster.

"Right. That's what I thought."

"Jasmine, why don't you tell me what you're talking about?"

"How is your father?" Jasmine spoke with slow deliberation.

"Dad's doing better." I turned right at the light and followed Springer Road closer to my father's house, saying nothing else.

I looked in the rearview mirror again, relieved to see that the red truck was no longer behind me, but there were headlights just turning the corner in this direction a little farther back. I held the phone to my ear, waiting.

I knew Jasmine was about to unload on me. Maybe even fire me. Well, she would certainly have to be the one to bring it up. I was already dealing with an entire city that hated me here. I wasn't going to go asking for more of the same from the other side of the country.

"Great, that's great to hear." She paused a moment. "Listen, I know we talked about this earlier, but do you think there's any possible way you could work it to arrive a few days earlier than you'd planned?"

What was she up to? "I'd like to—you have no idea how much I'd like to—but my father really needs someone here taking care of him."

"You just told me that he was doing fine."

"Yes, fine for a sixty-five-year-old man who just had his knee replaced. That doesn't mean he's ready to live on his own yet."

"Well, I think my news might change your mind."

"What news?"

"Good news. Really good news, actually. The Wadley Foundation is serious about making an offer on this place."

"The Wadley Foundation?"

"Oh yes, I told you about them, right? They had made inquiries earlier."

Yes, and you told me that they often fire the entire staff when they take over an inn. "But I didn't think you were interested."

"I didn't think so, either, at least not until I got a call from one of Steve's investment partners last night. How long have you known that was coming?"

"Jasmine, I—"

"How long?"

"I found out that it was a possibility the day before I left for Tennessee. But I talked to Steve earlier this week, and he told me that the deal still might go through. He also told me that Darin was going to call you days ago."

"Don't you think at least it would have been a good idea to warn me that this might be coming? Before I signed a contract for $10,000 worth of remodeling on my home—the home that there would be no reason to sell if this deal fell through."

"I would have told you if I'd known before you started. By the time I knew what you were up to, it was too late. There was nothing for me to do but hope things worked out at that point."

"Sounds pretty spineless to me." She paused for a moment, then continued in a controlled voice. "The Wadleys are doing a first official walk-through on Monday morning. Because of the increased difficulties I am currently experiencing with my son because of the remodel—a remodel I would never have contracted had you bothered to tell me the truth—I would think the least you could do at this point is get back here early and help me get this place ready for their visit."

To help her get ready for the deal that would cost me my job. At this point, I didn't know what I would do if that happened. The likelihood of finding another job quickly in this economy was slim, and there was no one left for me to turn to. Steve. Jana. Jasmine. Dad. I'd managed to alienate all of them. "You don't think you'll be able to handle it alone?"

"As we've already discussed, the Oates family is here through Sunday. They arrived last night in a *big* way, believe me. Without you here, I'll be forced to employ temps to pick up some of the slack."

Every year the Oates family stayed for a week in May. Since the place was small, they ended up taking over half the rooms.

There were three generations of Oateses who graced our inn for a week each year. The grandparents were quite well off and actually very gracious people. Their three children, however, had been raised with very little responsibility or manners and carried none of it into their adulthood. The grandchildren ran wild, destroying things everywhere they went.

There had been crayon drawings on walls, broken crystal lamps, and numerous other issues when they came. Starting my second year working with the family, back when I still worked for Jasmine's parents, we had taken all the valuables and put them away, putting cheaper replicas in their place, if anything at all. Even though we charged the family replacement costs when they broke things, and the grandparents paid without complaint, it was just easier to lose a lesser quality crystal lamp than the Waterford Kells table lamp, which they'd broken a few years ago. Anything remotely valuable or antique was put away and locked up.

"I really do wish I could be there to help you; believe me I do."

"Why is it that I suddenly find that hard to believe, given what I've learned about your loyalty—or should I say lack of it?"

"I'm on leave without pay. It's not like you're having to hire temps to do what you're already paying me to do."

"Yeah, maybe I'll even find one that I can depend on to be honest with me."

"Jasmine, I am sorry. You're right I should have told you. I expected them to call you on Monday, and then things started going downhill here. When I finally heard from Steve, he thought it had been taken care of."

"This is in your best interest, you know. You were the one saying you didn't want to spend two weeks with your father and wished you could get out of it. Now I'm giving you the excuse you need and you're not taking it."

"Jasmine . . ." I started to protest, but then I saw what she was saying. She did need my help. And certainly nobody else in Shoal Creek wanted me here. Dad was improving, if slowly. I was prepared to lose another week of salary anyway. Why not just hire someone to check in on him so it wouldn't fall to Jana? "I guess if it is possible for me to get back there early, I will. In fact, I'll start working on it and see what I can do." Yes, the more I thought about it, the more appealing the plan became. "In the meantime, you can handle it, Jasmine. Just lock everything up, and I'll get there as soon as I can."

"I'm counting on it. Hopefully you'll actually

come through this time, although I guess I can't really count on that, can I?"

When I pulled into the driveway, my father and Dylan were sitting on the side porch. Although the outside lights were off—turning them on this time of year asked for more bugs than anyone wanted to deal with—I could see their silhouettes in the faint light of the windows behind them.

I bounded up to Dylan. "Sweetie! You're moving around again."

He grinned. "Yep. I'm feeling better. Me and Grandpa are sitting here looking to see if lightning bugs are out yet."

"I'm so glad, honey." I sat down in the rocker and pulled him up into my lap and started gently rocking back and forth.

The smell of cigarette smoke still remained on the porch, although my father currently didn't have one lit. I kissed the top of Dylan's head, but something about the all-pervading smell surrounding us dug a memory from my childhood.

I must have been in the fifth grade at the time. One day each week a policeman would come to our class and talk to us about drugs and alcohol and tobacco, and how we should never use them. I had taken every word to heart.

One afternoon after such a class visit, my father had gotten angry at me for forgetting to feed the cat. "It's irresponsible. You've got to learn to do what you're supposed to do, to pull your weight. This is completely unacceptable."

I listened and cringed and listened some more. Finally, I'd had enough, so I said something to the effect of, "Well, you smoke."

"What?" I could still remember the look on his face. The feeling of power I got when my choice of words pulled him off his high horse, if only due to confusion.

"You smoke cigarettes. That's worse than forgetting to feed the cat."

He actually looked stunned for about two seconds before launching right back on the offensive. "Smoking is not a good thing; you're right about that. It's something that you should never start. Maybe it will someday affect my health, but it's just me I'm affecting so that's a choice I'm allowed to make. When you don't feed KC, then you're affecting not only yourself but someone else. Or some*thing* else at least."

The memory still stung as if it were brand-new. But it wasn't. It was a lifetime ago. My mother's lifetime. I looked toward my father and thought, "You weren't just affecting yourself, were you?"

Dylan turned to look at me. "What did you just say, Mommy?"

It was only then that I realized I'd spoken aloud. "Nothing, honey, just talking to myself."

My dad's decision affected a lot more than just

himself. My mother, when lung cancer took her life. Jana and me, when it took our mother from us. I didn't know how he could stand to sit here and continue to do this, knowing full well what he'd . . .

For the first time in years I felt my anger toward my father cool when I was thinking in this vein. Fact was, I was now in the same place. My decisions hadn't only affected me—they hadn't only affected my son—there were lots more people being affected by them.

Perhaps this is what Mrs. Fellows would call "coming full circle." Back to the place where I decided to hate and never forgive my father. Back to the place where I had to look at what had happened before and do something different this time. The only problem was, it was too late for all of us.

Chapter 21

Even though I'd never finished reading through yesterday's TalkBack, today I couldn't help but unroll the morning paper, one eye closed, because I just had to look. I suppose I was hoping to see a lot of chatter about the end of the school year, a mayoral scandal, or anything else that didn't involve me. Before I even made it to TalkBack, the headline of the editorial column got my attention. I started reading.

More Than One Side to the Story

There are many in this community who believe that failing to immunize your child is the wrong decision. A selfish decision, even. There are many in the international medical community who would agree with that.

Yet there are others who would disagree. Robert Kennedy Jr. is one such advocate. Mr. Kennedy claims to have transcripts from June 2000 conversations of top members of the Centers for Disease Control, the FDA, and the World Health Organization, along with executives from those drug companies who manufacture vaccines.

In these recorded conversations, the executives are heard to say that they would not give these vaccines to their own children, that they know they are dangerous. The whole series of meetings is more focused on how to cover this up, how to avoid catastrophic lawsuits, rather than how to make babies safe from the neurotoxin of thimerisol—a mercury-based preservative commonly used in vaccines at the time. Mr. Kennedy contends that greed led these companies to disregard the health of American children so that they could continue to turn a profit

It only takes one visit to the National Vaccine Information Center Web site to terrify anyone. I invite everyone to take a look and see what there is to see on the other side. Stories of vaccine contamination, and children injured and even killed by normal childhood vaccinations. Stories of government agencies who knew there was a problem, yet chose not to act.

Perhaps before we are so quick to judge someone for making a decision other than the one we feel to be correct—perhaps the one that truly is correct—let's at least take the time to understand what it was that led to such a decision.

I was stunned. More than stunned. It never occurred to me that the local paper might run such a column. Who else was on the staff? I looked at the byline to see who wrote it. Patti Fox.

Patti Fox? Why would she have written this piece that so clearly went against popular opinion? That so clearly went in my favor? Perhaps she felt as though the controversy would bring more TalkBack, and perhaps more business for the paper.

Whatever the reason, for the first time I could ever remember, I felt myself thankful to Patti Fox.

My confidence swelled that people really were seeing more than one side to this issue. I turned a couple of pages. Perhaps today's TalkBack audience would be more open-minded, as well.

The first message today was titled "Common Sense." My optimism faded beneath a fog of dread.

Common Sense

Here's my question: What was that mother thinking?

She took that child to a hospital while he was running a fever. A hospital! We're not talking nice airy park, we're talking an enclosed building, full of people who are there because they ARE NOT WELL. What kind of mother brings a child who is running a temperature into that environment?

I'll tell you. One who has no common sense. None. We're talking DUMB. DUMB. DUMB.

Now our hospital may have to function short-staffed because of that ignorance.

Anonymous

Ouch.

I folded up the paper and put it away. This was not productive. This was not healthy.

I poured myself a cup of coffee, determined to think about happier things. Dylan was getting better; things were going to be okay.

"Hey, Mama, we can leave the house today, right? Can I go to the park?" Dylan shuffled into the kitchen, his eyes brighter than they'd been in days.

I put my hand on his forehead. Didn't feel warm. "How are you feeling, darling?"

"Much better. So, the park?" He smiled up at me, giving me his cutest, most persuasive grin.

I could only imagine what might happen to us if we went anywhere in public right now, with Dylan's rash still so obvious, much less the park where there were likely to be a lot of children. I shook my head. "Even though you're feeling better, I think you ought to get some rest for the next few days. We may be headed home soon, and as soon as we get there, we'll go to the beach. How about that?"

"Aww, Mom, I really wanted to go to the park."

The acidity of the coffee suddenly burned my stomach. I poured the rest of it down the sink.

Chapter 22

I heard what sounded like a car in the driveway and pulled back the curtains. I'd never been so happy to see Jana's brown SUV. I ran out onto the porch to greet her, hoping her visit was a good sign.

It had been nine days, the day of Daddy's surgery, since I'd last seen her. Since then we'd avoided having Dylan near Hannah, thinking he might give her his cold. A cold. If only that were the case.

A frown line creased Jana's forehead as she climbed up to the porch. Her usual put-together in a windblown sort of carefree demeanor was totally absent.

"What's wrong?" I met her at the top of the steps.

"Aunt Jana, Aunt Jana, you're here." Dylan came bounding out the door. "Did you bring Hannah Rose? Doctor says I'm not contagious anymore."

"Not today, darling, I . . ." She stopped speaking and stared at my son. "Oh, my goodness." She put her free hand over her mouth, and I could see tears pooling at the corners of her eyes. "I had no idea. . . ." She stared at my son and shook her head slowly. "Oh, you poor thing. Does it hurt? Itch?"

"Nah." Dylan looked down at his arms as if just now noticing the rash. "It itched a little for a while, but not too much. You should have seen it a couple of days ago." The pride reverberated in his voice.

"Really?" I could tell Jana was taking deep breaths. She looked at me. "It was worse than this?"

I debated about whether or not to lie. Finally, I settled on, "Yeah, it was a little worse."

"It was really red and bumpy. Grandpa took some pictures. You should get him to show them to you." Dylan held out his arm, turning it over and over again so Jana could get the full effect.

Jana kissed him on top of the head. "You poor, sweet darling."

But I knew Jana was no longer talking about my son. She was thinking about Hannah, her perfect smooth baby skin. I knew she was trying not to picture that sweet face covered with red bumps, wondering if her little angel would ever return to normal again. I understood this, because it was the same thing I worried about Dylan. Would he be scarred? How long was he going to look like this? I still asked myself these questions even as he was starting to get better.

In spite of my fears, I'd done the research, reading through all the articles I could find. I knew what science told me. I reached over and touched my sister's arm. "It's just temporary. It will go away and he'll be just fine again."

She nodded, but her mouth had curved into a deep frown. "Of course." She ruffled Dylan's hair and said, "Do me a favor? Will you go inside and see if you can find Hannah's pink blankie? I'm pretty sure I left it upstairs in Grandpa's room the last time I was here."

"In Grandpa's room? Really? I don't usually get to go up there."

"That's right, isn't it? Tell you what, we'll make an exception just this once. Okay?"

"Woo-hoo." Dylan raced inside, oblivious to the fact that his aunt had just sent him away so he wouldn't hear what she was about to say. I was thankful that his insightful radar had not yet reached the level it would in a few years.

"So what's going on?" I waited only until the door closed behind him before I asked the question.

"Hannah woke up with a fever this morning."

The words grabbed me in a crushing fist. *Oh no.* I tried my best to remain calm, think through the possibilities. "Could it be another ear infection?"

She shrugged. "It's possible. The doctor doesn't want me to bring her into the office for obvious reasons. She said she'd stop by my house during her lunch and take a look."

"Times like this make it really nice to live in a small town." I tried to sound upbeat. "House calls and all. You don't find that in bigger cities."

Jana looked back toward her car. "Paisha Benter spiked a fever this morning, too." Jana's voice was a full octave lower than normal now, and little more than a whisper. "She was the baby that Dylan was playing with on the floor. Remember?"

"Yes. I remember." I pictured the sweet little baby all in pink, up on her hands and knees rocking back and forth, trying so hard to crawl, but not quite getting it yet. There could be no doubt that she'd been plenty close enough to contract his germs.

I could barely bring myself to think about a child so young getting so sick. At least with Dylan, he'd been able to tell me what hurt and how I could help him. With a nine-month-old, there would be no such luxury. It would be downright awful for them—all of them.

"Her father is working out of state and won't be back until next week. Her mother can't go into work because Paisha can't be left at day care.

She's having to take off without pay until her mother can get here tomorrow night."

"Is there anything I can do? I'd be happy to help baby-sit, anything you can think of."

She shook her head, searching my eyes with her own as if looking for something. "Somehow, I don't think that's such a good idea."

"I just wish I had the power to make this all better."

"I'm scared," she said, a single tear leaving its trail of sorrow down her left cheek, "that this is about to get really bad."

Chapter 23

I stared at my phone for a long time. Every ounce of my being wanted to call the one person I could *really* talk to when things got hard. But that little voice inside me kept reminding me I no longer had that right.

Still, before I even realized I was doing it, I hit speed dial and held my breath. The phone clicked on the second ring.

"Hi, Grace. How is Dylan?" Steve sounded tentative when he answered his phone. I'm sure he wondered what I was going to dump on him now, given our last few conversations.

"Much better. Fever gone, rash fading, appetite back up."

"Good. Glad to hear it." He paused for a

moment. "Are you still coming home on Saturday?"

"I . . . don't know."

"What do you mean?"

What right did I have to dump all my worries on him at this point? "It's just that . . ." No. This wasn't right. "Well, I guess I was just calling to check in."

"Uh-huh." He remained silent for a minute. "Now, why don't you tell me what this call is really about?"

"It was a mistake. I'm sorry. I have no right to call and dump all my issues on you at this point."

"Well, let's just pretend for this moment that you do have that right. Now, tell me, what's wrong?"

"I helped Jana with the babies in the church nursery last Sunday. Hannah and one of the other babies broke with a fever today. Not confirmed, but likely measles. Likely all six of those babies will contract the full-blown virus by the end of the week. I don't know what to do. Tell me what I'm supposed to do." And with the outpouring of what I'd been keeping back for too long, once again I was throwing myself on his mercy.

"I guess I'm not sure what your choices are."

"Jasmine wants me to come back to work early. Collin has had a lot of issues in the last few weeks; she's getting behind on everything." I decided not to bring up the subject of why she needed me back, because it could easily cause this conversation to disintegrate.

"Doesn't your father still need help?"

"He's getting better, able to get around without his walker now. He'll be allowed to drive soon." I grasped for something more convincing. "We've got some of our worst usual customers at the Blue Pacific this week—they totally wreck the place every time they're there. Jasmine really is trying to get things fixed up, but Collin has been in meltdown mode all week with the renovations."

"So what do you think you ought to do?"

"I'm trying to look at it from both sides—emotional and logical. The emotional thing is to stay here because of the potential for measles that I brought here. But in truth, even if Hannah does break with the measles, there's nothing I could do about it. I mean, I could be here to help with Dad. And to be with Jana. If Hannah is about to get really sick for the next week, because we are the one who brought the virus to her—shouldn't I stay here for as long as possible?"

"Okay, continuing in the emotional category, let me ask you this. If it were an unusual strain of the flu, or some other disease for which there is no vaccine, would you feel so compelled to stay?"

I thought about that for a moment. What if it

were another virus or disease for which I carried no overt guilt? "This is different. The measles has more of a potential for being serious."

"You think so? I don't know the medical truth to that, but I would think that the flu has the potential to be just as serious in a kid that age."

"Maybe you're right." At this moment I was thankful I'd gotten up the nerve to call him. I was beginning to have real hope that I could leave here early, and with a clear conscience. "Maybe I've done all I can do here."

"Perhaps. Let's talk about what brought you out there in the first place. You took two weeks off without pay, less than three months after investing almost every bit of your savings into the down payment for your condo. You couldn't afford it, why did you do that?"

"My father had knee surgery. He couldn't stay alone for a while after. Jana's house has too many steps for him to stay there, so I came here to help."

"All that may be true, but all of that was true three weeks ago and I never heard you mention going back there. What changed your mind?"

"Hannah has had so many ear infections in the last few months, I was trying to come give Jana some relief."

"And?"

"And, I was dying to see Hannah in something more than an Internet video or Facebook photos.

Dylan really wanted to see her. He talked about it all the time. I figured it would be a good time to give him what he wanted while also being helpful."

"And?"

"And what? That's it."

"I don't think so."

"What do you mean?"

"Think about it, Grace. Why else did you want to make this trip? To stay at your father's house for a couple of weeks?"

"I don't know what you're talking about."

"Oh, I think you do. All the reasons you mentioned are true, and all of those reasons helped give you the justification to do what it is you truly came there to do—and only you know the real answer to that one. What I'm saying is, you've got to look at all the pieces of this puzzle and decide what you think is best about coming back. Has the reason you went home in the first place been accomplished? That's the question you've got to ask yourself."

"The reason I came home in the first place is to take care of my father so my sister wouldn't have to."

"Grace, I've talked to Rob. I know there was more to the story. It's time to deal with your issues, don't you think?"

"You're being ridiculous."

"I don't think so. You have let the past eat you

up for so long. You knew deep inside you that you needed to spend some time with your father and learn how to somehow forgive him. You knew it even before Jana called and told you she was tired of carrying all the burden alone. You've got to let go of your anger so you can become part of your family again. And beyond that, you need to let go of your fear."

A quick flash of anger filled me. "I am strong. I am independent. I do not live in fear."

"Don't even try to go there, Grace. You know you. You've lived in complete distrust of anyone other than yourself since your mother died. Well, maybe that's not completely true. What your mother's death left intact, Chase Gaines managed to finish off."

"I don't know why I even bother to talk to you about these things. You are so ludicrous."

"Grace, look at the truth. You don't want to live the way you have lived for the last five years. In a cave so surrounded by self-protection that you can't or won't love anyone other than your son. You know Dylan needs more. Somewhere deep down you know that you need more and it terrifies you. I think you wanted to spend this time with your father because you saw reconciling with him as your last hope."

"It's a good thing for you that you're a much better architect than you are an amateur psychiatrist. I came here because my father needed help after surgery and I wanted to give my sister a break. Period."

"Well, if that is the truth, then I'd say you've accomplished what you set out to do. You should be able to come on home without too much of a problem."

"Then I guess I'll be coming home early."

"Let me know what time to be at the airport."

"Don't worry about it. I'll get a ride home."

And we were right back where we started. Or ended. We'd done this cycle so many times lately, I was having trouble keeping up.

Chapter 24

"Her fever is a hundred and one." I could hear my niece's screams in the background. "She started crying around midnight and hasn't stopped. She just cries and cries and cries. I can't seem to comfort her no matter what I do. The doctor stopped by yesterday and said her ears were clear."

My worst nightmare was coming true. "Have you had any sleep?"

"Are you kidding? Can you hear that?" The crying got louder for a few seconds, so I'm assuming Jana held the phone a little closer to Hannah. "I don't know what to do for her. The Tylenol and Advil aren't really bringing her temperature down much."

"Jana, why don't I come over there for a while? I'll walk around with her and Dylan can try to entertain her a bit, and you can lie down and get some rest."

"Dylan?"

"He's not contagious anymore—not that I guess it matters much at this point anyway. He loves Hannah so much, and he does seem to have the ability to perk her up."

"At this point, I suppose it may be our only chance to spend time together. I'd love a little company."

I felt the tears sting my eyes. "I'm so, so sorry."

"I know, I know."

An hour later, I pulled up at my sister's house, my father and Dylan in tow. Jana met me at the front door, her face pale, huge dark circles under her eyes. Hannah, who was crying inconsolably, was propped against her shoulder. "If you think she's fussy now, you should see what happens when I try to put her down." She bounced up and down in a rhythmic pattern. "You just don't feel good, do you, darling?" Hannah's crying perhaps softened a little, but it still was shrill enough to leave no doubt in anyone's mind that she didn't feel well.

"The poor thing." I looked at my sister. "And you must be exhausted."

She walked back inside, taking bouncing steps

in an effort to quiet Hannah. "My sweet darling, I can't get her to eat or drink anything. Even apple juice, which she'll usually suck down in about half a minute flat. I hope this stage doesn't last much longer."

"Hi, Hannah Rose, hey there, girl." Dylan followed Jana inside, pulling gently at Hannah's hand. Her crying turned into a mild whimper as she turned to look at him.

His rash had faded and turned a bit brown, but it still covered a good bit of the skin on his face, arms, and legs. "Don't worry, Hannah. You'll be all better soon. Just like me." Dylan coughed into his elbow, then stood on his tiptoes trying to get closer to his cousin. "We can be spotted together. I'll help you through it. Don't you worry."

As if on cue, Hannah started crying again. It was heartbreaking to hear, especially knowing that she hadn't seen the worst of it yet. She paused in her cries only long enough to cough, then resumed with full volume.

My father groaned as he lowered himself into an overstuffed chair. "That kid sounds just like her aunt Grace sounded the day we told her she wasn't getting a pony for Christmas."

"Hey, I wanted that pony. I deserved that pony." I had never been more grateful to my father than at this moment, with his attempt to bring humor into a situation that clearly had none. It took a great amount of energy to play along, but I wanted to do whatever I could to cheer Jana up, even if only a small amount.

"Sure you did. It had been a full three weeks since you'd had to stay after school for detention."

"The only reason I got detention was because that Kendra Jenkins was always talking about her pony and being all hoity-toity about it. I can't help it if my hands just reached out and shoved her down a couple of times. She was lucky it wasn't a punch to the mouth."

My father laughed. "Lucky is right. I've seen you punch mouths for less."

I looked toward my sister, hoping she was preparing to join in the conversation. Somehow everyone in the family was always willing to jump in on the Grace-was-such-a-wild-child conversation. Instead, I found her staring out the window, bouncing Hannah, and seemingly oblivious to the fact that we were even there, much less engaged in an attempt to lift her spirits. I reached out my hands. "Why don't you give Hannah to me? You go take a nap, or a hot bath, or whatever you think would make you feel better."

She looked at me blankly but did hand me Hannah, who started to cry all that much louder when I took the place of her mother. I could see the indecision on Jana's face. "She'll be just fine, Jana. A couple of minutes and she'll be fine."

"I don't know."

"Don't worry, Aunt Jana, I'll make her happy. Remember, Uncle Rob said I could be her nanny. Bring her down here, Mommy."

I sat in a chair, holding Hannah in my lap, and began to bounce her on my knees. Dylan got right in her face. "Bwww, bwww." Hannah stopped crying for a few seconds and looked at him. "Bwww, bwww. Remember?" He put his nose only inches from hers.

"Okay." Jana started down the hall, moving more like a zombie than the perky woman I knew and loved.

Ring.

Jana returned to the living room and picked up the handset. "Hello." She listened a bit and closed her eyes, nodding. "I was afraid of that." She dropped into a chair. "Okay, I'll give them a call." She pushed the button and set the phone on the end table. "Ryan and Emma both have fevers now. That leaves only Hunter and Kelsey, and no one has heard from them either way." Thoroughly defeated, she headed to the bath.

I took Hannah out into the backyard, thinking the warmth of the day might help calm her. Dylan followed close on my heels. "Let me play with her, Mama, let me play." Dylan coughed twice, then continued, "Please, it's my turn."

"Just a minute. Let me try to get her calmed down first. Okay?"

"Should I get the stroller? We could take her for a walk around the block."

"She can't leave her yard, honey. How about we play on the swing set?" Hannah had barely been home from the hospital before Rob was busy installing the latest greatest backyard play structure. I had laughed about it at the time, but now, looking at how he'd replaced one of the regular swings with a secured baby swing, I saw the genius of it.

"Why can't she leave her yard?" Dylan took a seat in the swing beside hers and used his feet to push gently off the ground.

"Well, because she has the measles, just like you did, and they don't want her to give it to someone else." I locked the safety belt around Hannah's waist and gave a gentle push. She continued to cry, but it seemed to lessen.

"Did I give the measles to Hannah Rose?" He looked at his cousin, his blue eyes huge with angst.

"Well, in a manner of speaking. She probably got the germs from you."

"I didn't mean to, Mommy."

"Oh, I know that, sweetie, and so does Hannah Rose, don't you worry. Remember how after the doctor told us you had the measles, we didn't leave the house? It's the same thing. Once you know you're sick with something that other people might catch, you just have to stay at home until you're not sick with it anymore."

"Why didn't I stay at home before I gave the germs to Hannah Rose?"

"We didn't even know you were sick then. Remember?"

"Okay." He chewed on his bottom lip. "Mama, what's a germ?"

"Well, it's a tiny little—"

"I'm surprised you have the nerve to show your face around here." The voice called from a distance away. I looked toward the house next door. I saw a woman I vaguely recognized standing on the back porch, fists firmly planted on ample hips.

"What's she talking about, Mama?" Dylan put his feet down and stopped swinging, focusing every bit of his energy into watching the scene that was unfolding.

"I don't know." I spoke loud enough for her to hear, then turned my back toward her.

"I'm talking about my niece, Kelsey Whyte, who was admitted to the hospital last night."

That turned me around. "The hospital?"

"Yes, she was so dehydrated it took them over an hour to get an IV in her little veins. Her fever has been hovering around a hundred and three, and she hasn't been able to eat or drink for two days."

I thought about what Jana had said about Hannah not drinking. Alarms started going off that I didn't want to listen to. I knew I should respond to this, to say something about how I hoped Kelsey got better, or maybe even that I was praying for her. At least something to the effect that I was sorry. But none of that would come out of my mouth. I just kind of choked and said, "Come on, Dylan, let's go inside." I grabbed Hannah out of the baby swing, bumping her leg against the restraint in the process, which brought her to a renewed bout of tears. Finally the screen door slammed behind us.

"What's the matter with you? You look like the headless horseman is on your tail." My father looked up from the chair, where he'd obviously been napping.

"Aunt Jana's neighbor is mad at Mama." Dylan wrapped his arms around my leg, and I realized he was frightened by the whole episode. "Her niece is in the hospital. They had to poke her with needles for a long time."

My father looked up at me, a question in his eyes. I bounced Hannah and shrugged. "Kelsey Whyte."

"Ah, another of the Mohicans has bitten the dust, eh? We knew that was going to happen, right?"

Jana's phone rang. She came walking down the hall in a terry robe with a towel wrapped around her head. "I feel better—it's amazing what a warm shower can do. Thanks." She sort of smiled at me as she picked up the phone. "Hello?"

"Sonja, I am not going to put up with any more of that kind of talk. You know it was unintentional. You know that her son has been sick—" She listened to what was being said on the other end of the line. "Oh, I didn't realize. Her kidneys? Really?" Jana walked over to me and reached for Hannah, took her in her arms and squeezed her tight. "Please keep me informed, and please tell Bev I'm praying for them." Jana hung up, the color drained from her face. "That was Sonja, my next-door neighbor."

I looked at her. "Yeah, we met."

Jana nodded once. "So I gathered."

"What about Kelsey's kidneys?"

"When they admitted her to the hospital, they drew some blood work. I guess one of the tests came back that there might be something going on with her kidneys. Sonja said it could just be because she's so dehydrated, but they won't be sure until this afternoon or maybe tomorrow whether or not there is permanent damage." She shook her head. "What a mess this is. What a complete and utter mess."

"Hopefully we're seeing the worst of it," I said. I had little faith that my words were true.

Chapter 25

My cell phone started singing Jasmine's ring tone. Maybe I wouldn't answer it. I just didn't need one more complication right now. *I wanna be a paperback writer. Paperback writer. Paperback, paperback, paperback writer.*

Jana, my father, Dylan, and even baby Hannah were all looking at me. Looking toward the phone in my hand, their expressions ranging from expectant to annoyed. At least Hannah was intrigued enough to stop crying for a minute. I slid the phone open.

"Hello, Jasmine."

"Hi, Grace. I'm wondering if you have made arrangements to get back here early. Like today, hopefully, tomorrow at the latest."

I looked at my sister, bouncing the once again crying baby Hannah in her arms, and I thought about Kelsey in the hospital with the same disease now claiming my niece. "Not yet, but I'll start working on it." How could anyone blame me for going back and doing what I could to save my job? I got up and walked out into my sister's garage so I could talk in privacy.

"Why haven't you been working on it before now? We were just talking about it."

"Jasmine, do you remember when I told you that Dylan was not feeling well last week?"

"Yeah."

"Well, it turns out, he has the measles."

"You're kidding me. That is so weird."

"It's more than weird. It's awful."

"I didn't mean that him having the measles was weird. What I meant was, my friend Tina—you met her, right? When she stopped by the office for a while? Her son Michael came down with measles a couple of weeks ago—right about the time you left for Tennessee, I guess."

Michael. Michael. "Was he the redheaded kid?" I pictured Tina's long wavy hair and Birkenstock sandals.

"Yes. They were spending a few days camping along the California coast and dropped in for a visit. He wasn't feeling well that day so they didn't stay long."

"Yeah, I remember. I met them as they were loading into the car. Dylan was with me that day. . . ." I thought back to what I knew to be the incubation period for measles. I started counting backward on my fingers. "That's what happened." I dropped onto the steps that led into the house.

"What do you mean?"

"Dylan caught the measles from Michael. The health department has been trying like mad to find out where he might have gotten it."

"Dylan didn't go anywhere near Michael, did he?"

"No, I'm pretty sure he didn't. But the droplets remain alive for up to two hours while they are airborne. I'm guessing Michael spent some time in the office?"

"Yes, he was playing with the magnetic building set I keep in there."

"Right, and that's where Dylan went only moments later. I'll bet Tina and Michael live in Oregon."

"Ashland." She said it with a hint of resignation in her voice. "Michael was one of the first American kids to get sick. They've traced the outbreak to some tourists from somewhere in Europe."

"How's he doing?"

"He's fine now. How about Dylan?"

"He's not contagious anymore and his rash is starting to fade. He's feeling much better."

"So then why can't you get here early?"

"I'm not saying that I can't. I'm just saying I haven't finalized the plans yet. Dylan has only been clear to travel since yesterday. Now my niece has it. She's just an infant—too young to have been vaccinated yet, and her mother would have vaccinated. Things can get a lot worse for her. I think maybe I need to stay here and help my sister, make certain everything is going to be okay."

"Let me get this straight. Dylan is fine, your father is doing better, your niece is sick with a disease that was a rite of passage for children until just a few decades ago, and you don't want to leave because you're afraid that she might be one of the rare exceptions who gets seriously ill?"

I leaned my back against the door that led to my sister's house. I knew that there was a lot of truth to what Jasmine was saying. I also knew that one of the babies my son had infected had already proven to be an exception. "There's one baby already in the hospital—a baby that was exposed by Dylan."

"Hospital? Why would he be hospitalized for the measles?"

"Haven't you been watching the news? Several kids in Ashland are in the hospital. The same story as here, I guess. The baby was admitted for high fever and dehydration."

"Thank goodness it's nothing too serious."

Nothing too serious? I supposed that by clinical definition high fever and dehydration didn't sound all that bad, until you'd lived it, that is. "She's sick enough to need a hospital. That should tell you something about it being serious enough. My niece has had the tendency to get ill easily anyway, and I'm afraid for her."

"But your staying there won't change things for her one way or the other. By contrast, your coming back early could be just the little extra I need to get this place sold. You owe me that."

• • •

Hannah finally fell asleep in Jana's arms, and though it took some doing, I convinced my sister she needed some rest, as well. Despite my promise to watch Hannah closely, Jana only agreed to sleep if she were near her daughter, so we fixed up a pallet on the living room floor for Hannah, and Jana curled up on the couch nearby. Within minutes, both were asleep.

The silence felt eerie.

I herded Dylan and Dad into the den for some more television. I'd given up trying to enforce the time limits Dylan normally obeyed at home. These were not normal times.

With *Bob the Builder* onscreen, I left the men to their show and crept back into the living room and sat beside my sleeping niece, so worried about what might happen to her. Had I been wrong? Was all this because of a mistake I made?

With nothing to do but sit in the quiet room and listen to the warring voices in my head, they became deafening in their noise. I needed to do something to keep my mind busy.

That's when I noticed Jana's laptop sitting on the far table. I tiptoed across the room and turned it on, thankful to see that it automatically connected to her home wireless. I started to look up more facts about measles, but determined not to do anything that would further my feeling of guilt. So I began to do some mindless Web surfing. I examined clothes I couldn't afford, and looked at reviews of books I wouldn't have time to read.

Then I went to American Airlines Web site, looking to see what kinds of flights might be available tomorrow. Not necessarily planning to do anything, mind you, just looking. There was one flight available late tomorrow afternoon, *if* I chose to change my tickets.

What was the right thing to do here? I looked toward my sleeping sister and knew she was glad that I was here, but I also knew she was harboring more than a little resentment toward me right now—as were many people in this town. Would it be better for all concerned if I got out of here?

I closed the laptop and stretched, then walked into the kitchen to get a glass of water. Today's *Shoal Creek Advocate* was sitting on the kitchen counter, folded neatly. In spite of myself, I flipped it open and went to the TalkBack section, a temptation I had resisted at Dad's house this morning.

The Truth About Vaccines

Unfortunately, today's society is more influenced by anecdotal stories than hard scientific fact.

Fact: The Wakefield study which

showed a possible link between the MMR and autism involved twelve children.

Fact: A subsequent study in Denmark of over 500,000 children showed absolutely no difference in autism rates in children who did receive the MMR and those who did not.

Fact: A study involving 1.8 million people in Finland showed absolutely no link between autism and the MMR.

Fact: Even Wakefield did not advocate ceasing to vaccinate. His stated theory was that splitting the vaccines into three separate shots and giving them over a longer range of time would be less toxic.

Fact: Eight months before this paper was published, he applied for a patent for a "measles only" single-virus vaccine. A conflict of interest if ever there was one.

Fact: Japan started giving the measles, mumps, and rubella as three separate shots in 1993. Autism rates in the aftermath did not fall. To the contrary, in the years that followed, autism rates in Japan appeared to rise.

Fact: Too many Americans base their decisions about these kinds of issues on video they've seen on YouTube, on a flawed and eventually retracted paper that studied all of twelve children, and on whispered stories from the friend of a friend.

Question: How many innocent people are going to suffer because of some parents' decisions to believe YouTube over world-renowned scientists?

Dr. Joe Earl Stern

How could the people of Shoal Creek not hate me after reading that article? Even knowing what I knew, I hated myself after reading it. I slid open my cell phone and placed a call. "Yes, my son and I have tickets on a flight Saturday. I was hoping to see about getting them changed to tomorrow afternoon."

"Wow, I cannot believe she's still asleep," Jana whispered as she sat up on the couch and stretched. "What time is it?"

I looked at my watch. "Three o'clock. You slept for a couple of hours."

"Wow." She looked toward her daughter. "I'm glad she was finally able to get some rest."

"I'm glad you were, too. You need to keep up your strength."

She nodded. "I do feel better. Thanks for coming over."

"I'm glad I could. Do you want me to stay here tonight and help you?"

"No, that's okay. I think Rob and I can handle it."

"How about tomorrow morning? I really want to see you a little more before I leave."

"What do you mean?" Her voice got gravelly as she sensed the truth.

I swallowed hard, trying to get up the nerve to tell her what I was about to say. "It turns out that Dylan and I are going to have to leave tomorrow afternoon. Jasmine needs me back at work. It's an emergency. She called and begged me to get back as soon as I could."

"How long ago did you decide this?" Her voice was hard now.

"She called a few days ago, but obviously I couldn't travel with Dylan until Tuesday, and I didn't want to leave until I knew Dad was going to be okay without me. He can get by without his walker now, and he'll be able to drive by this weekend. I'll stock him up with groceries and he'll be fine."

"Your boss needing you is not what this is about and you know it."

"Of course it is. She's trying to sell the bed-and-breakfast. A deal fell through, and now there's a new buyer on the way. She needs help getting ready."

"This is about things getting hard here and you running."

"That's not true."

"Yes it is, and if you're telling yourself anything else, then you're lying to yourself." I looked at her and saw her glaring—actually glaring—at me, something I rarely if ever saw from Jana. "Why don't you go ahead and leave now? Take your son and go back to California and stay there. The rest of us would be better off without you around. We need someone we can count on, and that person is obviously not you."

Tears were streaming down my face with the sting of her words. Still, I was angry enough that I was ready to call her bluff. I walked over to the sunken den and leaned down. "Okay, fellas, we're heading back to Dad's house. Come load up."

My father looked up. "Do what?" When he saw my face, he put his hands on the arm of his chair and pushed himself up. "Come on, Dylan, we've got to get moving."

"Aw, the show's not over yet. Besides, Mama said we were going to stay here and fix dinner for Aunt Jana."

"Plans have changed, Dylan. Now turn off the TV. We've got to get moving."

"You don't have to be so grumpy about it," he said, without ever taking his eyes off the television.

"Dylan, that is not an acceptable way to—"

Hannah started screaming from the living room. I looked at my sister. "Do you need—"

Jana walked away from me, not bothering to turn as she called out, "Show yourself out."

End of conversation.

Chapter 26

That night, I tossed restlessly without finding sleep for the longest time. Eventually my thoughts turned to Roger. I thought about his mother, Lisa, a member of Jasmine's support group—a group that called themselves parents of vaccine-injured children.

Roger was seven. He was referred to as "high functioning." In fact, most people who came in contact with him would not even consider that he might be autistic. Odd, yes; spoiled, likely; autistic, not really.

He was into major league baseball. And I don't mean into baseball in the way that your average sports fan is into baseball. The Dodgers were his favorite team, and he knew the stats in detail for every single player on the team, from the biggest stars to the player that had just been called up from the minor leagues. He knew stats from their college careers, which high school they played for, and all sorts of otherwise mind-numbing information.

One time Jasmine had asked me to drop something off at their house on my way home from work. Roger had shown me his room—the walls covered with charts he'd made. Intricate to the point where he knew more about the players than most of their coaches did.

Roger's father, Jeff, was a top performer at his financial firm, and in appreciation, his boss offered him Dodgers tickets. Not just any tickets. He held season passes in the prime seats not far behind the third-base dugout.

Roger was beside himself with excitement at the thought of seeing his favorite team in person. On the day of the big game, though, as they pulled into the parking lot, Roger began to twitch, a sign of growing agitation. There were lots of people walking through the parking lot, and crowds often bothered him.

The stadium was loud with the hum of so many people—people bumping into each other, people shouting across the way to each other. By the time they started down the stairs to their seat, Roger had gone into tantrum mode. A screaming, kicking, biting tantrum.

Since he was seven at the time, well past the age when most children have outgrown tantrums, I guess no one would be surprised that people weren't overly sympathetic. As Lisa tried to contain him, to keep him from hurting himself, she could hear the comments around her—"spoiled brat," "needs a good spanking," "needs to teach that kid some manners."

Thirty minutes later she finally got him out of the stadium and back into the car. The two-hour drive home was mostly filled with him kicking and screaming. They never again attempted another Dodgers game.

The phone rang at my father's house in the middle of the night. I scrambled from my bed and ran into the kitchen, bumping into the countertop as I reached the phone. "Hello."

"Hannah's being admitted to the hospital. I thought Dad would want to know."

The panic over my niece's well-being superseded the sting of the intentional omission. "Dehydration?"

"Her temp is almost 103 and she just wouldn't quit crying. We finally brought her to the emergency room about an hour ago. They're trying to get an IV in her now, but so far no luck."

"I'll be right there." I was already heading toward my bedroom, preparing to change into clothes.

"No."

"Jana, I know you're mad at me, but—"

"No. They only allow one person in the patient's room overnight. Even Rob has to stay in the waiting room."

"Then I'll sit out there with him."

"I don't think that's a good idea, either. The waiting room is full of Kelsey's family."

"Oh." Not exactly a crowd that would be happy to see me. "Rob needs someone to sit with him. I'm coming anyway." I knew that Rob's parents were on a month-long trip to Europe, and I didn't want him to face this alone.

"No. I mean it. You go ahead and get on your airplane. We'll be fine."

"Jana, I am going to come. I want to be there."

She remained silent for just a moment. When she spoke again it was in a much softer voice. "I'll call you tomorrow morning, okay?"

"But I want to be there, to help, something."

"I think the way you can best help right now is by giving us a little space." I felt the frustration in her voice.

"Okay, if you're sure that's what you want." I hung up the phone and laid my head on the counter. *This is awful. Awful.*

"What's going on?" My father shuffled into the kitchen in his boxers and T-shirt. "I heard the phone ring."

"Hannah is being admitted to the hospital for high fever and dehydration."

He nodded. "You heading out there tonight?"

I shook my head. "No."

"Why not?"

"She . . ." The truth was so painful, so completely awful, that I could hardly bring myself to finish the sentence. Somehow I managed to choke out the words. ". . . doesn't want me to."

"I see." He scrubbed both hands across his face, leaving his gray bangs standing straight out in the aftermath. "I guess that's to be expected, all things considered. What a mess."

"Yes it is." I stumbled into my room but didn't lie on the bed. Instead, I knelt beside it. "God, help them. Help me. Help us all." I buried my face in the sheets and wept.

Chapter 27

My father was already in the kitchen when I walked in. His eyes were red, his hair disheveled. "You sleep any?"

I shook my head. "Every time I closed my eyes I thought of Hannah and what she's going through. And Jana . . ." I choked on her name. "I can't stand the thought of not being there for her."

Dad leaned his forehead into his left hand and nodded. "One of us needs to at least go out to the hospital and check on things."

"I agree." During the course of the night I'd

come to the same conclusion, and I knew that one had to be me. "I'll go."

"You sure that's the best thing?"

"You're not supposed to drive yet. I could drop you off, but I really need to talk to Jana face-to-face."

He looked at me long and hard for a minute. Finally, he shook his head, something almost like approval on his face. "If you're sure that's what you want."

"It is."

"Good for you."

"I'll just go get ready." I hurried from the room, too stunned to think of anything else to say.

On my way out the door, I heard Dylan say, "You want to go sit out on the porch, Grandpa? I'll eat some raisins while you smoke your cigarette."

It was all I could do not to turn around, pick up Dylan, and take him with me. But I was going to face Jana. I wasn't going to run from this. So I walked out the door and got into the car, trying not to think about the poor example my father was setting for my son. Trying not to think about what toxins my son might breathe just by sitting near him on the porch.

I made the short drive to the hospital, praying that Hannah was better by now. That a little bit of IV fluid had made her well enough to go back home. Hoping that maybe my sister didn't hate me.

How was she going to respond to my unexpected visit? I still ached from her words yesterday, and showing up like this was only asking for more of the same. I supposed those words would be mild compared to what I might expect from Kelsey's family—I'd seen a good sample of that already, too.

I turned off the car in the hospital parking lot and didn't move. I could drive away from here right now, get on the plane this afternoon, and wait until all this blew over. There was no reason to put myself through this.

Yes there was. There were two good reasons. Hannah. And Jana.

When I walked through the main lobby, there were a couple of volunteers in their pink jackets at a desk near the front. "Can we help you find the right place, dear?"

"Pediatrics," I said, looking toward the signage, thinking I really didn't need their help.

"Pediatrics is a locked wing and only allows two visitors per patient at a time. We need your name and the name of the patient that you are going to see."

"My name is Grace Graham, and I am going to see Hannah Morgan."

The two women exchanged a glance. The one who had not yet spoken said, "Both her parents are back there with her, so you won't be able to go onto the floor unless one of them comes out. There is a waiting area outside the door where you can sit, but I think it is likely packed right now."

"All right. Which way to the waiting room?"

"Are you sure you want to do that?" It was less a question and more a warning.

"Yes, I'm sure. Now, which way do I go?" At the end of this day I would be leaving here. I had already braced myself to take whatever it was I might encounter in the next few hours.

"Turn right, go to the end of the hall, and turn left. About halfway down that hall you'll see an overhead sign pointing you to the pediatric waiting room."

"Thank you." I didn't look back as I hurried away from them. I pulled the cell phone out of my pocket and called Jana's. It went immediately to voice mail. I knew there were areas of the hospital where cell phones were not allowed, likely this very hallway where I was walking, as well as Hannah's room. I called 4-1-1. "Shoal Creek Hospital, please."

A few minutes later I was connected to the operator. "May I have Hannah Morgan's room, please?"

"One moment."

I heard the phone ringing on the other end. "Hello." Jana's voice sounded cracked and tired.

"Hey, it's me. How's she doing?"

"They finally got an IV going, so she's got some fluid in her, but her fever is 104 right now. They're giving her some medications in her IV, but I can't tell that anything's doing her a lot of good at this point."

"Well, I'm here. In the waiting room, or about to be. If you need to take a break and go get some coffee or something, I'm here for you."

I could hear Hannah crying in the background. I could hear Rob's voice as he tried to speak some sort of comfort to her. Finally, Jana said, "Thanks. I'll keep that in mind. I've got to go now." And she hung up.

I tried to tell myself that I understood my sister's anger—she was tired, she had a sick kid, she was worried and exhausted. Still, my whole chest felt as though it had been pounded with a sledgehammer. This was not my fault, and yet I felt as though my whole family—the entire town—was blaming me.

Why should I take the fall for something that was so obviously out of my control? Even as I had the thought, an image flashed through my mind of the standing stones in my dad's backyard. I supposed this was the beginning of my all-night march. *Please, God, let there be some hailstones up ahead. I don't think I can take an uphill battle without your help.* It surprised me how quickly I'd returned to praying in the last twenty-four hours, when it had been so long before that. I don't know what that said about my faith, and even as they came to me, I still didn't put a lot of hope in the results.

I wanted to curl into a ball right here in the hallway and cry and kick and scream. I wanted to force my way into my niece's hospital room and make them understand that I had made the right choices. I wanted to make them spend the day with Collin, to watch the old home videos so they could see what he had been like before the medical establishment loaded him down with all those neurotoxins. Then they would understand.

By the time I finished my little internal tirade, I saw the overhead sign and turned toward the pediatric waiting room. It was a medium-sized waiting area, with perhaps twenty chairs. More than half of these were filled by middle-aged adults, most of them overweight, and a half dozen children were playing with toys on the floor. The carpet was old and stained and I suspected that those kids on that floor were currently being invaded by all sorts of new and strange bacteria.

I walked to a chair on the end, thinking I would sit here for a while and try to finally make up my mind. Should I continue to stay here and wait, knowing there was little chance that Jana would even see me? Should I just go back to Dad's, pick up Dylan, and head home? I dropped into the chair and picked up a *People* magazine. On the cover was a full-body picture of a bikini-clad Rachel Wilson, a buxom blonde who had, until a month ago, been the Hollywood sweetheart. The recent scandals involving drugs and married men were currently making headlines and tarnishing her image, at least temporarily. I opened the magazine and started thumbing through the pages, not really caring what I read, just needing something to look at.

"That Rachel Wilson, she's something else, ain't she?" The woman sitting a couple of chairs to the right of me wore a sleeveless shirt that showed just how large the arms could be of a woman who was at least one hundred pounds overweight. Her bleached blond hair was piled on her head; she wore lots of makeup and big hoop earrings.

"Yeah, I guess so," I said, having no intention of having a conversation with this woman, about Rachel Wilson, or otherwise.

"Of course, it don't surprise me none. That's what happens to people when they move out there to Los Angeles. They forget about their upbringing and get all caught up in themselves and what is best for them. Don't care who it hurts in the process. Wouldn't you agree?"

The man sitting beside her leaned forward, elbows on knees, and waited for my response.

I gave none.

He began to stroke the stubble on his chin. "I don't see how you couldn't agree. I mean, look at this whole waiting room full of people. Why are they here? Because one person who didn't even have a college degree, much less a medical education of any sort, decided she knew more than all the doctors in this whole country—and refused to vaccinate her son. Now all of us are missing out on our regular lives to be sitting here in this waiting room, because a member of our family is in the hospital with a disease that she would never had been exposed to in the first place if everyone around her have done the right thing. Sweet little innocent baby. She's been so sick, got these little sores all over her tongue. You'd think that the person responsible for that would be in there begging her parents for forgiveness, wouldn't you?"

Angry heat crept up my shoulders, my neck, and all the way into my scalp. I was not going to let a couple of uneducated rednecks make me feel like less than the parent I was.

"No one is more sorry than I am about those babies getting sick. My son was sick, and my niece is sick now. But there was nothing uninformed about my choice. The question should be—which do you choose to believe? The eyewitness accounts of hundreds and thousands of families who have watched their children slip into oblivion within hours or days of receiving their vaccines, or to a scientific community who listens to all these stories and claims it is coincidence? That same scientific community would stand to lose millions and millions of dollars if vaccines were shown to be a cause of autism, so I think we can all agree that a conflict of interest exists at the very least."

"Correct me if I'm wrong"—the man seemed downright arrogant—"but aren't a good many of those parents with . . . what did you call it . . . eyewitness stories? Aren't a bunch of them in that group that is suing the government for millions and millions in that vaccine court I've been reading about? Say what you will about money being the motivation; it seems to me that point could be applied to both sides."

A woman from farther across the room said, "I don't care what all you tree-hugging yahoos do that affect your own kids, but what I'm saying is that you shouldn't be allowed to live among the rest of us. You were counting on the fact that most of us immunize our own children and do the right thing. That should keep your own son from getting sick from the disease, and you can just ride on the safety of our shoulders."

"You're selfish, that's what you are," a fourth woman chimed in. "I hope that Kelsey's parents sue you for everything you've got. You are the lowest form of society, as far as I'm concerned."

The entire waiting room had fallen into silence, every single person focusing full attention on me. Seemed that most, if not all, of the people in this room were here on account of Kelsey. I figured this was a group with whom there was no reasoning. I certainly didn't want to continue to fight for the next five hours while I sat out here just hoping that my sister would eventually come out and tell me what was going on with my niece. I looked back down at my magazine and pretended to be extremely interested in the pictures of Angelina Jolie at the ice-cream shop with a tableful of her adopted children.

"Yep, that's about right, isn't it?" one of the women said. "Ignore the problem and it will go away. Stick your head in the sand and don't even notice when it's your fault that a couple of innocent babies are in the hospital because of your selfish decisions."

I didn't look up. I tried as hard as I could to shut out the murmur of agreement and the subsequent mumbled slanders aimed in my direction.

"Your own family's mad at you, ain't they?" The first woman was speaking again. "That's why you're sitting out here all alone. They don't want no part of you because you done this to your own niece."

I wasn't certain what hurt most. The venom of the words, or the fact that they were true. I tried to focus on the picture in the magazine, but it was starting to blur around the edges. I blinked hard and tried harder.

"Her own family is right here." I jumped at the sound of Rob's voice right over me. I'd had my focus so turned down, I hadn't even seen him enter the room. I stood up and hugged him. "How's she doing?"

He glanced around at the hostile faces turned my direction. "Let's step out into the hallway, shall we?"

We walked outside the waiting room; then he nodded back toward it. "Sounds like you were taking quite a bit of heat back there."

Outside of the arena, standing here staring at the strained, pale face of my brother-in-law, all my righteous defense arguments melted. I felt tears roll down my cheek. "I guess I can't blame them. I'm mad at me, too." I didn't really understand the truth in that until the words came out.

My shoulders began to heave with the revelation. Somehow I managed to keep the sobs silent, but the tears gushed down my face. I used the palms of my hands to wipe them away but couldn't keep up with the torrent. "It's okay, kiddo." He put his arm around me and squeezed. "We all know that you acted with the best intentions." He leaned closer and whispered, "And don't worry about Kelsey. I just talked to her mother. Her kidneys are fine and she's been able to drink fluid. They're probably going to send her home this afternoon."

"I'm so glad." A small fraction of the tension eased with his statement, but there was a much heavier burden I carried. It frightened me so much I could hardly bring myself to ask about it. "How is Hannah?" I finally managed to squeak out the words.

"Not so good. Why don't you go back and see her for a few minutes? That's why I'm out here. I'll go get a cup of coffee and give you a little time with your niece and your sister."

"Okay. Thanks, Rob."

He squeezed my shoulders once more before he let me go. "Not a problem." He pointed at the locked door to pediatrics. "Just press the red button, they'll ask you who you're here to see, and you tell them Hannah. They'll buzz you in."

"Okay." I started toward the door.

"Grace?"

I turned back toward Rob. "Yes?"

"Your sister . . . she's not herself. Don't take anything she might say personally, okay?"

Chapter 28

The blinds were shut against the sun, leaving only narrow slits of light coming through. The overhead fixtures were turned off, and it took me a minute to focus clearly on the dark shadow hunched over the crib. I walked toward it. "Hi, Jana. How you holding up?"

She didn't respond. Didn't even move, just kept trailing her fingers across her daughter's face.

"Jana, I—"

"Shh." Jana didn't look up. "This is the first time she's fallen asleep since yesterday afternoon."

I went to stand on the far side of the crib from my sister, the sting of her words hitting their full mark and then some. By now, my eyes had adjusted and I looked down at sweet Hannah's face. Her face was pale. Even in this low light I could see that, and her breathing seemed labored. I could hear the sound of the rattling that always seemed to accompany babies when they got a runny nose. This particular runny nose, I knew, came from the measles. From my son. Bottom line, from me. Hannah coughed twice but didn't wake up.

I looked down at that suffering, sick little baby and my tears dried up in a jolt of adrenaline-fueled fear. That defenseless, sweet baby. So completely vulnerable, so completely dependent on us, and we were all helpless to help her, really. What if what we did for her, what the doctors did for her, wasn't enough?

Rob was right. I couldn't take the fact that Jana was angry with me personally. Next week, when this was over and everyone was getting well, clearer heads would prevail. For now, I just needed to keep my mouth shut and wait.

I stood there quietly, listening as Hannah coughed occasionally, but otherwise remained still. Wanting so much to hug my sister, but knowing this was not the time.

A few minutes later a nurse walked into the room. "Mr. Morgan is back."

I nodded. "Good-bye, Jana. I'll be praying," I whispered, then followed the nurse out the door, down the hall, and outside the locked doors of the pediatric ward.

Rob was waiting there. He put one hand on my shoulder and said, "You go on back to the house now, take care of Dylan and your father. I'll call you if anything changes here. Okay?"

"My flight's not until early evening. I could wait for a while, stay close by, in case you need something."

He shook his head. "I know you want to help, but I think the best thing you can do for us right now is to stay out of the way for a while."

"Okay." I couldn't imagine anything hurting more than this. The person I loved most in the world, next to my son, was in great distress, and the way I could best help her was to stay out of her way.

"Grace, hopefully this will all be over soon, and we will all move forward. It's just going to take a while. Okay?"

"Thanks, Rob."

He nodded. "Give that boy of yours a big hug for me."

As I started down the hallway, I could see into the pediatric waiting room, see the very same people who had been there with me only moments before. Only this time, they were standing in a circle holding hands, heads bowed and eyes closed.

Praying.

I looked at my watch. Eleven o'clock. We needed to leave for the airport by two, which gave me time to pick up a few more supplies for Dad. I called him from the parking lot. "Hey, it's me. I'm on my way home but thought I'd stop and pick up a few things. Is there anything you need for me to get for you?"

"I called in a refill of my pain meds this morning. Do you mind stopping by the pharmacy and picking it up for me?"

"Sure." I actually looked forward to this trip.

Maybe I'd see what kind of tea Dawn could make that would help relieve a guilty conscience.

I had to park halfway around the town square. I walked past the Square Forty diner, unusually empty as the breakfast crowd had vanished and the incoming lunch crew hadn't yet arrived. There was a sign in the window, "Taking donations for those affected by the measles outbreak." This stopped me cold for just a moment.

I walked inside, and sure enough, right there on the counter was a large clear plastic jug. It simply said "Measles" on it. I pulled out a ten-dollar bill, stuck it in, and turned to go.

"Much appreciated. You staying for lunch?" A waitress had appeared behind me.

"No, not this time."

"Well, thanks for the help. Those poor families. Between the quarantine parents having to miss work and the kids that are in the hospital, this is a real financial hardship on all of them."

"Glad I could help out." I practically ran from the restaurant.

I walked into the pharmacy to see that there were a couple of people in line ahead of me. I got behind them, trying my best to be inconspicuous. It had been long enough since I lived here that I hoped there wouldn't be anyone I knew, anyone who might recognize me.

When I got to the counter, Dawn smiled at me. "Hey there. How's your son?"

I realized then that although she knew I'd had a sick son, she didn't know I was *that* mom.

"He's feeling better," I said, and let it go at that.

She offered a sympathetic smile. "Have you got a prescription for him?"

"No, I'm here to pick up a refill for my dad. Charles Graham." I was certain that my sick kid combined with my father's last name would spell out exactly who I was, but if she put it all together, she gave no sign of it.

"Alrighty, let's see what we've got here." She turned and began thumbing through a bin of white pharmacy bags. "Here we go. Got it ready. You need anything else?"

"No, I guess that's all for now." Another donation can marked "Measles" sat next to a display of mints and gum on the counter.

"Your father has a ten-dollar co-pay."

"All right." I pulled a twenty out of my wallet.

She gave me a ten in change and I put it in the bucket, shaking my head. I could never add enough money to absolve my guilt.

I turned to go, and Dawn said, "Hey, if you have a minute, since you're a tea drinker, I thought I'd run something past you."

"Really? Some tea?" I looked at my watch. Eleven twenty. "I don't have a lot of time."

"It won't take long and it might be just what you need."

I doubted seriously she had anything close to what I needed, but at this point I needed any bit of help I could get, even if it amounted to no more than some dried-up plants. "Okay." I followed her over to the herbal tea area.

"Have a seat right here, and I'll whip you something up." She turned her back to me and began scooping things together.

"This is a blend I read about that's supposed to give you a calm spirit. I don't know about that, but it tastes amazing." She put a cup beneath a hot water faucet. "It's a green tea base with wild rose petals, Italian bergamot oil, and holy basil." I heard the whishing sound as the cup filled almost to the top. She dropped the infuser ball into the cup, then set it in front of me before she took the seat beside me.

"There was a time, just a few years ago, when I had made some decisions that seemed right at the time, I was convinced of that. In the end, they cost me everything and everyone I loved. I felt so trapped because I didn't really have much left in the way of a support group."

"I could join that club." I took a sip of the tea. It really was amazing.

"Most people do to some degree or other." She smiled. "You know what I found out?"

"What?"

"Move forward no matter how hard it is, do what's right no matter what it costs you, and trust

God that somewhere in the process, He'll give you the chance for a new start. A do-over, if you will. Those past hurts can be repaired; they'll leave scars, but if you'll stay the course, if you don't give up, it can happen."

A do-over. I felt the urge to ask Dawn if she had some standing stones set up somewhere. What I actually said was, "Thanks." I kind of choked on the word.

She reached out and squeezed my arm. "I don't know why, but somehow I just felt like you needed to hear that today."

"You have no idea." I drank the last of my tea and tossed the paper cup in the trash. "Thanks, Dawn. This is a winner."

Chapter 29

When I got home, Dad was asleep in his recliner and Dylan was asleep in front of the television. Between Dad's painkillers and Dylan's illness, this was an all-too-familiar scene.

I tiptoed out the back door and went to stand by the old crab apple tree. I thought about what Dawn had said, and what Mrs. Fellows had told me about coming full circle. I thought perhaps it was too late for me. I was like the generation sentenced to wandering the wilderness for forty years. Chance over.

"Well, now, here you are again." Mrs. Fellows

walked out toward me, her steps a bit uneven. "Thinking about starting over, I'm guessing."

I shrugged. "Wishing it wasn't too late for that, I suppose." I looked at her, then had to look away. "I changed our flight home. We'll be leaving in just a few hours. I thought it best for all concerned."

"I see." She pulled off her glasses and wiped them on the hem of her shirt, then put them back on her nose.

She wanted to say something. I could see it in her eyes. She'd been as kind as the people at the hospital were cruel, so finally I just said, "You have another story for me?"

She smiled. "Grace, after your mama got sick, seems to me you lost faith in everyone but yourself. That year, I know it was your last year of high school when most girls are dreaming of proms and college, you were busy caring for your mother and your house, and at some point the happy-go-lucky, over-the-top, carefree girl we all knew and loved just disappeared. You refused to rely on anyone. Not your father. Not anyone who tried to help you. And I'm guessing by what's going on right now, you don't trust the medical establishment at all."

"I'm not alone on that last one."

"I'm not saying you made the wrong decision. Fact is, I've never read up on it one way or the other, or spent any time praying about it. What

I'm saying is, just like the Israelites, you've got to learn that you can't trust common sense, or even what you think you know to be true. God's the only one you can depend on. Not yourself. Not what seems obvious to us. Remember I told you that the Gibeonites had tricked the Israelites into signing the treaty?"

"Yes."

"Well, now I'm going to tell you exactly how that happened." She smoothed her tan pants and pinched the crease between her fingers as she talked. "The Israelites were told not to make a treaty with anyone in the land. So when a delegation came to visit them, with clothes tattered and torn, and moldy bread their only remaining food after such a long journey, they were obviously from far away. In fact, the Israelite men even sampled the provisions—the bread was indeed moldy. So they agreed to a treaty, swearing their allegiance, without bothering to stop and ask God about whether or not they should do it. You know what the problem was?"

"What?"

She quit playing with the crease in her pants and looked directly at me. "That delegation wasn't telling the truth. They were actually from nearby."

"Wouldn't the fact that they lied nullify their deal?"

"In an American court, perhaps, but under God's law and after His name had been invoked in the promise . . . these people were stuck."

"So you're saying all that trouble—the all-night march and everything—could have been avoided if the people had just asked God before they made the decision in the first place?"

"Yep. Sometimes what looks like common sense isn't what God wants for us."

"When Mama was sick I prayed all the time that He would heal her, and He never even came close. Never even a slight improvement."

"I didn't say He always gives you what you want. I imagine you don't always give your son everything he wants, either, even though at times what he wants is not a bad thing, it's just not the right thing."

"It doesn't make sense to me."

"The reason Gilgal was necessary, the reason the people needed to start over, was because they didn't trust God in the first place. They saw the *giants* who were living in the land and thought there was no way they could take them. They were right about that, but God was and is big enough. They didn't ask Him. They made a decision based on their own common sense. Maybe that's what you're doing right now, huh? Looking at the giant size of the situation and thinking there's no way to deal with it."

"But life is so hard."

"And it always will be this side of heaven. What I'm saying is, He's the One, the only One, you can rely on. Not yourself. Not whether you stay here now or get on back. Not any lifestyle you might choose, no matter how healthy you may believe it is. If you don't learn to trust the One who created it all, then nothing else really matters. You give that some thought." She stood and shuffled back toward her house.

Chapter 30

I loaded Dylan's duffel on top of my suitcase, then closed the trunk. I walked around the car and opened the back passenger's-side door. "Okay, Dylan, it's time to go."

"Grandpa, I don't want to leave. Tell Mama we need to stay. Tell her, Grandpa. We never even got to show her—"

"Your mama needs to get back to her job, little man. That's just the way the world works. Don't you worry, though. You can come back and visit me anytime. There will be plenty of time in the future for the rest of our project."

Dylan wrapped his arm around Dad's leg, and Dad bent down to return the gesture. When he straightened up, there were tears in his eyes. "You be a good boy, now, you hear me?"

"Okay." Dylan wiped tears from his eyes as he

climbed into the car. "Good-bye, Grandpa, I love you."

"Love you, too, buddy."

Nothing could have prepared me for the shock of those words—coming from my father—directed toward my son.

I spent an extra moment double-checking Dylan's car seat before I stood up to face my father. He was blinking fast, as if something was in his eyes, and the two of us simply looked at each other. The wind stirred my hair across my face—the same black stick-straight hair I'd inherited from my dad, at least until his turned gray. One of the few things we had in common. "Well . . . good-bye, Dad." I held out my right hand and he shook it.

"Good-bye. Thanks for being a good nurse."

"You're welcome."

I walked around to the driver's side of the car. As I opened the car door, this exit suddenly felt so final. I wondered if I would ever be back here.

"Gracie?" my father asked, just as I was about to climb inside.

"Yeah?"

"Take care of that boy for me. He's a fine young man. Keep up the good work."

"Um . . . thanks." I sat down in the car and backed out of the driveway as soon as I could get the car started and in gear.

Halfway down the first block, Dylan said, "Mama, why are you crying?"

I couldn't explain to him what I didn't really know myself. I finally managed to say, "I guess I'm not very good at good-byes."

The Nashville airport had four lines of self check-in machines. All four lines were backed up with what appeared to be a college group all traveling together. After each new person checked in, a red light would flash on the machine. It would take several minutes before an airport employee came to check on the situation. Over and over I heard him say, "Oh, you're traveling internationally. I need to see your passport."

After this same scenario repeated itself countless times, I was ready to scream at him, "Every single one of these sixty people in line in front of me is traveling internationally. Why don't you just stand here and look at their passports now, instead of making us all wait through this every single time?" But I didn't say anything. I simply held my son's hand and waited our turn. Our turn to go home.

"When can we go back and see Grandpa? And Hannah Rose? I want to come back to Tennessee real soon." He'd asked the questions ten times in the car and six times already since we'd gotten inside.

"What do you want to do when we get home, Dylan? You want to go to the beach? We could take your bucket and dig a moat and a castle."

"Nah. Me and Grandpa do stuff that's way more fun than that. I'd rather come back here."

"What did Grandpa mean, about your project?" I looked at him, that part of the conversation just now registering with me.

Dylan shook his head. "It's a secret."

I wanted to tell him that we would likely not be back here for many years to come and he might as well tell me and let us both enjoy it, but I didn't. No reason to make this any harder than it was already.

"Look at those things." He pointed to several rows of glass display cases. "Mama, what is that?"

I'd never been more thankful for a change in subject. "It's a traveling art and historical display that's here at the airport through the end of the year. I read about it in the paper last week." I pointed toward a glass case that held a musket and a coonskin cap. "I think that's maybe what Davy Crockett used to wear."

"But what's that one?" He pointed farther down the way.

I strained to see inside the tabletop glass case. "Oh, that's a replica of Stonehenge. It's a very famous place in England. I seem to recall that no one really knows who placed those rocks there or why."

"It's funny that they would stand stones up like that, isn't it, Mama? It kind of reminds me of the tree in Grandpa's backyard."

"What?" The question no more made it off my tongue until I was hearing Mrs. Fellows's words about fresh starts and do-overs. But it was too late for me. I couldn't do it over; my son had the measles and he'd passed them around. There was nothing to be done over about that.

I had come here with such hopes of restoring my family. Now I was leaving with not one bit of it still intact and no illusions that it ever would be again.

Jana had been right, I guessed. It seems that I did always leave when the going got hard. Or in this case, the going got impossible.

That's the very second that it hit me. What it was I needed to do over. No, I couldn't undo the damage that had already been done. What I could change was my response to the trouble. Instead of running away, I could come full circle. And in this version, I was going to face the all-night march and stand firm in the head-on battle. Even if I lost everything.

This was it for me. My chance at a do-over and I was about to miss it. I tugged at Dylan's hand. "Come on, son."

"Where are we going? We're next in line."

"We're going home. Back to Grandpa's house."

• • •

As soon as we were on I-65 and headed back to Shoal Creek, I called my father. "Hey, it's me."

"Is everything okay?"

Perhaps in many families it would not be considered an unusual thing to call right now—to confirm safe arrival at the airport, to offer thanks for the visit, whatever. From the worried tone in my father's voice, anyone could guess that this was not true of our family. "Yes." I looked in my rearview mirror and changed lanes. "Well, no. Have you heard anything more from Hannah?"

"I just talked to Rob a few minutes ago. He said there wasn't much change. I'll call you if anything major happens."

"I don't think you're going to need to do that." I hit my brakes to avoid a car that changed lanes in front of me. A horn blared behind me.

"Why?"

"We're on our way back to your house. I can't leave right now. I promised you I'd be there for two weeks—"

"I can manage on my own."

"I know you can, but this isn't the right time to leave Jana, either. Not with Hannah so sick, not with things between us like they are now."

"I see." Neither of us said anything more. I kept the phone pressed against my ear and continued in silence.

Finally, he said, "I'll make sure the porch light is on for you."

"Thanks. I guess we'll be there in about an hour."

"See you then."

And that was the end of the conversation. Somehow, I'd thought that coming full circle would be a bit more climactic than that.

Of course, there were still two other conversations I needed to have. One was with Jana, and that I'd save until tomorrow. The other was with Jasmine. I needed to call her and tell her things had changed. Coming full circle meant not running from things when they were unpleasant. And I figured this phone call would be unpleasant.

She picked up on the third ring.

"Hi, Jasmine, it's me."

"Hey. Tell me you're back in town and on your way here. The place is in total chaos and you've got work stacked a mile high on your desk."

"That does make me wish I was there. . . ." My attempt at sarcastic humor fell short. Better just to get to the point. "Which brings me to the reason I'm calling. I won't be back early. In fact, I delayed my flight an extra week."

"Are you kidding me?"

"My niece is in the hospital. She has measles. I plan to stay here until I know that she is okay.

Given what Dylan experienced, I'm expecting that to take about a week."

"You've already taken two weeks off work, when you had no time coming. I don't think it is reasonable for you to expect a third week."

"Jasmine, to tell you the truth, I can't afford a third week. I can't afford another day. But here's the thing—I'm going to do the right thing, even if it's not the best thing for me personally." The uphill battle was fully underway now. I hoped the path didn't get much steeper. I didn't think I could make it.

"You know it's in your best interest to get back here early like you promised. You know that. But when you start talking about not being here on Monday as originally planned, then you're starting to cut into other people's best interests—and the best interest of your job. If you choose to stay away, then you may force me into making a choice to replace you."

"Jasmine, I would think that you of all people would understand the situation I'm in."

"What do you mean?"

"You're the one who convinced me not to vaccinate. Now an outbreak of measles amongst innocent babies who were exposed by my son has started. Many would argue that by not fulfilling my obligation to vaccinate, I am responsible for this. How can I shirk the responsibility to stay here and do what I can?"

"What exactly do you think you can do there? Your responsibility is to take care of your son. You did that by choosing not to allow the doctor to inject him with a bunch of foreign chemicals and heavy metals. Your sister's job is to take care of her baby as best she can, and I'm sure she and the highly trained doctors can handle that just fine without you. You need to get back here and do what you are supposed to do. If you were really serious about doing what is best for your son, this decision would not even be a discussion now."

Half of me wanted to slam down the phone, hard, and let her hear exactly what I thought of her opinion. The other half agreed that she was right. "I'll see you as soon as I can."

"You're making a mistake."

"You're probably right, but it's a mistake I've got to make."

I hung up the phone, my emotions torn. She was right. What good could I do here? Jana wasn't even speaking to me. I was hardly being a help to her.

Still, it surprised me that Jasmine showed so little sympathy for my plight. She of all people.

Then the truth of the matter began to form and solidify in my mind. If it hadn't been for Jasmine, her maniacal insistence that vaccines were harmful, wouldn't this have been a much different trip home? And if it hadn't been for her friend with a measles-infected son who came to visit, would my choices have mattered? Wouldn't Dylan have spent the entire time playing with his cousin Hannah, completely healthy? And wouldn't Jana and Rob and I even now be talking about how this trip had gone by too quickly and we weren't ready to be apart yet? And yes, maybe even my father and I would have come to some sort of peace.

Jasmine had been the start of every bit of the problems this week. If I couldn't get back there to help her, then it was her own fault.

Chapter 31

After tossing and turning for the second straight night, I dragged out of bed at first light. Without even considering what I was doing, I went out to sit in the backyard. To look at the stones. To think about the commitment I made. Had I been crazy? This was likely to get awful for me and for Dylan. Why hadn't I left when I got the chance?

Because it was time to take the chance offered to me—a chance to do things differently. To fight as hard as I needed to fight for the right outcome. A time to pray to God for the strength to do that—and maybe ask for a few hailstones along the way.

"God, I've been mad at my father for years

now. As much as I've always known he didn't hurt Mama on purpose—would never have hurt Mama on purpose—it was his fault just the same. Now I find myself in the exact same situation. I would never have made any of those children sick. As much as I'm still convinced that measles is a better option than a life of autism, I find myself in the position of having caused something I would never have purposely caused. And now everyone hates me for something that wasn't really my fault."

Even as I prayed the words, a part of me knew better. It *was* my fault. This whole thing was my fault. Good intentions or not, right reasoning or not, my niece was in the hospital because of a decision I'd made.

I fell to the ground. It was time to quit hiding behind the reasons and look the reality full in the face. What if it had been diphtheria? Or polio? What then?

I sobbed and sobbed and sobbed. Regardless of motives, I was the cause.

My father was the cause of my mother's illness, too. Is this how he had felt all these years? All this time while I'd been angry, hating him even, perhaps he'd needed my support and love every bit as much as I needed support and love now. I had failed him when he needed me most.

On the other hand, he'd never attempted the

uphill battle to fight for my forgiveness. Never once asked for it. Never faced my anger head-on. Perhaps that was what I would have to do with Jana. I hoped I had the strength to see it through.

"Okay, God, starting here, starting right now, I'm going to forgive my father. I'm going to move forward and try to salvage what I can of our relationship. I'm going to do everything in my power to help my sister and work toward earning her forgiveness. Please forgive me for doubting you for so long; help me to keep marching forward. I'm going to trust you with the results and pray that you'll send the occasional hailstone to help me out a bit."

At some point, I got up. For a long time I stood out there, just staring, thinking about the commitment I'd made. The commitment to start again. Just like the Israelites had done all those many years ago.

I heard the screen door slam at Mrs. Fellows's house. She came walking toward me, wearing a long gown and robe. "You're back."

"Yes I am." I looked away from her and shrugged. "I came to realize that I had more than a little in common with the Israelites. Always wanting to turn back when the road ahead looked too hard."

"Honey, we all do, and that's a downright shame. Who knows where He might have led us if we'd just followed in faith?"

"Yes, I'm going to try to do that now."

She nodded her head. "It's a good thing when you start again."

"I sure hope so." I truly wasn't convinced, but I wanted to believe. More than I could ever remember wanting anything.

My father was awake when I went inside. He was sitting at the kitchen table looking at the newspaper, which he lowered slightly and looked over when I walked into the room. "How's Mrs. Fellows this morning?"

"Good. She's good."

He nodded. "You want a section of the paper?"

"I . . . don't think I do."

"I'm hearing talk that Patti's editorial got a lot of people riled up. Rumor is, a whole bunch of people threw their papers on the sidewalk right in front of the door to *The Advocate*."

"Oh no." I sat down and dropped my face into my hands. "How many more people's lives can I mess up?"

"That Fox girl is the one who made the choice to write the article. You're not responsible for other people; you're responsible for yourself."

I looked at my father. Right then and there I saw my future if I were not willing to make a different start right now. I didn't like that thought. "That's not true. The choices I make affect so many other people. Dylan's measles is a case of that. My choice has affected Hannah, and other babies, too." His expression remained absolutely blank, and I wondered if my words even registered with him. "Perhaps that article helped change one person's mind about me, and I appreciate it very much." Even if I'd never particularly cared for Patti.

"I guess so." He turned the page to the sports. "Rick's Barbecue is hosting a fund-raiser for The Lady Wildcats today. Fifteen percent of the proceeds go to help pay their way to the state championships. I don't suppose I could convince you to drive through and pick us up something for lunch?" He eyed me warily over the top of the paper.

Several retorts came to mind, but somehow I managed to bite them all back. I held out my hand. "Can I have the TalkBack section?"

"Here you go." He handed me the back section of the paper.

Conspiracy of Fools

I find it interesting that yesterday's absurd article mentioned the National Vaccine Information Center. I went to this site yesterday just to see what it was about. Want to know what I found?

The small print at the bottom.

It says, ". . . we make no representations or warranties of any kind, express or implied, about the completeness, accuracy, reliability, suitability, or availability with respect to the Web site or the information, products, services, or graphics contained on the Web site. . . ."

Does anyone but me find this more than a little disturbing? This is supposedly one of the sites where we should get our information? It goes on to say they will not be ". . . liable for any loss or damage, including, without limitation indirect or consequential loss or damage, or any loss or damage whatsoever from any activities arising out of or in connection with the use of the Web site."

So basically it seems to me that beneath all that legal gobbledy-gook, the site is saying the government health agencies are all a bunch of liars and we shouldn't listen to them. That we can't trust them, even, and they should all be held accountable for this group's theories about what caused their children's developmental disorders. But if you read the fine print, this group is openly admitting we can't trust them, either. They say that health agencies should be held responsible for their actions, regardless of what kind of science backs them up, but they themselves are not responsible for any problems people might encounter for following the advice given on their Web site.

Give me a break! This is the problem with America today.

"I'm going to write a letter to the editor right now."

At this point it wasn't about convincing people that I was right. This situation was way too far gone for that. I simply wanted to stand in defense of Patti, who had stood in defense of me. Perhaps I'd never liked her, probably never would, but it was time for me to break my silence.

My son had the measles. I hate this fact.

He was miserable. I am miserable because of this. He exposed several other children, who are now sick with measles. There are many people angry with me right now and I understand their feelings. In fact, to a large degree, I share them.

I also understand that several people in this community are angry with the editor of this newspaper for printing articles from the opposing viewpoint of vaccines. I beg of you, all of you, to consider that there might be a time when you are on the unpopular side of a decision. Wouldn't you want someone to at least help people understand that there is another side to your story? If you are angry about the coverage of this, please throw your papers on my lawn, not back at The Advocate. Not at the person who may someday be your only chance to be heard.

I could explain to you all why I made the choices I did, but at this point it no longer matters. My choices have affected many of you, and for that I am sincerely sorry. Whether or not you accept

this, please know that you and
your families are in my heart and
prayers.
  Sincerely,
  Grace Graham

I read and reread the letter over and over.
Finally, I closed my laptop and looked at my
father. "I'm going to Krystal for a minute."

"Having a craving?"

"Very funny. I'll be right back."

I sat in the parking lot, read it through once,
then hit Send. I was pretty certain she wouldn't
publish it, but I felt like the truth needed to be
out there. If I wasn't willing to tell it, then who
would?

As I started out of the parking lot, I thought of
my earlier conversation with my father this
morning. Maybe it was time to offer a bit of an
olive branch. I picked up my cell phone and
dialed his house. "Hey, I was thinking that while
I'm out, I'd pick up some barbecue for the fund-
raiser. What is it that you like from there?"

And it was a nice compromise, I supposed. I
was sure I could come home with grilled chicken
and unbuttered corn. The coleslaw and potato
chips? Well, it *was* a compromise.

After lunch—which, I have to admit, was
delicious—I knew it was time to go back out to

the hospital, to face Jana. I looked at my father as I loaded the last of the glasses in the dishwasher. "Do you want to go?"

"We can't leave Dylan here alone."

"He could come with us."

He looked toward the den, then back at me. Checking, I assumed, to make certain we weren't going to be overheard. "I don't think it's a good idea to take him."

"Kelsey's family should be gone by now, so that won't be an issue. Jana is plenty mad at me, but she won't take it out on Dylan."

"Both are probably true, but he still has what's left of his spots. He shows up out at that hospital and everyone there is going to know exactly who he is. I just don't think it's a good idea."

"I hadn't thought of that." I nodded. "Do you want me to drive you, then? We could just drop you off for a while."

He shook his head. "I'll stay here with Dylan. You go do what you need to do with your sister."

"Okay." I picked up the car keys, with every bit of me screaming to turn and run. "Wish me luck."

I made for the door, determined to see this through. In spite of the fact that I really did think it might kill me.

A few minutes later I stopped at the front desk. I told the lady who I was and who I was there to see. She simply nodded and pointed me in the right direction. I called Hannah's room on my way down the hall.

"Hello." Rob sounded tired.

"Hey, it's me. Listen, I didn't leave town after all. I'm here—like here in the hospital. I'd really like to come and talk to Jana."

I could hear the sound of voices in the background. Sounded like a nurse talking to Jana. Rob exhaled noisily into the phone. "I'll see what I can do."

"Thanks."

The waiting room was mostly empty this time. There were two couples sitting together against the far wall, but if they had been here yesterday, I didn't recognize them. I supposed they were just some other parents with a child, or a niece, or a friend's child, who was sick. I nodded at them and sat in the opposite corner.

I thumbed through a year-old copy of *Southern Living*, noting that the roasted chicken recipe looked good. After that I picked up a more recent copy of *Parent* magazine. There were several articles about whether or not baby food from a jar was safe to give an infant, or whether the mother should home cook all the baby's food. Having mashed everything by hand for Dylan, I was disappointed to see that the magazine didn't take a stronger stand in that direction.

I looked at my watch. Two thirty. Over an hour had passed and no word.

By three thirty the other people in the waiting room had all taken their leave, and I'd gone through a whole stack of magazines. Maybe this was just a waste of time. It was pointless to sit out here if she wouldn't even see me. I stood up and walked over to the lone window in the room. It overlooked the parking lot, which was perhaps half full this afternoon.

"I'm glad you stayed." Rob's face had a couple of days' worth of razor shadow, and his eyes were hollow.

"Me too." I walked toward him. "How's Hannah?"

He shook his head. "She's not doing so well. She's having some trouble breathing, and they've started giving her breathing treatments. Not a lot of fun, but it does seem to help."

I nodded. "Good."

"Listen"—he rubbed his hand through his hair—"this is probably not the best time for you to see Jana. Why don't we wait a day or two, until Hannah gets better. I just don't think anything good would come of you seeing each other right now."

"Oh. Okay. Thanks for telling me."

He nodded.

"Rob?"

"Yeah?"

"I really am sorry. For everything."

He reached out and hugged me. "I know."

But he didn't know. He couldn't. Because he wasn't the one who had wrecked everything.

Chapter 32

Dinner—which was more grilled chicken, since it was the one thing we all seemed to agree on—sat on our plates, mostly untouched. Neither Dad nor I had an appetite or apparently anything to say, so we sat quietly and moved the food around without eating. Dylan, however, couldn't sit still.

"Hey, Grandpa. What do you want to do tomorrow? Should we walk down to the creek?"

Dad glanced at me, then looked back down at his plate. "I don't know. The water's up a bit now; it might be a little too dangerous."

What? Had it really only been a week ago that he'd called me an unreasonable, overprotective mother? I knew he didn't consider the creek dangerous. This comment had been made for my benefit, and mine alone. Dad was trying, too.

I thought perhaps now would be one of those opportunities for a mini do-over. "You know what, Dad? I think it's probably okay, if you're sure your knee is up for it. Maybe I'll walk down with the two of you just to check it out."

My father looked up, clearly surprised. "Well,

okay, then. Why don't we look out in the garage and see if we can scare us up a couple of fishing poles. We could bring home some dinner for tomorrow night."

"Yeah. That's what I'm talking about." Dylan was already pumping air fists. "We're going to catch us some river monsters, right, Grandpa?"

I wasn't sure whether this comment alarmed me or amused me to a greater degree. "Son, I think you've been watching a bit too much television since we've been at your grandpa's house. I doubt seriously that there are river monsters in Shoal Creek."

"Well, sure they would call them creek monsters, but they're big fish all the same. Right, Grandpa?"

My father nodded. "Sounds about right to me. There's got to be a few Shoal Creek monsters down there somewhere. It's up to us to catch them."

He was a good sport—at least where Dylan was concerned—I had to say that about him. And he was the only grandparent Dylan would ever know. I reached over and squeezed my father's hand. "Thank you."

"For what?"

"Being so adventurous."

A flick of surprise went across his face. "You're welcome." He cleared his throat and looked down.

I thought I might have seen the glisten of a tear falling from his cheek, but I couldn't be sure.

Ring.

Dad pushed back from the table. "I'll get it." He was hobbling toward the phone before I even had the chance to tell him I could get it. "Hello." He leaned against the counter. "I see. I see. Okay, what can we do? Okay, call me when you get there."

He dropped into a chair and hung up the phone. "Hannah's got pneumonia. They've had to put her on oxygen, and they are transferring her to Nashville by ambulance right now."

Oh no. Oh no. No. No. No.

"Hi, it's me." I stood looking out the window at my father's backyard, wishing I were talking to someone who actually cared, rather than to Steve's voice mailbox. "I just wanted to let you know that Hannah has pneumonia. Measles pneumonia. They're transferring her to a bigger children's hospital in Nashville. It's really scary, and terrible here right now." My voice cracked, but I forced myself to keep going so the machine wouldn't cut me off. "There's no reason to call me back. I just thought you'd want to know. Maybe you could be . . . praying for her. That's really all we can do right now.

"I also wanted to say . . ." I thought of all the times he'd comforted me when times got hard.

269

Of how many times he'd forgiven me when I'd flown into a jealous rage over nothing. ". . . that I'm . . ." *Beep.* "Sorry." I hung up the phone, knowing that as with everything between us, I'd been too late.

Chapter 33

My father tossed the Sunday paper on the table. "I think you'll want to see this."

"Somehow, I don't think I do." I laid my head on the table, not needing to use imagination to know what was being said about me there.

"No, really, this time I think you do. Pay special attention to the article at the bottom of the page."

The Science of Non-Vaccinators

I took a deep breath and started reading, fully prepared to read a slanted story about the bogus science behind those of us who refuse to vaccinate.

By now, the 1998 *Lancet* article by Dr. Wakefield and its later retraction have been discussed, argued, and debated plenty. Here are some other facts you may not know:

In February of 2008, the United States government conceded that a combination of nine shots at her 18-month checkup "aggravated" an existing mitochondrial condition in a young girl, whose identity has been sealed to protect her privacy. The unnamed girl was developing normally until days after her well-baby shots, at which time she began to exhibit decreasing responsiveness and other symptoms of autism, including loss of language skills, incessant screaming, arching, loss of "relatedness" and other traits of autism.

A recent survey of over 1500 American parents demonstrated that 25 percent of them believe that some vaccines can cause autism in healthy children.

Although there are numerous examples of results to the contrary, before we as a city declare this a "good" and "bad" issue, I think we all need to understand that there is enough gray area that perhaps a bit of grace could be offered to those

on the opposing side—whichever side that may be for you.

Only after I'd read the article did I look up to see who had written it. Patti Fox? Again?

I looked at my father. "Why do you think she'd write this article if she's already taking flak for the one she wrote earlier in the week?"

He shrugged. "Search me. Your letter to the editor is in there, too."

"I'll be right back." I walked out my father's front door and down the street.

When I reached the Fraker house, I hurried up the sidewalk to the front porch and pushed the doorbell. No answer. Of course there wouldn't be. It was Sunday morning; she was likely at church. The same church my father and sister attended. The same church whose babies I had infected. The same church whose members had been praying in the waiting room for Kelsey, mere moments after they'd shunned me. The same church where I wouldn't dare to show my face right now.

I turned and started toward my father's house knowing one thing for certain. I would be back.

Shortly after I returned, the phone rang. My father answered with a grunt, listened in silence for a few seconds, and hung up.

"That was Rob." He rubbed his temples

between the thumb and middle finger of his left hand as he set the phone back on the counter.

"What's happened?" I whispered the words.

"Hannah has been moved to the pediatric critical care unit. Rob says she's not doing well at all."

"What did you say about Hannah?" Dylan came into the kitchen, dressed for fishing and skipping rocks, looking every bit as innocent as he was. "Is she feeling better? Is she coming over?"

"I don't think so, sweetie."

"Are you sure? 'Cause if Hannah Rose is coming over, maybe she can go down to the creek with us. I know she's too little to fish, but she could play on her blanket and watch. Couldn't she, Mama?"

"I think she's still a little too sick for fishing," I said, choking the words out through a throat that was closing. I looked at my father. "We've got to go up there."

He nodded. "You're right, I think. It'll make for a pretty hard day."

"I know." I knew that we would be stuck in the waiting room for hours, but I also knew there was no way I was staying here while Hannah was fighting for her life there. I was certain my father would feel the same way, regardless of whether or not his knee hurt. Since Nashville was over an hour away, Dylan would not be recognized there.

"What about him?" My father nodded toward Dylan. "You know they're not going to let him back there."

I pulled him up in my lap. "Sweetie, Hannah Rose has gotten very sick, and they've had to take her to a hospital—one far away. We're going to drive up there so we can be nearby, okay? Mostly it's going to mean lots of sitting around in a boring waiting room and just waiting to see how she's doing, but it will have us nearby in case Aunt Jana and Uncle Rob need us. You can be a big boy and do that. Right?"

" 'Course. I am a big boy and I'd do anything for Hannah Rose."

"That's what I knew. Okay, go to your room and find some books and things that you can play with while we're there and put them in your backpack. I'll grab a few healthy snacks and we'll leave as soon as possible. Okay?"

Unfortunately, despite Dylan's best intentions, he was still only a four-year-old, and twenty minutes into the hour-long drive he was already wiggling with boredom. Things weren't going to get better from here, because this was going to end in a multi-hour sit in a waiting room. It was going to be a long day for Dylan. For all of us. At least this waiting room wouldn't be packed with parents of a sick baby that all hated me for it. I could focus on keeping Dylan entertained and not worry about the drama.

For the first time I could ever remember, I cherished the fact that my son was going to be a handful today. It meant that he was healthy.

Dear God, please give Jana many, many, many days to be frustrated with Hannah in the future. Please keep her little lungs moving, keep her heart beating. Please, God, please. The prayer ran through my mind over and over and over.

Chapter 34

The lobby at Children's Hospital had a three-level train set, with multiple points that could be activated by onlookers simply by pushing the appropriate button.

"Wow, look at that!" Dylan ran over and pressed his face to the glass.

"I'll watch him. You go ahead." My father nodded toward the desk across the lobby.

"Thanks. I'll be right back." I approached the lady at the desk. "We're here to see Hannah Morgan. She's in the pediatric critical care unit."

The woman typed something in her computer. "She's only allowed three visitors at a time. If both her parents are up there, only one of you can go in." She nodded toward Dylan. "Unless he's a sibling, he'll likely be restricted, but you can ask the nurse."

"Thanks."

We were given visitor passes to stick on our

shirts and were then pointed toward the elevator. We rode in silence. Even Dylan had gone quiet and still.

When we got to the waiting area, a lady in a green jacket was sitting behind the desk. "Name of the patient?" she asked.

"Hannah Morgan."

"Both her parents are with her now, but one of you may go in." She pointed at three different doors ahead of us, one green, one red, and one yellow. "Hannah is in the green section. If you get lost in the hallways back there, just look for your color and it will get you back to where you need to be."

"Thanks." I looked at my father. "I think Jana would rather see you right now."

He nodded briskly, not bothering to argue the obvious. He went to the green door, rang the bell, and waited until a nurse in Tweety Bird scrubs came to let him in. The door closed and latched behind him, separating those who were allowed and those who were not. I wondered if it also separated those who were welcome and those who were not.

"Let's see, Dylan, do you want to do some coloring?"

"I'll draw a picture for Hannah Rose."

"That's a good idea, sweetie. I'll bet they can put it up on the wall in her room, or something." I found myself fantasizing about the scene at a family Christmas a few years down the road, when we all sat around and reminisced about this year. The year of the measles. The year that we all came through a little banged up, but in the end, we survived with nothing more than the memories of the battle left behind. At least, that's what I prayed for.

I looked at Dylan, who had begun the process of drawing a horse, and realized there was someone else who was equally vested here. Usually, Dylan was an impatient artist and would produce copious drawings in any given hour. Today, however, he drew with precision and great care. Thirty minutes into it, he was still working on the horse, which I must say was taking on a nice dimension, considering the fact that it was being drawn by a four-year-old.

"That looks really nice, honey." I leaned over and studied his work.

"I want to do my best work for Hannah Rose. I bet she feels real bad right now. I felt real bad last week, huh?"

"Yes, you did, sweetie."

Just then, Rob came walking into the waiting area. There were black circles under his eyes, and his long-sleeved blue button-down was as wrinkled as I'd ever seen it. I jumped up and threw my arms around him. "How is she?"

He hugged back. "It's pretty scary at this point. They've got an oxygen mask on her face, but her oxygen saturation is running lower than they like and her respiratory rate is close to sixty."

"What does that mean?"

"It means she's having to breathe extra fast to make up for the lack of oxygen. Once the rate hits sixty, they won't let her eat or drink anything by mouth. They say the likelihood of her aspirating is too high. They're talking about intubating, but they want to avoid that if they can. I guess the next twenty-four hours will be critical."

It took every ounce of strength not to collapse into a chair.

"Look, Uncle Rob, I'm making her a picture." Dylan held up his work for inspection.

"Yes you are." Rob looked over my shoulder. "That's some fine artistic ability on display right there, buddy."

"Do you think I can give it to Hannah Rose?" He looked up, all wide-eyed and innocent.

"I'm not sure about that, but we'll look into it. Okay? They usually don't let kids your age visit patients unless they are siblings."

"What's a sibling?"

"You know, a brother or sister."

"Well, I'm Hannah Rose's brother. Maybe not exactly, but in spirit we are."

"In spirit? What kind of talking is that from a four-year-old?" Looking at the exhaustion on his face, I could only imagine how much effort this lighthearted conversation with his nephew was costing him. I'd never loved Rob more than that very minute.

"What's wrong with that kind of talking? Don't you think she's my sister in spirit?"

"I sure do, buddy. I'm just surprised that you see that so clearly."

Dylan looked as if he was trying to decide whether he was receiving a compliment or a criticism. The light smile on his face told me that he was choosing to believe the former but wasn't wholly convinced.

Rob looked at me. "Why don't you go and see your niece? I'll spend a little time with my favorite *artiste*, Dylan."

"Are you sure?"

He nodded. I started to turn and he touched my arm. I looked toward him. "She may not want to see you."

I knew the sadness in my eyes must mirror his, but his eyes also carried a hint of accusation. Did mine carry guilt? I was pretty certain they did.

I rang the bell at the locked door and soon was led into a large, colorful room with dozens of little rooms off the center, each covered by a sliding glass door—most of which were open.

Not Hannah's. Even the door was different—wooden with a large window. There was a bright yellow sign hung on it: Contact and Air Precautions. The nurse opened a cart that was parked right outside the door. There was a stack of something yellow and folded inside, and a collection of face masks. "You need to put one of these on, and a mask." She handed me what I now saw was a yellow paperlike gown and a mask. "Take both things off and throw them in one of the containers before you go out of this room."

"Okay." After I suited up, she led me through the door, which opened to a tiny area with a sink. Another door led into Hannah's room.

I took a deep breath before I pushed the second door open. When I walked into the room, there was Hannah, lying completely still in a little crib. She was wearing nothing but a diaper, because there were tubes and lines all across her body. There was a large oxygen mask covering most of her face, secured with tape. Her arm had a large flat board taped to it that looked almost like a splint, and IV tubing came out from the tape. I assumed this was to keep her arm stable so she didn't pull out the IV by accident.

Jana was standing at the crib side. She didn't look up at me. My father was sitting in a seat against the wall, his leg stretched out in front of him. His expression was grim.

"Hi, sweet girl," I whispered softly to the unmoving lump of my niece.

Her breathing was fast, so fast, and I could see the little muscles around her rib cage working, struggling at the base of her ribs. In spite of the mask, with each contraction there was an audible squeaky kind of wheezing sound, with a rattle like loose phlegm. Even her head was bobbing in the effort to get a deeper breath. The urge to cough became almost overwhelming as if my own body were trying to cough her airways open. And even in this low light, I could see the stain of red starting to march across her face. The rash had announced its arrival.

Her ID bracelet was wrapped around her ankle, and on her other foot there was some sort of clip with a light in it. My dear, sweet little niece was covered with tubes and wires.

"Oh, dear God, please help her." I whispered the prayer, trying to block from memory the lack of effectiveness in similar prayers over my mother's hospital bed.

My father lumbered up from his chair. "You know what, I've got to stretch my knee out. I think I'll go out and check on Rob and Dylan." He hobbled from the room, but he turned to give me a meaningful gaze before he left.

I waited until I heard the sound of the second door closing, and finally took a deep breath and dove in. "How you holding up?"

She rubbed her hand up and down Hannah's pinkie finger, then the ring finger, then the middle. When she got to the thumb, she had to do a modified version because the wrapping holding the board on Hannah's arm partially covered her thumb. Jana kissed her fingers then and touched them to Hannah's forehead, pausing long enough to see if it felt warm before returning to the pinkie finger. She gave absolutely no indication of even knowing I was in the room.

"Please Jana, I know you're upset right now, but can't you understand that I want to help? That I'm worried sick about Hannah? That I would take this all on myself if I had that choice?"

She looked up at me then, her eyes red from crying or lack of sleep, or both. "Oh, really? Your previous choices would contradict that."

"You know it never entered my mind that something like this would happen."

"Why not? There are news programs about it all the time. Some doctor from the CDC standing there saying that parents like you are putting children like mine at risk. You apparently listened to enough information from parents with absolutely no medical training to make your decision. Did you never even bother to listen to what the true experts say?"

"I've listened to plenty of experts—people who are living with the consequences."

The door squeaked open and a thirtyish-year-old man wearing a yellow gown and a surgical cap walked in. "I'm from respiratory therapy, here to give Hannah her breathing treatment."

"I guess I should go." I started to leave.

"No," Jana rasped. "Stay. Stay and just see what your niece is having to go through because of you."

The man looked up at a monitor on the wall over the bed. "Looks like her oxygen sats are falling again."

Jana nodded, biting her bottom lip. "I know."

"Well, I'm going to do anything in my power to help keep those numbers up." His tone was reassuring if not promising.

I looked at him. "She's breathing so fast."

"Yes, it's her body trying to accommodate for the lack of oxygen she's able to use from each breath. Actually, that's sort of a good thing. If the respiratory rate starts dropping at this point, it tells us she's gotten too tired to keep up the fight."

"What would that mean?" I was pretty sure I didn't want to hear the answer.

"We'd have to sedate her and intubate. We'll avoid that if we can, but if this little darlin's body just can't keep up anymore, we'll help her out as best we can."

He looked at Jana. "I'm going to suction her now. Do you want to leave the room for a minute?"

Jana shook her head. "No. I'm not going to leave her." She didn't move from the side of the crib, but she did turn her head away.

The respiratory tech removed the oxygen mask so he could stick a tube into Hannah's lungs. She started making a gagging sound almost immediately, only in a screechier, more air-starved way than I had ever heard a gag before. The baby couldn't breathe.

"You're choking her." The words ripped from me.

He didn't even look up. He simply spoke in a very calm voice. "She's okay. There's lots of secretions in there. I'm just sucking them out. It sounds awful, but it's helping her."

The gurgling of thick liquid made me feel sick to my stomach, while everything inside of me wanted to jerk that tube out of her before it choked her. Hannah was clearly fighting against it, fighting for air. It went on forever.

Finally, he pulled the tube away. "All done now." He attached the mask back over Hannah's face. "I didn't see any blood in the secretions. That's the good news."

By the time he finished, tears were pouring down my cheeks. Hard pressure pushed through my stomach, causing the bile to burn all the way up my throat. I ran through the first door and into the middle room. I jerked off my mask and got sick into the sink, heaving long after there was anything left to come out.

I rinsed out the sink, then my mouth, and turned around, embarrassed. The Tweety-

Bird–wearing nurse entered the area, reached up into the cabinet and pulled out a bottle of spray, and doused the sink with it.

"I'm so sorry." Humiliation burned through me. "Please let me take care of this."

She patted me on the shoulder. "It's okay, sweetie. You wouldn't be human if seeing a sweet little thing like this suffer didn't bother you."

"I guess so." I walked back into the room, where once again, Jana continued to watch over her daughter but refused to acknowledge my presence. It was relieving that Hannah's breathing did sound a tiny bit less rattley after the treatment. At least, that's what I tried to tell myself.

I walked back over to the bed. "I'm sorry, Jana. I'm sorry, Hannah. So very sorry. And I'm going to be here until this is over. I'm not going to run away this time, even if you both prefer that I would. I'm here for the long haul." I turned and walked from the room.

Chapter 35

My dad walked into the waiting room, his jaw clenched tight. He'd been in with Jana and Hannah the past hour and looked exhausted. He dropped into the chair beside me, rubbed his hands across his face, and stared at the wall.

"Anything new?" I whispered the words, not wanting Dylan to hear us.

"Hannah's breathing rate has decreased. They say it's because she's just too tired to keep struggling so hard, so it's time to put a breathing tube in. They're sedating her now, although to tell you the truth, I can't see there's much need for it. She barely moves at this point."

"How's Jana taking it?"

"Not too good, which I'm sure you can imagine. They've asked her to wait outside the room while they do it. Rob had to practically carry her out the door."

"Is she coming out here?"

He shook his head. "Nah. She's standing right by the door waiting for the okay to go back in."

"Bless her heart." I looked toward the closed doors of the unit. "Oh, Dad, what are we going to do?"

"Not much we can do at this point, except pray that she gets better and the doctors know what they're doing." My father looked as tired as I'd ever seen him.

"Is Hannah Rose okay?" Dylan climbed out from under the row of seats he'd been playing beneath. I'd long since given up keeping him still and in a chair. At least he was contained this way.

"They're having to put a tube in her to help her breathe better. It'll give her body a chance to quit trying so hard." I tried to make it sound like a good thing, an upbeat, positive development.

"Oh. So she can sleep better?"

I thought of the fog of sedation that they would put her under in order to keep her still. "Yes, I definitely think she'll sleep better now."

"That's good, then." He climbed back under the chairs and started back to work on his Lego village.

My father looked at me. "You want to go back and see if it's over?"

I thought about it for a moment. "Yes, I think I will."

When I was let into the unit, I did not see Jana or Rob outside Hannah's door, so I gowned up and went inside. I pushed open the door and found my sister and brother-in-law standing over a limp baby Hannah. She had clear tape all over her face and mouth, holding the tube in place; a large blue and a large clear tube came from the device over her upper lip, as well as another smaller clear tube running out from it. Her breathing was more rhythmic now, her chest moving with the swish of the ventilator. It would have been peaceful except for the fact that she lay so still. Almost as if . . .

"Did you come in here to see what you've done? Well, take a good look." My sister's voice had lost every bit of its southern sweetness. Now it was almost a hiss.

"Jana, I . . ." I looked at her haggard face; I looked at my unmoving niece. "I came here because I want to help."

"Maybe you could help more back home in California. I think we've had enough of your kind of help here."

"I'll . . . be in the waiting room if you need me."

She didn't answer. And this time Rob didn't follow me out. I walked through the doors and nodded toward my father. "I guess she'd prefer it if you were back there."

"Okay." He stood up and hobbled back toward the door, leaning on a cane for support. Jana had always been Dad's favorite; it looked like from here on out, he was also hers. The last person who had really been "mine" now hated me. The worst of it was, I didn't blame her.

After a sparse lunch of soup and fresh fruit in the cafeteria, Dylan and I returned to the waiting room yet again.

Fox News was playing on the television overhead. Hour after hour I stared at it mindlessly, looking over every now and then to make some sort of appropriate comment about Dylan's drawing or latest Lego structure to at least affect interest, before settling back into my chair and disappearing into numb disbelief. I sat out here wishing for something to distract me.

There was nothing that could take away from the reality.

At eight thirty, Rob and my father came walking out to us. "Visiting hours will be over at nine, and only parents will be allowed then. Do you want to go back there one more time?" Dad asked.

I looked at Rob and didn't see anything like encouragement on his face. I shook my head. "Not this time. I think it's probably easier for everyone if I'm not around."

Rob looked at me, his eyes almost flat but not quite. "You know she loves you."

"Yeah, I know."

"Mama, he said measles."

We all turned to look at Dylan. "Who said?"

"That man on the news. He said something about measles; I didn't hear what."

We all looked toward the television, which had now gone to commercials. The three adults remained rooted to our spots, each of us thinking a solitary thought, no doubt. *Please let it be good news.*

The announcer came back on. "Folks, we have tragic news to report from that measles outbreak in Oregon. We'll go live right now to Kiersty Foster."

The reporter nodded her acknowledgment of the pass-off. She stood outside what was obviously a hospital, the wind blowing her long curls in a wild dancing pattern. "Yes, Shep. Here in Ashland tonight, officials are reporting the first death due to measles-related causes. This is the first measles-related death in this country in over a decade. The victim was an infant, six months old, who came into contact with the disease at her older brother's day care, where over a dozen schoolmates were infected.

"I am told the baby's brother did not get sick, because he had, in fact, been vaccinated. The infant was in the room during the time that an infectious child was present, and it went from there. The family has asked that the media respect their privacy while they grieve their loss."

"Kiersty, can you tell us what exactly caused this infant's death?"

"They're telling us there will be a press conference within the hour to discuss specific details, but we know there are currently at least five measles-infected children in this hospital. According to sources, most if not all of them have pneumonia. This has yet to be confirmed as the cause of death, however."

"Thank you, Kiersty. We'll come back live when the press conference starts."

We all stood there, staring. Mouths open. *Please, God, no. Please, God, no*. Rob reached up behind the flat screen and pushed the power button. The screen faded to black. "I think that's more than enough of that." His face had gone stark white. He turned and walked out of the waiting room without another word.

God, I'd really appreciate it if you'd send something like those hailstones and help us win this battle. Keep her breathing, keep her little heart pumping, keep her tiny little brain safe from the high fevers. God, please don't take her away from Jana and Rob. And me.

"Mama, did they say that baby died from measles?" *And Dylan. Please don't take her away from any of us; we all really need her. Please, God.*

"Get your stuff together, Dylan. We'll talk about it later."

"Is Hannah Rose going to die, too? Is that why she's in the hospital, 'cause she's dying?"

"Of course not. Now, get your things together." I picked up random crayons and began shoving them down into the box.

"How do you know, Mama?"

"I just do." Even as I said it, I knew the typical mommy answer wasn't going to cut it this time. Not for any of us.

Chapter 36

Dylan was crying by the time we made it out of the hospital, through the parking structure, and into our car. "I don't want Hannah Rose to die."

"Honey, she's not going to die. She's sick right

now, but the doctors here are taking really good care of her. She'll be all better soon."

"Did the doctors not take good care of that baby who died? Is that it?"

"I'm sure they tried, honey."

"Are they trying harder with Hannah Rose?" He was sobbing now. "They got to try harder."

"Don't you worry, Dylan," my father said. "Hannah's doctors are the smartest ones around. They'll keep a close eye on her and she'll be just fine. You wait and see." The false enthusiasm in his voice was as bright as I'd ever heard him sound.

I chanced a glance in his direction and I could see that his jaw was clenched tight. He, too, was fighting to hold it all together.

I turned on the CD player, which already held one of Dylan's sing-a-long favorites. I was hoping it would distract him enough to calm him down, but it did not. For the first time I could ever remember, I regretted my decision to abstain from all the electronic goodies most parents use at a time like this—Nintendos, portable DVDs, and whatever today's new gadget might be. Dylan was working himself up more and more, his cries shredding through what was left of my soul. It had been a long day and I knew he was exhausted.

We drove past a billboard for Nashville Shores Water Park. It showed kids about Dylan's age, sprawled across inner tubes riding the Lazy River, smiling and laughing. A few hours ago, I could have pointed out this sign with even a hint that we might someday make an appearance there, and he would have been beside himself. Now, I knew there was no point. Nothing mattered anymore. Even my son knew that. It took almost half an hour of all-out crying before he fell asleep in the backseat.

As we neared our driveway, my father leaned forward in his seat. "What the . . ."

I looked to see what he was talking about. His front yard. It was buried in a sea of what I knew were dozens of copies of *The Shoal Creek Advocate*. "I guess I got what I asked for."

"No! No! Nooooooo!" Dylan's screams cut through the house at just after midnight. "No! Noooo!"

I raced into his room, my heart pounding with fear. "What's wrong, Dylan? What's wrong?" I placed my hand on his forehead, dreading that he might be getting sick again. He was sweaty, yet cool. "What hurts, honey? What's wrong?"

"I did it! I'm the one who did it!" His shrieks were loud and hysterical.

"What did you do?"

"I made Hannah sick. It's all my fault. She might die and it's because of me." He began to kick and thrash in the bed. "I hate myself, I hate myself. It's all my fault."

I finally gathered him in the same lock hold I'd seen Jasmine use on Collin when he was in a complete meltdown. I could feel him thrashing against me, but I held him firm enough that he wasn't moving much. "Shh, baby, shh. It's all right. It's just a germ; it's not your fault. You can't help that."

He struggled for a few minutes, then stopped. "It's because I'm a fraidycat, isn't it?"

"What do you mean?"

"Cory and Tyler and Drew all talk about how much their shots hurt when they go to the doctor. I always pray and pray that you won't make me get one and you never do. If I hadn't prayed like that, I wouldn't have caught measles and neither would Hannah Rose. It's all my fault, Mommy."

"No, honey, it's not your fault at all. Mommy made up her mind before you were born not to let the doctors give you shots. So, see? It wasn't because you prayed; it was because of a decision Mommy made."

"But why?" He began to still in my arms, gulping deep breaths as he slowly began to calm.

"Well, there are a lot of people who believe that vaccines might actually make children unhealthy. I didn't want to take that chance."

"You mean, like the vaccines might give you the measles?"

"No. A different kind of unhealthy. You know

how Collin doesn't really talk much? And he gets really upset a lot?"

"Yeah."

"Well, that all seemed to start after he got some of his vaccines. I didn't want to risk that with you, so I chose not to take the chance."

His crying had turned into soft hiccuping by now. "But . . . I made Hannah Rose sick."

"The *virus* you had made Hannah Rose sick."

"But I wouldn't have had that virus if I'd gotten a shot."

"That's probably true."

"Mommy?"

"Yes, sweetie?"

"Would you hate it too much if I was like Collin? I think I'd rather do that than hurt Hannah Rose."

I rocked him against my shoulder, saying nothing. There was nothing to say.

Chapter 37

"The boy's sleeping in late today." My father nodded toward Dylan's closed door. "I guess all that screaming he did last night wore him out."

"I guess." I stared out the back window.

"Well, I'm going out on the porch for a bit. I'll see you in a while."

Despite my best intentions, I felt the usual flair of annoyance. He'd learned absolutely nothing.

All these years after his choices had killed Mom, he was continuing to make the same . . . "Dad, I'm going to walk down the street. Keep an ear out for Dylan if he wakes up. Okay?"

"Sure."

I walked down the sidewalk toward Patti's house. She would likely be gone to work already, but we'd made it home too late to come over last night. I rang the doorbell, not expecting an answer.

The door swung open and she was standing there in a sleeveless blue sweater and white denim skirt. "Hi, Grace. How are you?" Her concern sounded genuine.

"I'm hanging in there." I suddenly lost my thought process to continue.

"I heard your lawn got a few new additions yesterday. Sorry about that."

I shook my head. "I'm sorry for you. And grateful. And that's why I came down here this morning. I wanted to let you know how much I appreciate the fact that you've chosen to tell both sides of this story. I know that there are plenty of other newspapers who would have milked the anger of the town for everything it was worth."

"Oh, you are more than right about that one. I can speak to that one firsthand." She paused for a minute, then gestured inside. "You want to come in for a minute?"

"No, I don't want to hold you up. I know you're trying to get ready for work."

She smiled. "Well, I am the boss, so no one's going to fire me if I come in a little late. And there are a couple of things I'd like to talk to you about."

"Okay."

I followed her inside. I glanced toward the right at the living room. Dark brown shag carpet, worn furniture—the kind of thing you generally see in a college apartment. It wasn't much different than my own, but given the fact that Patti was single, had just bought a newspaper, and I had always heard that she came from a family of some standing back in Nashville, her modest living surprised me. She led me into the kitchen where she poured coffee into a blue mug that said *The Shoal Creek Advocate* across it in white letters. "Cream? Sugar?"

"Just a splash of milk."

She reached into the canary yellow refrigerator, which looked to be almost as old as this house. "There are a couple of things I want to tell you."

"Okay."

"First, there is going to be an article in *The Advocate* today about Dr. Wakefield—the doctor who wrote the original article alleging a possible link between MMR and autism."

"What about him?"

"A few years ago he filed a lawsuit against a reporter. His name was Brian Deer, and he was an investigative reporter who uncovered several things, including the fact that Wakefield's control blood samples—the ones from healthy kids he used as a comparison—for the paper he wrote were drawn from children at his own son's birthday party. They were paid about five dollars each. Then there was the fact that Wakefield had already been paid $750,000 by attorneys filing a class-action lawsuit against the MMR vaccine. And the fact that he'd applied for a patent for a measles-only vaccine months before this paper was filed. A vaccine that could have made him a rich man if health departments—or frightened parents—demanded it instead of the combined MMR."

"Did Dr. Wakefield win the lawsuit?"

"No. In fact, by the time it was over, the suit was shown to have so little merit that Dr. Wakefield was required to pay the legal fees for Brian Deer."

"Oh." I took a sip of the coffee, but it burned all the way down to my stomach. I shook my head. "At the time I chose not to vaccinate I didn't know any of this. I didn't know about the study in Finland, or Denmark. All I knew is that I worked with a woman whose son went from bright and outgoing, to a shell of a child, all within days of receiving his vaccines. She has a support group of several other mothers; they call their children vaccine-injured. All of them have a similar story."

Patti nodded and stirred her coffee, although I was certain that the sugar had long since dissolved. "I know what you mean. It's easy to look at cold, clinical medical studies and get little from them, but one real-life instance of a problem speaks volumes." She traced her finger over the handle of her cup. "Do you know Daphene Steepleton?"

"No."

"She was at the walk-in clinic the day you took Dylan in."

"Oh, wait . . ." A memory flashed through my mind of the waiting room at the walk-in clinic. "Well, there *was* a Mrs. Steepleton in the waiting room with us that day. I remember them calling her name. She let us go in front of her."

Patti nodded. "That's the one. She was diagnosed with measles this morning."

"You're kidding me. It never occurred to me that adults might be affected."

"Apparently she was in the generation that got a measles vaccine but no booster. They say it still has about a ninety to ninety-five percent success rate, but the problem is, she has rheumatoid arthritis and takes fairly strong immune suppressants to combat that. Her body isn't able to fight off a disease like a healthy person could. She's one of those who depend on herd immunity, because her own body is not strong enough to fight off highly contagious diseases."

"Oh." I rested my forehead in my hand. "She was so nice. Let us go ahead of her because Dylan was feeling so bad. I feel just awful about this."

"The anti-vaccine contingent never talk about people like Mrs. Steepleton, or your niece, Hannah, do they?"

"No. No they don't." I lifted my head to look at her. "Judging from what you've just told me, I gather that you do not agree with parents who don't vaccinate."

"Not particularly. I think a lot of well-intentioned parents have listened to the wrong people for too long."

"Then why have you made such a point of telling my side of the story if you don't agree with it?"

"Do you remember anything about me when I came here?"

I shrugged. "It's a small town, you were the new girl, of course I remember." I could still clearly visualize the beautiful, sophisticated blond girl walking onto campus at the end of our junior year. Her clothes were trendy, she was so poised, so self-confident. The boys had fallen all over themselves trying to get close to her—including my at-the-time boyfriend, Jared. Turned out, he was the one she chose.

"I'm sorry about Jared. I knew the two of you were dating, I knew what I was doing was wrong, but I'd just come through such a storm in my life I felt that it was okay for me to do the wrong thing to make me feel better. I guess I was trying to make up for what had been done to me." She took another sip of coffee. "I used that excuse for a lot of the things I did back then. Especially to you. I want to tell you how truly sorry I am for that."

As I wasn't ready to offer blanket forgiveness, I tactfully redirected the conversation. "What wrong had been done to you?"

"We lived in Nashville, in a beautiful home, and lived a beautiful life by most people's standards. I attended the top private school, we took nice vacations, we had it all. Until one particular Friday when I came home from school and found my father asleep on the couch." She closed her eyes tight. "I can still see his right hand resting across his forehead, his left hand hanging down to the floor.

"I knew then he must be sick, because my father was never home in the middle of the day and I'd never, ever seen him take a nap. There was an empty glass on the table and a couple of prescription bottles, so I figured he must have been to the doctor's and gotten some medicine. Just as I started to tiptoe past him and into the kitchen, I noticed a piece of stationery on the floor beside him. I reached down and picked it up. It started with the words, *To my dear family,*

I am so sorry. That's when I noticed he didn't seem to be breathing."

She wiped at her eyes and shook her head. "I called 9-1-1 and they came and told me what I already knew. It took me an hour to track down my mother—she'd been called unexpectedly to a charity board meeting that afternoon—so I just sat there beside my father in that big house, full of assorted paramedics, firemen, and policemen, and wondered what I was supposed to do next."

Patti's father had committed suicide? I never bothered to talk to her long enough to find out that part of the story. "I had no idea. I am so sorry." I thought about my own life at that time and understood fully the grief of the loss of a parent. "I lost my mother our senior year."

She nodded. "I know. I remember how much I envied you."

"Envied me?"

"I can still remember the line of cars parked down this street and all the nearby streets, after her funeral. I didn't go to the service or anything after it, but I'd be willing to bet there were a lot of people standing around talking about what a wonderful person she had been."

"Yes."

"That's what I envied."

"Your father . . . ?"

"Turned out that my father had been running a Ponzi scheme. Long before Bernie Madoff made this a household term, my father had been doing basically the same thing."

I remembered a bit about the Madoff case. A New York investor who had pocketed millions, or maybe billions, of his investors' money while sending fraudulent updates to his investors about their earnings. By the time someone figured it out, many people, institutions, and even charities had lost everything.

"In the note my father left behind, he said that the walls were closing in and he knew it wouldn't be much longer until it all collapsed. He thought it would make things easier for our family if we didn't have to watch the trial, to have to live with the stigma of a father in prison." She shook her head and stared out the window. "Of course, we still lived with the stigma. Just a different kind. Most of the people who had been our friends had invested money with my father. Several of them lost almost their entire life savings."

She pulled out the spoon and carried it to the sink. "Needless to say, there weren't a ton of people standing around my father's funeral talking about what a lovely person he had been. I would guess that the few people who came were thinking, 'I can't believe what a liar and fraud that guy was.'" She returned to the table and dropped into her chair. "We lost our home and most everything else. That's why Mom decided to move here. The cost of living was less; no one really knew us. We could start over."

"Makes sense."

"I suppose it does." She shook her head at some distant memory.

"I had no idea about any of that. All I saw was the pretty girl who swooped into town and took over the school."

"And I saw you as my biggest rival. Not just with Jared, either. I had always been the teachers' darling, especially when it came to literature and journalism. It was pretty evident that Mr. Baumgartner favored you. So . . . more than once I turned in recycled papers—ones that I had written for my class in Nashville, that had been graded and returned. I incorporated all my previous teachers' suggestions, so it made it appear that I was a better writer than I was."

She stared out into her backyard, which needed a good mowing. "I put on plenty of airs, I know that, hoping the kids here wouldn't catch on. They'd caught on plenty fast in Nashville." Patti shook her head. "That was one of the darkest moments of my life. And there was no one who cared to tell my side of the story, or my mother's.

"Yes, I'd been raised in privilege; yes, my father's trickery had earned that privilege, but I hadn't been a part of it. I'd grown up doing volunteer work just like my mother—who is as wonderful a person as I've ever known. No one cared that we were just as innocent as the other people he deceived. And that's . . . well, that's why I promised myself when I became a newspaper editor that I would see to it that those without a voice would have one. Someone like you right now."

"Even someone you've never particularly liked?" I gave her a look that dared her to contradict me.

"Someone I never took the time to get to know well enough to determine if I liked her or not." She smiled wryly. "Yes, I agree with the other side of the vaccination argument than yours, but to me this story was like coming full circle. I had a chance for a do-over, not in my own life, per se, but the opportunity to offer someone else what I never had."

I looked at her. "Full circle? A do-over? That's right. Mrs. Fellows told me you'd asked about the standing stones."

She laughed. "Guilty. I found her little stone configuration intriguing, and being a newspaper gal, I couldn't help myself but ask about it."

I stood up and extended my hand. "Thank you. For being willing to tell both sides."

She took my hand and shook it. "I'm glad I got the chance."

Chapter 38

I could smell the smoke as I neared the house. My father's all-pervasive habit even had the nerve to infringe its disgusting smell on the outdoors.

I thought about the backyard and the stone circle around the tree. The place where people started over. They pushed through hard, impossible circumstances to do the right thing, even though they didn't want to. Even though maybe it wasn't really their fault.

As much as the smell and the memories pushed me away from the side porch, something else drew me forward. I changed my direction and walked around the corner of the house. My father was sitting in the rocking chair, his eyes closed, and he rocked, a cigarette in his hand. How many times had I seen him just this way over the years?

The memories of my senior year, when I'd come home from school to find him sitting out here just like this—knowing that my mother was inside the house in a hospital bed—because of what he was doing . . .

How many times had I wished he'd had the cancer instead of her? He was the one who *deserved* it. Now I was ashamed of the thought. But at the time, the injustice of it caused me to rethink everything I'd ever believed in.

I walked up the couple of steps and sat down in the chair beside him. He opened his eyes as soon as he heard me. "I'm done. You want to go inside?"

I shook my head. "That's okay. You look comfortable."

He had his right leg extended up on a foot rest, but with the left he made small rapid rocks. Finally, he said, "So what was all that screaming about last night? Bad dream?"

"I wish." I locked my hands behind my head and bent forward. "Nothing's quite as simple as bad dreams at this point, is it?"

"I s'pose not." He continued to rock, moving more or less in time with the birds singing in the trees around back.

Finally, I looked up at him and released my hands, although I continued to rub my neck with my left hand. "He was crying because he thinks Hannah is going to die, and he thinks it's his fault."

"His fault?" My father looked at me, and there was no denying where he placed the blame.

I couldn't help but flinch. "He says he was afraid of getting shots and every time his friends talked about getting one, he would pray and ask God to make me not let the doctor give him one."

My father expelled a short, hard laugh. "Well, I guess that's one prayer that got answered."

"Oh, Daddy."

I rocked back and forth and my mind flipped through the various problems currently confronting me. There were too many to settle on just one. Then I remembered the part about Joshua and Caleb being the only two spies who were willing to move forward. It was time to commit. Whether or not the rest of the camp chose to follow was not my responsibility; my responsibility was to do the right thing. Period.

"I'm going back to Nashville today. Do you want to come with me, or is the trip too hard on you?"

He cocked his head to the side. "You mind my asking why you'd want to do that? You know your sister isn't going to see you. And it's hard on Dylan sitting still in that waiting room for all that time. Why put yourself through that? You know Rob will call us the minute anything happens—good or bad."

"I know he will, I know. It's just that Rob's family won't be back in town until late tonight, they don't have anyone else up there with them. I want Jana to know that someone is there for her. I know she's mad at me, hates me, even. But if she should all of a sudden need her sister, decide that she needs me there with her, well, I'm going to be there. It's the right thing to do. And, if she wants to scream at me and get it all out of her system, I'll be there for that, too. Might just be what she needs."

He nodded, pulled his right leg off the stool, and rocked hard for a couple of strokes until he was able to launch himself easily out of the chair and into a standing position. "All right, then. I'm up for it if you are."

I went inside and began packing some snacks for Dylan for the day. I had left his backpack on the kitchen counter last night, and it still contained all his coloring supplies and the travel set of Legos, so he was essentially packed and ready. I hated the thought of waking him up, but it was almost nine o'clock and we needed to get moving.

Very slowly I turned the knob to his bedroom door, then just as slowly pushed the door open. I knew it would squeak if I didn't use the utmost care. I peeked my head inside and found Dylan sitting up on the bed, coloring a picture. "Sweetie, I thought you were still asleep, you were so quiet in here. How long have you been awake?"

He shrugged. "Don't know." He continued coloring without further comment.

I walked over to see what he was working on. It was a drawing of a person with arms extended straight, and in those arms was a white blob with a head sticking out. I knew instantly what it was. Hannah. Wrapped in her blankets. "Who is that holding Hannah, sweetie?"

"It's me." He drew a round mouth on his face. "I'm talking to her."

"Really? What are you saying?"

"That I'm sorry."

"Honey, I've told you, it wasn't your fault. It's not even mine. It's a complicated kind of thing that even grown-ups have a hard time understanding."

"Don't matter, really. I didn't mean to hurt her, but I did. That's a good reason to say I'm sorry." He looked up at me with innocent blue eyes. "Don't you think?"

Chapter 39

During the drive to Nashville, I spent the entire time thinking about what Dylan had said. Yet somehow I balked at fully accepting the blame for this. I wouldn't run away from the consequences, but I knew too many parents who were living with another truth. How could I pretend I would make a different choice if it meant risking that for my own son?

Then, of course, there was Hannah. While I wouldn't risk my child for a stranger, would I have risked him for my niece? Well, it didn't matter what I would do or wouldn't do differently now. The fact was, the decision had been made and it was too late to change that now. And, perhaps because of that, Dylan was a happy and healthy little boy. But, definitely because of that, Hannah was in the hospital with a tube down her throat, the only thing that was keeping her breathing.

We pulled into the parking lot and made our way into the hospital and to the waiting area. "Please, can I go see Hannah Rose? Please, I've just got to talk to her for a minute."

"I don't think so, Dylan, but we'll see." I was certain the hospital staff wouldn't allow it, and I was perfectly prepared to ask the question and get the answer in front of Dylan so that he could see that I wasn't the bad guy.

Just as we were walking up to the waiting area, a nurse came walking out of the pediatric critical care. It was the nurse in Tweety scrubs who had been with Hannah yesterday, and when she noticed us, she came walking over. She nodded toward my father and me. "Two of you can go back right now, if you want. Mr. Morgan just went down to get some coffee. I'm headed that way on break myself."

"Can I go back and see her?" Dylan blinked his huge chocolate eyes, framed by long dark lashes. "I know she's not my real sister, but we're all each other's got, me and Hannah. I'm the one that made her sick and I have to see that she's okay."

"She's pretty sick right now. There are lots of tubes and things. It looks pretty scary."

Dylan nodded and blinked. "She got that from me. It's all my fault, every bit of it. I got to tell her I'm sorry so she'll know I didn't do that on purpose."

The nurse looked at me, a question in her eyes. I shrugged. "Dylan encountered one of the children from Ashland and subsequently got sick. He's the one who exposed Hannah to the measles and he feels like it's his fault."

Dylan pulled at the nurse's scrub top. "Please. I got to tell her I'm sorry. I can't stand for her to not know that."

"How would you feel about him going in there?" The nurse waited for me to respond.

"Please, Mama, please."

I looked at my son's pleading eyes and then looked at the nurse. "I think it's the only way he'll find peace."

She nodded and bent down eye to eye with Dylan. "Well, I tell you the truth, the rules are that only brothers or sisters are allowed, but you know what? I think we might be able to make an exception in your case. Just for a quick visit. But here's the deal." She leaned a little closer. "You're going to have to wear a mask and a yellow gown over your clothes. It's very important that Hannah doesn't come in contact with any other germs than what she's already got, and it's important that we don't bring any of her germs out into the other rooms."

Dylan nodded. "Okay. I had to wear one of those already, back when they poked me with a needle."

"Right. It'll be the same thing." She looked at me. "You need to come in with us in case he gets upset." I supposed that she'd seen enough of my interactions with Jana yesterday to know that there were issues, but this was spoken as an order, not a request. She took Dylan by the hand and led him toward the door of the unit, where she swiped her ID badge to unlock the door. It clicked open and soon we were standing outside Hannah's little room.

The nurse pulled out one of the gowns and handed it to me; then she began to wrap one around Dylan. It could have gone around him twice, but somehow she managed to tie it up so that it all worked. "Stay put now while I get you a mask."

She reached deeper into the cabinet and pulled out three masks, one of which she handed to me. She helped Dylan put on the second one. "It's very important that you keep your mouth and nose covered. Okay?" Dylan nodded and for the first time a bit of worry crept in his eyes. "You have to be brave, okay? She needs to hear your voice and know that you're okay."

Dylan nodded. "I will."

The nurse put on her own mask and we walked through the first door, closed it behind us, then pushed open the second. "That didn't take long." Jana looked up then and gasped. "Dylan?"

"Hi, Aunt Jana. They told me I could come in

313

just for a minute and talk to Hannah Rose." He walked directly up to Jana. "But I guess I need to talk to you first."

"What do you need to talk to me about, sweetie?" Her voice sounded tired and halfhearted.

"I know you're probably real mad at me and I know I deserve it. I'm sorry. I didn't mean it, really I didn't." He reached up and rubbed his eyes. "But if you don't ever want to speak to me again, I understand."

He turned then, while Jana simply stared, and beneath her mask I'm pretty sure her mouth was hanging open. Dylan walked right up to Hannah's crib. "Hi, Hannah Rose. Hey there, girl."

She didn't move. By now the rash had spread down onto her trunk, and her bare stomach looked raw and patchy.

"I know you're too sick to hear me, and I guess you're too little to understand even if you could. But I'm the one who made you sick. It's all my fault. My germs." He took a moment, seemingly to compose himself. "I'm pretty sure you're going to be okay. See, I prayed that Mommy wouldn't make me get my shots, and she never did. I prayed that Mommy would come to Tennessee so I could meet you, and then we needed to come take care of Grandpa after his surgery. But now, I prayed that God would make you better and let me die if someone needs to die. I'm pretty sure He'll answer me. He always has."

He leaned closer to her and wiggled his fingers, although he didn't try to touch her. "You're such a pretty girl, such a big girl. I love you." The baby talk voice disappeared and he straightened up, noticeably lifting his shoulders. "You're worth it."

He turned then and looked at me. "I'm ready to go now." He reached up and took my hand and led me from the room.

Chapter 40

When we stepped back in the waiting room, my father looked up from the magazine he was reading. He looked from Dylan to me to Dylan again, then closed the magazine. He didn't say a word; he just looked at us, as if wondering what had changed.

I finally burst into tears. Loud, sobbing tears. The kind that embarrass you when they're happening but there's nothing you can do about it. The kind that embarrass everyone in a two-mile radius—thankfully there was just my family in the waiting area. Dylan came over. "What's the matter, Mommy?"

"Oh, Dylan." I wrapped him in my arms and cried on his shoulder. I took loud sobbing breaths and absolutely could not regain control no matter how hard I tried. This went on and on; I just couldn't stop.

Finally, I managed to pull myself together enough to look at my son—who was obviously now clearly freaked out about his mother's meltdown. "Dylan, I can't believe what a big person you are."

"Huh?" He looked down at himself as if to confirm whether or not he'd grown.

"Grown-ups are so much smaller. We spend so much time defending ourselves and blaming other people that we forget how to truly love someone selflessly, the way you love Hannah Rose." I pulled a Kleenex from the box on the table and wiped my eyes.

"Well, if you think you're gonna be okay without me, I think I'll go on back and see my granddaughter." My father quickly left the room without looking back. How could I blame him?

Dylan fell asleep almost immediately on the drive home. My father stared out the window in silence. He was worried about Hannah. I knew he was. We all were.

"Rob's parents will be at the hospital tomorrow."

I nodded, remembering that they had been in Europe on vacation. After they found out Hannah was sick, it had taken them several days to arrange flights home. "I know Rob will be glad to see them."

And then we simply fell into silence. Not a word exchanged between us for the rest of the drive home.

The scene with Dylan in Hannah's room replayed over and over in my mind. It never failed to amaze me what a wonderful young man he was becoming, but nothing had prepared me for what had happened. He'd asked Jana for forgiveness in such a grown-up way—much more so than I, and I knew it. And when he talked to Hannah, so matter-of-fact, so confident in his faith that God was in control, so willing to give up his own life for his cousin that he loved.

My father and I, in contrast, had sat in silence and bitterness for years. Dad had certainly never asked for forgiveness like Dylan, but I hadn't been much in the way of a grown-up, either. That's when it hit me. I wanted to grow up to become more like my four-year-old son.

When we got home, I carried Dylan to his room. I turned down the bed with one hand while balancing Dylan on the opposite hip, then gently laid him down. He rolled over onto his side but never opened his eyes. I pulled the covers up, smiling at the red Ferrari that was nestled directly by his chin. Dad was making an effort. Perhaps I needed to be more like my son and make a bigger one of my own.

I walked down the hallway but saw no sign of

my father. But I had known that I wouldn't. I knew exactly where I would find him, and I would have known it even if I didn't detect the faintest whiff of smoke.

When I walked out onto the porch, he glanced up briefly while taking a long drag on his cigarette. He turned his head away from me to blow out. "Everything okay?"

"Don't I wish." I sat down and started rocking.

"Isn't that the truth." He took another puff but said nothing more.

I rocked slowly back and forth, debating what I was or wasn't going to say. Finally, I decided it was best to move forward while I still had the inclination. "Dad, there's something I think I need to tell you." My mouth went dry. I wasn't sure I was going to be able to do this.

"Yeah? Like what?" He stubbed his cigarette out in the large ashtray beside his chair.

"All these years, I've blamed you. For Mom, I mean. It's been eating me up inside. And, fact is, I know now, actually deep down I've known all along, you would never have hurt Mom on purpose, just like we would never have hurt Hannah, I suppose. I just want you to know that I'm sorry I've spent so much time being angry at you, and I . . . forgive you."

He sort of snorted. "Well, all right, then."

I waited for him to say more. He didn't. Not one single word. What he did do was pull another cigarette out of the pack, put it in his mouth, and light it with his lighter.

I'm not sure what I'd expected here, but it was definitely more than this. Some acknowledgment of responsibility at the very least. Instead, I got nothing. My anger started to burn toward him again, but I remembered Gilgal, I remembered Hannah, and I prayed that God would help me let it go.

"I'm going to get a shower." I walked into the house without bothering to look back.

Later, when I got out, I went into the kitchen for a glass of water. I could see the light coming from beneath the guest room door, and I thought I heard my father talking to someone. I tiptoed down the hall, wondering if something was wrong. I was getting ready to knock when I realized that the sound I heard was not talking, it was sobbing. My father's sobbing, but he was talking, too.

In spite of myself, I put my ear to the door and listened. Every now and then, I would hear his voice. "I'm sorry. I'm so sorry." He said it over and over and over.

Chapter 41

I dreamed about that morning when I had stood with the white plastic EPT stick in my hand, staring at the double lines across the window. Positive. It couldn't be true. Chase and I had used precautions so something like this wouldn't happen. And now, barely a month into my second year of college, my goal of free living and having fun was over.

That night, Chase and I both worked the late shift at the ocean-front restaurant where we'd met the past year. I had cleared the last of my tables and cleaned my station when he came up behind me and wrapped me in his arms. "You want to come over tonight?"

And I did. I wanted the comfort of his love and support. He was all I had in the world. "Mmm. Sounds good."

"I'll grab some beer and we can go sit on the beach first. There's a full moon tonight." He disappeared behind the bar and came back with two plastic cups topped with foam. He handed one to me. "Here's to us." We touched the cups together and he threw back a good swallow. Then another. He looked at my still full cup. "What's up with you?"

"I probably shouldn't drink this."

"Don't worry, Charlie's in the back." Our boss

had a strict rule about underage drinking by employees. Since I was only twenty, I fell under this rule—not that I hadn't broken it every time I found an opportunity.

"It's not that. I guess I'm not supposed to drink anymore. You see, I found out today, I'm . . . pregnant."

"What?" He tossed back the rest of his beer and took the one from my hands.

"I'm pregnant."

He drank about half the cup's contents before he said, "Who's the father?"

How I managed to remain upright after the blow from this question would always remain a mystery to me. There had never been anyone but Chase. Never. "You are."

He shook his head. "You can try that line on someone else, because I'm not buying it." He walked from the restaurant and never looked back. Not at our relationship. Not at me. Not at our baby.

My father's response, when I finally got the nerve to call him, was more or less what I'd expected. "If you're going to live that way, you can pay for your own college from now on. I'm not paying for wild partying. I was paying for an education."

So I drove out of the city of Santa Barbara, away from my job, away from my school, just trying to escape from it all. Somehow I ended up on a deserted stretch of beach just outside Ventura. I sat there and cried and cried and cried.

After I'd finally spent every last tear, I began to look around. I was stunned when I turned to look behind me. There was what appeared to be a giant Victorian mansion, sitting on a neatly manicured lawn, bordered by a white picket fence. I walked across the sand to get a closer look. Absolutely stunning. I noticed a sign on the fence gate, so I walked closer. *Guests of the Blue Pacific Inn Only* it read in white letters against a navy blue background. I stood there for a moment, considering climbing over the fence because I was really curious about the place.

"Can I help you?" An older woman, sophisticated-looking in an unpretentious way, walked over to me. She wore a white linen tunic and pants, and a wide-brimmed straw hat bordered by a blue ribbon. Apparently she'd been sitting beneath one of the trees bordering the property.

I shook my head, embarrassed to have been caught. "No thanks, I was just admiring the place." I was certain at that point that I looked a mess. My eyes were red from crying; the sand was clinging to my wet cheeks.

"I'm glad you like it. My husband and I own it. You want to come look around?"

I shook my head. "That's really nice, but I've got to get going."

"Are you sure? Do you have time to do me a really fast favor? Our chef has been experimenting with different recipes for muffins and scones. Would you be willing to come take a quick taste test?"

"I . . . guess so."

She held the gate open. "You live around here?"

I shook my head. "I go to Santa Barbara City College, or at least I did."

We approached the three-story building with dormers, a cupola, and grape arbors. "This is the most beautiful place I think I've ever seen."

"I think so, too."

As I followed her inside, I had the distinct impression that there was more going on here than I could see. Turned out I was right. I found out months later that she had seen me crying on the beach and just couldn't shake the impression she needed to do something to help me.

After I'd tasted some of the most delicious breakfast breads I'd ever tasted in my life, she said, "So, tell me, what is your major?"

I shrugged. "I guess I don't have one now."

"What do you mean?"

I looked at my feet. "I just found out I'm pregnant. My boyfriend, or should I say ex-boyfriend, doesn't want any part of it. My father has told me he won't pay for my school anymore. So my focus now is going to be finding a job."

"That's funny. We've been looking for an on-site receptionist. There's a small apartment out back in the carriage house that is included with the position. Would you be interested?"

Just like that. To someone she'd just met. And that was the kind of woman Mrs. Fulton was.

When I awoke, thinking about all they'd done for me, I realized that over the years there had already been some hailstones thrown on my behalf. Mrs. Fulton had "felt like" she should come help me; Patti had "felt like" she should buy the paper just months before this all happened. I'd been so busy with the uphill of that battle, I'd never really thought about the extraordinary provision in the midst of it.

"Thank you, Father. Please keep those hailstones coming."

Chapter 42

The phone rang early the next morning. I ran in to pick it up and saw Private Caller on the caller ID. Probably Jana or Rob. "Hello?"

I could hear a baby's screams in the background. Short, bursting cries.

"Jana? Rob?"

No answer but the baby's continued crying.

"Who is this?"

"How can you live with yourself, knowing what you've done to our children?" The man's raspy voice shook with anger. "Pack up your granola and get back where you belong."

The line went dead.

I sat there staring at the phone, my hand shaking. It started ringing again almost immediately. Private Caller. My whole body shook as I simply waited for it to stop ringing.

"What are you doing? Answer the stupid thing, for crying out loud." My father thumped into the room and reached across me for the phone.

"Dad, don't—"

"Hello." He looked at me for a few seconds, then nodded. "Well, that sounds good. Uh-huh, uh-huh." He waited again. "All right. I'll talk to you in a bit. Thanks for calling." He hung up and looked at me. "That was Rob."

"What'd he say?"

"Hannah's oxygen levels are up; her blood tests are looking better. They started weaning her off the vent early this morning. If she continues to tolerate it, they may be able to try turning it off maybe tomorrow. Looks like she might be past the worst of it."

I collapsed against the counter, relief washing over me. "Thank God. Thank you, God." I'd never meant the words more.

"They had to turn the ventilator back up." Rob's voice sounded . . . broken. It was the only word that applied.

"What happened?" I asked.

"They started weaning her, and at first it was looking good. But then, everything went south."

I pictured my little niece with all those tubes in her body, gasping desperately for her next breath. "Should we come up there? We'll be up there in a heartbeat if you need us."

"No, my parents are both here. There's not much we can do at this point besides wait it out. I'll call you if anything else comes up. For now, just sit tight."

"Okay. Just know we're praying for her. And the two of you."

"Thanks, we could all use it." The line clicked.

I looked at my father and shook my head. "They had to turn the ventilator back up."

He rubbed his forehead. "That kid never seems to get a break, does she?"

I heard the sound of Dylan's coughing as he came down the hall. "How's Hannah Rose?"

"She's hanging in there, buddy, but she's not ready to be off the breathing machine just yet."

"I got to pray harder." He turned and walked back to his room. A couple minutes later I peeked in. He was beside his bed, on his knees, hands folded. I walked in, knelt beside him, and prayed my heart out.

Twelve hours later, we got the call.

"They were trying to wean Hannah from the

vent again, and she actually started breathing on her own, over top of the ventilator. They turned it off, took it out, and she's holding her own pretty well. The doctor says she might even be home in a few days."

"Oh, Rob, I'm so relieved. How is Jana?"

"She actually fell asleep on the cot in the room. I think it's the first time she's really slept since this started."

"Give both of them a hug for me, okay?"

"You can bet I will."

I hung up the phone and turned to my father and Dylan, who both sat waiting for news. "Hannah is off the respirator, holding her own. Looks like she's definitely turned the corner."

"Yeah! Yeah!" Dylan jumped in the air and pumped his fists. Finally, he looked at me. "What does that mean exactly?"

I ruffled his hair. "Well, for one thing, it means we're heading home."

I picked up the phone to see if I could move our flight up to tomorrow.

Chapter 43

"Hannah's finally coming home from the hospital tomorrow, and you're leaving town today." My father hadn't liked it when I made the arrangements last night, and it still bothered him a day later. He shook his head as if this were the most foolish thing he'd ever heard of.

"Gosh, Dad, it almost sounds like you want me around." I shrugged. "They need me back at work. I would say I wanted to stay for a while so I could help Jana, but I think she still needs some space. I'm not running out on her; I'm respecting her wishes. The least I can do is give her that."

"Good-bye, Grandpa. I love you." Dylan threw his arms around my father's waist.

"I'm going to miss you, buddy. You come back soon, you hear? We've got to get some fishing in, and we've got to finish our project."

"You got it." Dylan smiled up at him.

"Okay, you two, it's time to come clean about this project. What is it?"

My father nodded toward the detached garage, then looked down at Dylan. "Should we show her?"

Dylan nodded. "Yeah, I think she's ready."

The two of them led me inside the place where I expected to see a lawn mower and a weed eater, and those things were there. They were just shoved against the wall to make room for . . . what was it? "Uh, what is that?"

"It's our grass house." Dylan's chest puffed out as he said it. "Grandpa and I have been sneaking out here and building it every time you left the house. Even when I was pretty sick and Grandpa was still on his walker we worked on it. Didn't we, Grandpa?"

Dad looked at me, gauging my reaction. "We sure did."

"A grass house?" It was only the frame of a building, so I had no idea what its final intention was.

Dad nodded toward it. "We knew how you felt about climbing trees, so we decided that instead of a tree house, we'd build a clubhouse that we could put on the grass. We were calling it our grass house."

"Dad, it must have been excruciating for you to work on this."

He shrugged. "Wasn't nothing."

I hugged Dylan tight. "It's beautiful. I love it."

He wrapped his arms around my neck and I stood up, carrying him on my hip. I looked at my father, completely stunned. "Good-bye, Dad." I sort of petted him on the shoulder—the closest we ever really came to a hug.

"See ya."

I looked at him then, and I knew there was something I had to say. "Dad, I . . . love you."

His expression told me he was more shocked to hear that than I was to say it. He simply looked at me, unmoving, for what seemed like forever. Then I noticed a hint of moisture on the rims of his eyes. He grabbed me and wrapped both Dylan and me in a hug so tight it hurt. A lot. "I love you so much." His voice shook when he said it. "So much." He released me then and pulled back. He looked toward my car and nodded. "You best get moving or you're going to miss your plane."

"You're right." I loaded Dylan into his seat.

"Can I ask you one thing?" My father had come up behind me. "I don't mean to make you mad or anything, but I'm really curious about something."

"What?"

"If you had it to do over again, would you give Dylan his shots?"

I looked at my father, at the sincerity of the question on his face. "I've been thinking a lot about that, and to tell you the truth, I'm not sure. One thing I do know is I'd spend some time praying about it, rather than just sampling the provisions."

"Huh?"

I laughed and hugged him one last time. "You'll have to get Mrs. Fellows to explain that one. Bye, Dad."

"Bye." He stood in the driveway and waved until we were out of sight.

"Mama, this looks like the way we go to the hospital. See, there's that man on the horse that we always pass."

I glanced toward the statue of the Confederate general who appeared to be shooting at someone. Me, perhaps? He would be in good company at this point. "The hospital is near here, darling, you're right."

"Can't we go say good-bye to Hannah Rose? It doesn't seem polite not to—you always make me say good-bye when we're leaving somewhere. Remember? 'You gotta have *good manners*.'" He said the last two words with enough exaggeration that I had no doubt how he felt about them.

"We don't really have time, Dylan. We've got to return the rental car and then get checked in for our flight."

"Please. It won't take long to say bye, will it?"

I looked at the clock in the dashboard. Two forty glowed at me in pale blue light. In truth, we did have time for a very quick visit, but Jana didn't want to see me. Besides, Rob's parents were there; they didn't need us now. "I just don't think we can do it today. I'm sorry, darling."

"You don't sound sorry." I didn't have to look in the rearview mirror to know that his arms were crossed and his bottom lip turned out.

"That was an amazing clubhouse you and Grandpa have been making. I can't believe you kept it secret from me all this time."

"Yeah, it's cool." The acknowledgment was delivered in a pouty tone.

"Maybe at Christmas we can come back and you can work on it some more. Okay?"

"Really?" Now he was perking back up. "Really?"

"No promises, but I think we'll look into it."

He sat silently for a while, sort of mumbling something under his breath. "Hey, Mama? What did that mean—that thing you said to Grandpa about . . . stamping pigeons?"

I couldn't help but smile. "*Sampling*. And not pigeons. *Provisions*. Basically, it means that instead of doing what seems to be the smart thing to do, I would spend some time praying to God about it and seeing if that's what He thinks is right."

"Did you do that about saying good-bye?"

"What?"

"To Hannah Rose. Is that why you won't go to the hospital now, because the pigeons told you not to?"

The question stunned me. And worried me, too. If my four-year-old managed to see through me so easily now, what would he be like in a few years? Yes, less than an hour after I'd made that statement to my father, I was once again trying to do things my own way without bothering to ask God about it.

I tugged at Dylan's hand, but it was hardly necessary. He was in a bigger hurry than I was. He walked past the train in the lobby without a second glance. "I can't wait to see Hannah Rose, can you, Mama?"

"Remember, I told you we probably won't get a chance to see her."

"But Grandpa said she's not in intensive care anymore. I can visit her now, right?"

"But there is other family in town; the room will be full and noisy. They might not want us in—"

"Grace. Grace, is that you?"

Rob's parents were coming down the hallway toward us. "It's so good to see you." Rob's mother gave me a hug. "We didn't know you were coming here today."

"We weren't really planning to, but we were on our way to the airport and decided to make a quick stop."

"Good for you." She bent toward Dylan. "Haven't you grown up since I saw you last?"

Dylan hid behind my legs. I touched the top of his head. "It's okay, honey, these are Uncle Rob's parents."

Dylan leaned out just slightly. "Really? Where is Uncle Rob?"

"He's in the room with your aunt Jana and our granddaughter. We came down to get a bite to eat."

"Okay. Bye." Dylan had already darted out from behind me and was moving toward the elevators, obviously delighted by the fact that he wasn't going to have to share Hannah with any grandparents.

"Good to see you," I called over my shoulder as I let my son drag me down the hall.

A moment later, we pushed inside Hannah's room. She still had an IV line in her arm and the light clip attached to her toe. Her breathing still looked labored, but it was better than before.

Rob got up to give us both hugs. He pointed to Jana—asleep in a recliner beside the bed—and put his finger over his lips. He picked up Dylan and whispered very softly, "I didn't know we'd be seeing you today."

"Me and Mama prayed about pro-pigeons and decided it was what God wanted." He whispered this in a very matter-of-fact tone, then leaned to look around Rob's shoulder. "How is she?"

"Better. Both she and her mama are asleep, but you can go over to her crib and look if you'll be really quiet." He set Dylan on his feet.

"Okay. Got it." Dylan leaned forward then back with each step as he demonstrated his best tip-toeing technique.

Rob came over and gave a quick squeeze around my shoulders. My eyes burned with the pressure of unshed tears, but I forced them back. "I'm so sorry, Rob, about all this."

He kissed the top of my head. "I know." He pulled away and nodded toward Jana. "Do you want us to leave the room so you can wake up your sister and say good-bye?"

I looked at her—neck at almost ninety degrees as her head rested on the right chair arm. I wanted to talk to her so badly, but she needed rest. Now was not the time. This was not the place. I shook my head. "She needs the sleep and we need to get moving. Will you tell her I was here? That I love her? That I . . ."

Rob nodded. "I'll tell her."

We flew into Los Angeles and rode the Air Bus back to Ventura. By the time we got home it was almost eight o'clock at night—this was ten o'clock by the Central Time Zone we'd adjusted to. I was exhausted, yet Dylan, who had slept a good bit of the plane ride, was amped. All I wanted to do was to get him in bed so I could collapse.

"Mama, you want to play cards? Mama, can I have Billy over tomorrow? Mama, let's do something."

I thought about what I wanted to do—sleep—and I thought about what needed to be done. Something I didn't want to do, something that was not going to benefit me in any way, yet it was the right thing to do. "You know what, Dylan? I need to run over to the Blue Pacific for a little while. You can come with me, how about that?"

"Aw, Mom, that doesn't sound like fun at all."

"You know what, buddy? I agree with you. I don't think it sounds like fun, either. But Jasmine really needs me there to help out. I think it's the right thing to do."

"Oh-kay." He rubbed his toe along the carpet. "If I have to."

We pulled up and I walked into the office to find my desk stacked high with invoices. I walked into the storage room and found several items still put away from the Oates family visit. I wondered why it was that they hadn't been returned to their right place. When I walked into the living room, I saw the reason.

The walls were being repainted. I was assuming there had been crayon markings—or worse—here. I heard the sound of footsteps behind me. "What are you doing here?" Jasmine's voice sounded more surprised than angry.

"I came in to see if you needed help getting ready. It's pretty obvious that you do."

"Why would you do that? After what I said to you?"

I could have told her about Gilgal, about Patti, about my father. I could have told her that this was my chance to come full circle and help her family in their time of need. Instead, I simply said, "It seemed like the right thing."

Chapter 44

The next morning I awoke with the keen sense of what I needed to do. But it was going to be hard. And I hoped I wasn't going to come out of it looking like a fool. Or, more of one than I already had.

I dropped Dylan off at preschool early to make certain I had time to do this. Then I made the half-hour drive to Santa Barbara, parked outside the small craftsman-style house, and walked up to the porch and knocked.

Steve answered almost immediately. "Hey." He leaned against the doorframe and simply looked at me. I think he was trying to decide whether this was a friendly visit or the other kind.

"Hi," I said. "There's something I need to say to you."

"Okay." He held the door open wide and motioned for me to come inside.

I closed the door behind me and said, "You were right." I stopped for a minute and took a breath trying to collect myself. "About a lot of things, really. But during all this I came to realize I had lost my trust in everything and everybody—except myself. Guess what? I found out I'm not always so perfect, either. I suppose what I'm trying to say is . . . you were right and I was wrong." Why was this so hard to say?

He looked at me evenly for a couple of seconds, and I began to realize that he was about to send me packing. Then he burst out laughing. "You're so cute when you're apologizing."

I didn't back away from him, nor did I move toward him. I needed to keep my focus if I was going to get this all out. "It's more than just apologizing. I'm going to learn to believe again. To have faith. Faith in God and faith in people."

"I like the sound of that."

"Do you think you have a little bit more patience in there for me while I figure all this out?"

"I've been patiently waiting all this time for you to figure out that you needed to figure it out. I'm not going to abandon ship now."

I wrapped my arms around his neck. "That's what I like to hear." He pulled me into his arms and touched his lips to mine. I decided I just might enjoy this process of learning to believe again.

"This place is immaculate. You run a tight ship." Jaron Wadley ran his hand over the office doorframe as he made this proclamation.

"Thank you. We work very hard at it. Not just my family, but also the people who work here." Jasmine nodded toward me as she said it.

And we *had* worked hard. *Very* hard. Over the course of the last forty-eight hours we had worked most of them, getting the Blue Paradise ready. We'd done well.

Jaron looked at me, then looked away. "I am sure that is true." He nodded Jasmine toward the door. "Shall we go talk potential deal points over lunch?"

"We can do that right here." Jasmine's voice was firm. "I really don't have time for lunch; I need to pick up my son soon."

"I just thought . . ." He looked at me.

"Mr. Wadley, Grace has worked here for the last four and a half years. She runs this office and knows the particulars through and through. There's nothing you can say that will surprise her."

"Right." He nodded. "I think we will likely be prepared to make an offer in the next few days. This piece of property is exactly what we've been looking for."

My heart sank. I'd just done my job well enough to work myself right out of a job.

Jasmine nodded calmly, but I could see the excitement in her eyes. Finally, things were going to work out for her. "There is one particular point I think you need to be aware of before we consider moving forward with this deal."

"What's that?"

I looked at Jasmine, wondering the same thing. "Our employees are like family to us. We would insist on a contractual clause that they all be kept on."

He shook his head. "We don't do that. We usually like to move our own people in after we purchase a property."

"Really? Oh, right, I knew that. I must have forgotten." She shook her head and stared at the floor, which had to be somewhere above where my heart had fallen. "I must have forgotten all about that." She sank into her desk chair and picked up the silver frame that held Collin's picture. She stared at it for a full minute, then stood up and extended her hand. "It was nice to meet you, Mr. Wadley. I'm sorry we weren't able to do business together."

His formerly neutral and controlled look melted. "Well, I . . . I'm sorry you feel that way." He cleared his throat and seemed to regain his confidence. "I'm sorry we can't do business together. You have my card. Call me if you change your mind." He turned and walked from the room, and I think he fully expected her to be calling him soon. Truth be told, so did I.

After I heard the front door close behind him, I looked at Jasmine. "Why did you do that? You need to sell this place. You need to get Collin the treatment he needs."

She nodded thoughtfully. "Yes I do, but as someone I admire very much once said to me, 'It seemed like the right thing to do.'" She walked from the room without further comment.

Epilogue

Jasmine held the phone to her ear with one hand and covered her mouth with the other. "Really?" She shook her head. "I see. All right, then. Thanks for calling." She hung up, then dropped into her chair.

I was just packing up my things for the day, Steve beside me waiting to take me to dinner, but I knew I couldn't leave her like this. I was guessing it was Collin's caregiver on the phone. These calls were not uncommon and almost always bad. "What's wrong?"

"I . . . don't think anything is." She kind of smiled, but still looked shaken. "That was my real estate agent."

"What did she want?"

"Jaron Wadley called her. He's prepared to agree to my conditions and is planning to make an offer by the end of the week."

"Why?" I could remember the determined look on his face when he left that day two weeks ago. His way or no deal.

"Apparently there's a rumor that someone else is getting ready to make an offer on the place. Jaron really wants it, and doesn't want to risk a bidding war. Since guest reviews were consistently strong, he felt he could trust the people running it to keep on."

"You're kidding me." Now I dropped into my own seat. "That's terrific news."

Jasmine shook her head. "I could still get Collin started in that program by the fall."

"Is there someone else interested in buying the place?" I certainly hadn't heard anything to that effect.

"Not that I'm aware of."

We sat there and looked at each other in disbelief. Each afraid to believe that it might be true. How could this have happened?

Suddenly, Jasmine leaned forward on her desk. "You know what? Steve, I'm thinking this has your name all over it."

"Who, me?" Steve looked just a little too innocent. "I don't know what you're talking about."

"Oh, really?" I stood up next to him. "I'm saying you do. Now spill."

"Well . . ." He grinned and rubbed his chin. "I did mention to someone last week that my group had been talking a lot about making an offer on this place. Of course, I didn't mention that it had fallen through; I simply said we'd been talking about it. Who would have guessed that the person I mentioned this to happens to know Jaron Wadley?"

"*You* did. *You* knew it."

"No comment." He tried to keep a straight face but didn't quite succeed.

Ring.

I picked up my handset, still grinning up at him. "Blue Pacific Inn. May I help you?"

"It's me." Jana's voice was so low I could barely hear her, but my heart jumped with the sound of it. It had only been two weeks, but it seemed like forever since I'd last heard her.

"How's Hannah?" I saw Steve and Jasmine exchange a quick glance; then they walked out of the office together without another word.

"The spots are almost gone. Still coughing, but she's feeling better every day."

"That's what I've heard from Dad. I'm so glad."

"Here's the thing . . ." She waited a couple of heartbeats before she continued. "I know you made the decision you thought was best for your son."

"Yes."

"And, well, what I want to say is . . . when I thought Hannah might not make it . . ." Her voice cracked and I knew she was taking deep breaths trying to keep herself from crying. "Well, I said and did some things—"

"It's okay. You don't have to say another word. I understand."

"I guess what I called to say is, Rob is thinking about coming to some conference in Los Angeles next month. He wants Hannah and me to come with him. I was thinking we might drive up the coast and spend a day or two with Dylan and you."

"Really, Jana? I would love that so much. And I can't tell you what it would mean to Dylan."

"I can't wait to see him again. That kid's got quite the heart."

"Yes, he does."

"Well, do you think you might be able to set us up with a room somewhere? We were thinking a bed-and-breakfast on the coast. You know of anything like that?" Just the attempt at teasing brought up a well of happiness inside me.

"I know of a really great place called the Blue Pacific. There is a rumor they may soon be under new ownership, so you may find the place in a bit of transition when you arrive."

"Really? Rob said that deal fell through." Jana's voice became serious. "What happened?"

What did happen? I thought about it for a moment—about how many things had fallen into place for us—before I answered with the truth. "There was a hailstorm."

"What are you talking about?"

I smiled. "It appears as though things are going to work out after all."

"Okay, well, that's terrific news, then, for all of you. So you can maybe reserve a room for us?"

"I'd say you can count on it."

"All right. I guess we'll see you next month."

"I'm looking forward to it."

We hung up, and I stared out the window at the gorgeous Pacific coast. I knew that Jana and I had a long way to go before we would be back to our old relationship again. But I also knew we were moving in the right direction, and even if it were an all-night march and uphill battle, in the end it would be worth the fight.

Acknowledgments

Father in Heaven—Thank you for continuing to bless me in my dream. You knew what this year would bring long before I knew I was going to write this book. I thank You for Your perfect plan.

Melanie and Caroline Cushman—for giving me a reason to smile every single day

Ora Parrish—your amazing strength and enthusiasm keep me going on the hardest days

Leah, Carl, Alisa, Lisa, Katy—the coolest family ever

Gary and Carolyn, Kathleen, Brenna, Kristyn, Judy, and Denice—for the love and support during the darkest year of my life

Carrie Padgett, Mike Berrier, Shawn Grady, and Julie Carobini—you are so much more than writing buddies

Jim Rubart, John Olson, Jenn Doucette, and Katie Vorreiter—my fellow Winklings

Lori Baur—you've been a great support this year, marketing wise and otherwise

Dave Long—thanks for pulling, pushing, and otherwise moving me in the right direction

Dr. Heather Hindo, Dr. Diane Brown, and Dr. Sara Stern—for taking such good care of Melanie—and for patiently answering my questions about measles

Questions for Conversation

1) How do you personally feel about vaccinations? How do you feel about people with the opposing viewpoint?

2) Do you believe a smoker should be held liable for tobacco-related diseases in non-smokers with whom they have close contact? Do you believe non-vaccinator parents should be held liable if their child passes on a preventable disease?

3) Where is the line between personal choice and corporate responsibility?

4) Can you think of a time in your life where you got a "do-over"? Did you apply what you had learned from past mistakes to do something differently?

5) Can you remember a time when someone, like Patti, reached out to help you, in spite of the fact that it was not in his/her best interest?

6) Is there a time in your past where, in retrospect, you see that a few hailstones

were thrown on your behalf, but in the thick of the battle you were too busy to notice them?

7) What is the issue or topic you feel you need to learn to see the "other side" on? (Not to change your opinion but to gain a new perspective.)

8) Do you think Jana will ever be able to fully trust and forgive her sister?

9) Has your child or a child close to you ever unintentionally shown you something new about faith?

KATHRYN CUSHMAN is a graduate of Samford University with a degree in pharmacy. After practicing as a pharmacist in Georgia, Tennessee, and California, she left her career to stay home with her daughters and has since pursued her dream of writing. Kathryn and her family currently live in Santa Barbara, CA.

Center Point Publishing
600 Brooks Road ● PO Box 1
Thorndike ME 04986-0001 USA

(207) 568-3717

**US & Canada:
1 800 929-9108**
www.centerpointlargeprint.com